Kingdom of Heirs

Book Two of The War-Torn Kingdom

by Timothy L. Cerepaka

An Annulus Publishing Book

Annulus Publishing, Cherokee, Texas, 2016

Published by Annulus Publishing

Contact: timothy@timothylcerepaka.com

Cover design by Elaina Lee of For the Muse Design

ISBN-13: 978-0692719930

ISBN-10: 0692719938

Acknowledgement

I would like to thank my uncle, James Wilhite, for helping me get this manuscript into publishable shape. I'd also like to thank the rest of my family for supporting me while I wrote this novel. You guys rock.

Chapter One

Twenty-three years ago ...

S CREAMS OF PAIN AND *fear tore through the Low Woods, only to be quickly silenced by mad laughter and the sound of metal cleaving against flesh. A woman was begging for mercy from the rogues killing her and her companions, only for her cries for mercy to be immediately silenced by the sound of a sword cutting through flesh.*

And a baby was crying, crying in fear, and it kept crying long after the last of the rogues had left ...

The young hermit known as Tiram suddenly awoke. He looked around at his surroundings, at the tall and ancient trees on every side, but he saw and heard nothing except for the chirps of the birds in the trees above. He yawned and rubbed the sleep out of his eyes, wondering if he had simply had a very vivid dream. He almost always did whenever he spent the night in the Woods away from his cabin. Although Tiram did not know for sure, he had always believed that there was something about the Low Woods that made his dreams more vivid than they normally were.

Tiram glanced at the sword at his side. The blade—a magical sword called Gildshine—was still where he had left it on the dewy grass the night before, untouched by any hands. Still, he picked up his weapon and lay it in his lap, listening again for any sounds in the Low Woods that should not be there. There had been something about that dream that had not been quite right, but he did not know for sure what—

Then Tiram heard it. A baby, crying somewhere in the distance, but close enough that he knew that it was not a dream or some kind of strange animal noise. It sounded exactly like the crying baby in his dream.

But more alarmingly, he smelled smoke, too.

Rising to his feet, Tiram took a quick swig of honey beer from his flask to awaken his senses before taking off through the thick trees and undergrowth of the Low Woods. If there was an abandoned baby nearby and a fire, then Tiram had to act fast. He thought of himself as the protector of the Low Woods and part of being the Low Woods' protector was putting out any fires that started, whether by other humans or by nature.

A few minutes later, Tiram burst through the trees onto a pathway that cut through the Low Woods and stopped at the gruesome sight that lay before him.

Six corpses—mostly men, with one elderly woman among them—lay scattered around the path. An overturned cart lay just off the path, with its canvas burned off and one of its wheels missing. The smoke was coming from the burned cart and one of the corpses, a man who looked like he had been burned alive. The men wore the armor of the Knights of Lamaira, but Tiram did not understand what five Knights of Lamaira and an elderly woman were doing out here in the middle of nowhere, far away from the capital city of Tain, although he could guess at the identities of their killers.

Probably the Marauding Blades, Tiram thought. *Vicious*

bandits, they are. They even make other bandits look peaceful.

But Tiram could still hear the baby crying. It sounded like it was coming from the dead elderly woman, so Tiram ran over to her corpse and bent over it once he reached her.

The woman was lying on her stomach, but Tiram noticed that her arms were folded underneath her like she was protecting something. Although Tiram hated touching corpses, he nonetheless grabbed the old woman's body and turned it over, revealing a baby boy swaddled in fine velvet blankets. Aside from the tiny burn on his forehead, the baby boy appeared uninjured, but he was still crying his lungs out anyway.

Tiram, having had some experience with babies before, immediately scooped up the baby boy in his arms and started to rock him back and forth, all the while saying, "It's okay, it's okay. There's no need to cry. You're safe now."

Much to his surprise, the baby actually did stop crying. He looked up at Tiram with big dark eyes, eyes that did not look quite human to Tiram, but he was unable to explain what was different about them.

"There," said Tiram, smiling despite himself. "See? You're safe now. And lucky, now that I think about it. Somehow you survived when these big strong Knights did not. I wonder how that happened?"

Then Tiram heard a moan and looked down at the old woman. She had elaborately done curls and gold jewelry woven through her hair, making her look like royalty. Most of the jewelry had been ripped out of her hair—no doubt by the bandits that had done this awful thing—and her face was beaten in several places and her nose was clearly broken.

But she had moaned, which meant she was still alive, so Tiram leaned over her, still keeping the baby safe in his arms, and said, "Are you still alive? Miss?"

The old woman opened her eyes. They were gray and cloudy, yet she looked straight at Tiram like her vision was fine. She reached up with one weak, burned hand and said, in a weak voice, "Please … protect the young *shelmai* …"

Tiram had no idea what 'shelmai' meant, but the old woman seemed to be referring to the baby. So he said, "I can help you. I have a cabin a few miles from here with food, water, and medical supplies and—"

"No …" the old woman croaked. "Don't bother … my time has come …"

"What do you mean?" said Tiram. He glanced around at the dead Knights lying around them. "Are you dying? Why were you and five Knights out here all by yourselves in the middle of nowhere?"

The old woman coughed. "His majesty … King Riuno … is dead …"

"The King of Lamaira?" said Tiram, unable to believe his ears. "What? How?"

"It … does not matter," said the old woman. She hacked and wheezed. "Please … just protect the *shelmai* … he must survive …"

The old woman's words trailed off and her eyes became lifeless. She stopped moving, stopped breathing. She was dead.

Tiram stood up and looked at the baby boy in his arms. The baby, the *shelmai*, as the old woman had called him, was sleeping soundly within his arms now, as if he sensed that he was going to be safe now.

Tiram still had no idea who the old woman was or what was so special about the baby boy, but he did understand that King Riuno was dead. He didn't know how or why, but he doubted that the old woman would have wasted the last moments of her life telling him a lie.

And if the King is dead, then Lamaira will not survive long without him, Tiram thought grimly.

Tiram shook his head. The fate of the Kingdom was not important at the moment. Right now, he needed to focus on getting this baby to safety and searching the corpses of the woman and the Knights for any clues as to their identities or purpose for coming here. Then Tiram would take whatever the bandits had left, bury the bodies, and worry about the future in the morning.

So Tiram turned and walked back into the trees of the Low Woods, intending to take the baby, the *shelmai*, to his cabin. And the baby slept softly in his arms all the while.

Chapter Two

Twenty-three years later ...

ON THE FIRST DAY of fall, Keo of the Sword dodged a slash from a man clad in silver armor. Seeing an opening, Keo slashed at the soldier with his sword Gildshine, the blade striking the soldier's side, but all that seemed to do was enrage the swordsman, who pulled his sword back and tried to strike Keo again.

Keo ducked, avoiding the Knight's sword, and tried to slash at him again with Gildshine, but the soldier blocked the blow with his shield. This forced Keo to back up, while the Knight advanced on him with his shield before him and his sword in one hand.

"Foolish spy," said the Knight, his voice somewhat muffled through the metallic visor covering his face. "Think you can sneak into West Lamaira without us noticing? You think us greater fools than we really are."

"I've *told* you," said Keo, not bothering to hide the annoyance in his voice anymore, "we're *not* Magician spies."

"And I am the reincarnation of King Riuno," said the Knight sardonically. "Taste my blade of death!"

The Knight charged Keo suddenly. But Keo, seeing an opportunity, stepped out of the way, allowing the enemy Knight to run past him. In one smooth motion, Keo slammed the flat of

Gildshine against the back of the Knight's head, clanging his blade against the Knight's helmet. He put enough power into the blow that the Knight fell onto the ground unconscious, dropping his weapons around him.

Panting, wiping the sweat off of his forehead, Keo nudged the Knight just to make sure that he was down. When the Knight did not move, Keo sighed in relief and then looked around at the rest of the battle going on around him.

On the opposite side of the battlefield was a young, blonde-haired woman in a green tunic, who used the winds to assault the Knights of the Old Kingdom fighting her. That was Maryal of the Wind, one of Keo's three traveling companions, and despite her petite form, she was holding her own against the burly Knights fairly well, probably because of her magic.

Closer to Keo was an older man, perhaps in his fifties, fighting two other Knights, but the older man—Keo's other traveling companion, Dlaine of the Fist—did not have any weapons. Instead, he fought with his hands, moving with great dexterity for a man his age, landing the occasional blow but otherwise keeping out of the reach of his two opponents, who were having a hard time keeping up with him despite being at least half his age. That was probably because of Jola, the invisible Magician, casting fireballs and making their weapons jerk around in their hands, which was probably the main reason why Dlaine had lasted so long against them.

Their battle took place on the border between South Lamaira and West Lamaira. The party of four had intended to travel through the Cloudway Pass, which was located on the small mountain chain on the border, to reach West Lamaira, but when they crossed over into that country, they were immediately ambushed by a group of West Lamairan border patrol Knights who believed they were spies sent from South Lamaira. It wasn't true, because Keo and friends were actually wanted criminals in their home country, but so far the Knights had not bothered to listen to their protests, hence the battle that had erupted between both sides.

And they clearly are not going to listen to us no matter what, Keo thought. *But that doesn't change the fact that I need to end this fight quickly so we can continue heading to the Restorationists' capital city, Tain.*

So Keo moved to help Maryal with her opponents, but before he could get very far, he heard something heavy spinning through the air and looked to his right just in time to see a heavy metal ball and chain flying toward him.

Alarmed, Keo ducked, allowing the flail to go flying over his head, and then looked to see yet another Knight standing several feet away, dragging the ball back to him. This Knight, however, was much larger than the other Knights, about a head taller than any of them, and he looked even more eager to murder Keo than the others were.

"Lucky move, spy," said the Knight, his voice deep and rumbling behind his visor. "But luck will not be on your side forever, you know."

"How many times do I have to tell you guys that we're *not* spies?" said Keo in annoyance. "We're just peaceful travelers trying to reach Tain."

"Oh, so you are dim enough to tell us your destination?" said the Knight. "I never had much respect for Magician spies like you, but I didn't realize just how justified that that lack of respect truly was."

Before Keo could protest once more that they were not spies, the Knight hurled his ball and chain at Keo again. This time, it came almost too quickly for Keo to dodge, but he managed to dodge it at the very last second. He slashed at the chain with Gildshine, cutting through it and sending the metal ball flying.

But as soon as Gildshine cut through the chain, the Knight threw it aside and drew his own sword from his sheath. The Knight charged at Keo and swung his blade at him. The Knight's broadsword flew through the air toward Keo, who blocked it with Gildshine, but then the Knight suddenly forced Keo back, putting all of his weight into forcing Keo down to the ground.

Keo gritted his teeth and, finding his footing, pushed back against the Knight. The two pushed against each other, neither giving the other any openings, and it was all Keo could do to keep the Knight from forcing him down. They were so close that Keo even saw the Knight's blue eyes through the slit in his visor, which were focused in anger.

Then Keo, realizing that his enemy was too focused on pushing him back to do anything else, ceased pushing back against the Knight and stepped to the side in one smooth motion. The Knight—who had been very busy pushing back against Keo —suddenly staggered forward, giving Keo the opportunity to slam Gildshine against his back and knock him to the ground.

But as soon as the Knight hit the ground, he rolled over and back onto his feet, but he did not attack right away. Instead, the Knight watched Keo carefully, his shoulders lowered, his panting audible through his visor.

"It appears I underestimated you, spy," said the Knight, his voice somewhat breathless. "You are clearly a much better fighter than I thought."

"My friends and I merely wish to travel to Tain," said Keo, turning Gildshine in his hands. "If you let us go, we will not break any of your people's laws or cause any unnecessary trouble."

"And you underestimate my own intelligence," said the Knight. "But you Enforcers have always been dimmer than we Knights of the Old Kingdom, so perhaps I should not be surprised."

The Knight took a fighting stance, likely to continue to attack Keo, but before he could move, a sudden rumbling in the earth caught them both off-guard. Keo and the Knight looked down at the ground under their feet, listening to the rumbling coming deep from within the Pass itself.

"What is this?" said the Knight, looking up at Keo. "A trick?"

Keo shook his head. "I don't know, but—"

Keo was interrupted when the ground cracked underneath the Knight's feet. Immediately understanding what was about to happen, Keo ran forward and tackled the Knight, sending them both stumbling across the ground as something burst through the earth, right where the Knight had been standing mere seconds before.

Rolling off of the Knight, Keo looked at what had burst out of the earth, blinking away the dust that the wind had blown into his eyes. He at first thought that the creature pulling itself out of the earth was some kind of freakishly huge mole, because it had large claws clearly meant for digging, in addition to the mole-like head and body, although the strange drill-like appendage on its nose was certainly unusual for a mole.

But as the mole-like beast emerged from the earth, Keo noticed that its eyes were as red as blood and its teeth were razor sharp. Even before the beast turned its large head to look at him, Keo understood exactly what this creature was and that he and everyone else here were about to have a very bad day.

"What in the name of the Good King is that?" said the Knight, sitting up and staring at the beast as it fully emerged from the earth, standing a good ten feet tall. "I have never seen a mole that big."

"It's not a mole," said Keo, not bothering to hide the dread in his voice.

"Then what is it?" said the Knight, looking at Keo in confusion. "Have you seen it before?"

"Not this particular creature, but I've faced its brethren before," said Keo. "It's a demon."

The Knight looked at Keo in astonishment. "A demon? But they were sealed away a thousand years ago by the Good King! How can this thing be a demon?"

"I'll explain later," said Keo as he held Gildshine in an offensive position. "For now, we need to kill it before it kills us."

"But you and your friends are spies," the Knight said. He sounded torn, like he wasn't sure who was the bigger threat: Keo or the demon. "Why should we ever work with enemy spies?"

"Because that thing will kill all of us if we don't kill it first," said Keo. "Trust me. I've fought a few demons recently and they don't care what country you're from or what you believe. They'll kill you just the same."

The Knight scrambled back to his feet, but rather than fight

Keo, he took up a fighting stance next to him and said, "Very well. We will work together to kill this thing, but as soon as it is dead, we will resume our previous conflict."

Keo looked at the Knight in disbelief, but then shook his head and said, "All right. But we might need the help of your men, so you should tell them to stop fighting my friends so we can focus on killing this thing."

"What will you do in the meantime?" said the Knight.

"Distract it," said Keo. "Now go!"

The Knight nodded and then ran off to go gather his fellow Knights, while Keo ran to fight the mole-like demon, which was blinking at the bright sunshine above. Its vision was likely still adjusting to the light of the surface, which would give Keo the opportunity he needed to strike before it had a chance to defend itself.

Keo swung Gildshine at the demon, but the demon blocked the blow with its long, drill-like horn and tried to stab Keo, but he dodged its horn easily and slashed at the demon's eyes. The sword cut through the demon's left eye, causing it to scream in pain and staggered backwards, covering its eye with one of its shovel-like claws.

But it still slashed at him with its other claw, forcing him to jump backwards to avoid getting slashed. Instead of charging toward the demon, however, Keo backed up, thinking about how he was going to kill the demon, which was now nursing its wounded eye.

He could give up half of his energy to give Gildshine the ability to cut through anything, which would allow him to kill the demon quickly and easily, but that would leave him unable to defend himself from the Knights afterward. Yet Gildshine's magical ability was the only surefire way to kill a demon that Keo knew of.

Unless I access the fire within me again, Keo thought, remembering the golden flames that had enveloped Gildshine about a month ago when he had been fighting the demon known as Plague of Wrath. *But I don't even know how I did that the first time, so how can I access it again?*

But Keo had, for quite some time now, wanted to try that again. He recalled that his rage against Plague for harming Dlaine and Jola had driven his ability, but right now Keo did not have that rage flowing through him. He focused on it briefly, but the fire in his soul seemed to have gone out completely, because he could not feel it at the moment.

Just as Keo thought that, the demon finally finished nursing its eye. It then took a step toward Keo, growling, but before it could move close, a powerful gust of wind tore through the area. Keo was almost blown away, while the demon, which took the brunt of the attack, was knocked off its feet, although it got back up quickly enough, only for its body to burst into flame. The demon roared in pain, its roar loud enough to be heard over the burning flames covering its entire body.

Surprised, Keo looked around. He saw Maryal, along with the Knights she had been fighting, running over to him, and he also spotted the Captain Knight from earlier leading Dlaine, Jola, and their enemies toward him as well.

"Did you guys do that?" said Keo, pointing at the demon, which was still on fire and roaring in agony.

"Jola did," said Dlaine, skidding to a stop beside Keo. He

grimaced when he saw the demon. "Damn it. I thought we wouldn't see another demon for another couple of months at least."

Maryal stopped beside Keo as well and said, "How do we beat it?"

"By slaughtering it like a lamb," said the Captain Knight suddenly. He pointed at the burning demon with his sword. "Brave Knights of the Old Kingdom! Slay this foul beast that has taken the form of the noble mole! Show it no mercy!"

Before Keo or the others could tell the Captain Knight that that was a bad idea, the seven other Knights yelled a battle cry and ran to fight the demon. At the same time, the demon stopped thrashing about and then opened its mouth, barely visible through the flames. The fire was sucked inside its mouth, like water going down a drain, until soon all of the flames had disappeared inside its mouth, although the demon's skin was still smoking from the fire. Yet the Knights continued to charge toward the demon as if nothing had changed at all.

Keo at first did not know what the demon was going to do until Dlaine suddenly shouted, "Move, you fools!"

Even before those words left Dlaine's mouth, the demon opened its mouth and unleashed a gigantic burst of fire at the incoming Knights. Thankfully, most of them were smart enough to separate and avoid being melted alive, except for one Knight, who took the full brunt of the fire. He screamed as the flame melted his armor and his skin, staggering about as he struggled to remove his armor before suddenly falling on the ground, instantly dead.

As for the other Knights, they surrounded the demon on all

sides, because the demon had apparently used up all of the fire in that one attack. The Knights started slashing and stabbing at the demon, but their swords merely bounced off its flesh and it did not even pretend to be injured. Instead, the demon stabbed one of the Knights straight through with its drill-like nose and then knocked the rest of them away with its claws. The Knights landed on the ground and did not get up, although they appeared to be unconscious rather than dead.

"What?" said the Captain Knight in alarm. "How come none of my men could even lay a scratch on its hide?"

"Because demons cannot be killed harmed by normal weapons," said Keo. He nodded at Gildshine. "You need a magical sword like this one to kill it."

"Then why haven't you slain it yet?" said the Captain Knight in annoyance. He pointed at the demon with his broadsword. "Kill that damned beast right away!"

"Because my sword's magical ability leaves me exhausted and unable to fight if I miss, so I have to be careful about using it," said Keo.

"Even so, it is plainly clear that your sword is our only option if we are going to make sure that this battle does not turn into a slaughter," said the Captain Knight. He stepped toward Keo, his free hand twitching. "If you will not do it, then perhaps I will take your sword from you and use it myself."

Keo shook his head. "All right, all right. I'll use it, but I need you guys to distract the demon while I get Gildshine's ability ready, okay? I will only have one chance to hit it and I don't want to waste it."

"Of course," said Dlaine. "Distraction is what we're good at.

Follow my lead, everyone."

Dlaine ran toward the demon, as did Maryal, and surprisingly enough, the Captain Knight as well. Perhaps the Captain Knight wanted to avenge his fallen men or maybe he simply recognized that the demon was the bigger threat right now to the 'Old Kingdom,' as he called it, and thus it made sense for him to work with Keo's friends to distract the demon.

The demon, for its part, seemed annoyed that more humans were going to attack it. It tried to stab Dlaine when he got close, but Dlaine dodged it easily and then another fire blast from Jola struck it in the face. The demon howled in pain, but before it could react, Maryal waved her hands and blew dust and dirt into its eyes, causing it to once again paw at its eyes before the Captain Knight slashed its face with his broadsword. The broadsword did nothing to actually harm the demon, of course, but it did make the demon angrily swipe at him, which the Captain Knight blocked with his shield before stepping out of its range.

While the others did that, Keo focused on accessing the fire deep within him. He knew that he probably should have been focusing on using Gildshine's actual ability instead, but he remembered how powerful that the fire within had made him feel and he was not going to let that feeling go just yet. Besides, if he could access the flame, then he would not have to suffer from the usual exhaustion he felt whenever he used Gildshine's ability.

At first, Keo did not feel the flame at all, but soon he felt something warm deep inside his soul. It was the fire from the Citadel, the one that had helped him beat Plague of Wrath. It didn't feel quite as powerful as before—probably because he wasn't as angry—but he grasped it just the same and pulled.

Immediately, fire coursed through his veins and Gildshine exploded into golden flames. Like the first time he had done it, Keo now felt like he could beat anything.

Grasping Gildshine in both hands, Keo ran toward the demon, which had now turned around to follow the Captain Knight, who it seemed to have taken a special hatred of for some reason. Its back was to Keo, which was exposed.

So Keo raised Gildshine and drove it into the demon's backside.

Or *tried* to. As soon as Gildshine's blade touched the demon's back, the golden flames suddenly sputtered and died and the fire in Keo's veins vanished. Gildshine's tip harmlessly bounced off the demon's hide, but before Keo could react to that, the demon whirled around and slammed its drill nose into his side.

The impact was enough to send him flying. Keo landed hard on the ground, temporarily stunned by the blow, though he still held onto Gildshine. Ignoring the pain in his side and his back from where he had fallen, Keo tried to find the fire inside him again, but he couldn't feel it at all now, like the fire had left.

Just as Keo came to that horrifying realization, Dlaine shouted, "Keo! Watch out!"

Looking up, Keo saw the demon running toward him with its drill nose aimed at him. The others were all shouting at Keo to get up, which Keo did, albeit not as quickly as normal because of the pain he suffered from the blow he had taken.

Keo then focused on Gildshine, telling the sword to take half of his energy so it could become powerful enough to cut through anything. In less than a second, Keo felt his energy transfer from his body into Gildshine itself, felt the sword become sharper than any substance in the world.

The demon was still charging at him, but Keo did not run. Instead, he dodged the demon's drill horn and then brought Gildshine down on the demon's neck as hard as he could.

Gildshine cut through the demon's neck as easily as melting butter. The demon's head rolled across the ground as its body crashed, black demon blood leaking out of the stump where the head had been. Like with all demons, its body soon turned into dust, and then that soon vanished into the earth, leaving no trace of the demon's existence whatsoever.

Keo sighed in relief at the demon's death, but as soon as that sigh escaped his lips, complete and total exhaustion abruptly hit him like a sledge hammer. As usual, he stabbed Gildshine into the earth to support him, but this time he must have been more tired than usual, because he felt his consciousness rapidly slipping even faster than normal.

The last thing he saw, before unconsciousness overtook him, was Dlaine and Maryal running toward him. Then everything went black and he saw no more.

Chapter Three

WHEN KEO NEXT AWOKE, he found himself lying on a simple white bed underneath a white sheet. He was staring at the wooden ceiling of the room he was in, with a window open just above his head, allowing the cool fall air and warm sunshine to pour through.

Blinking, Keo looked around the room he was in. It was a small, square room, with a desk opposite his bed and a door between them. His boots, worn and ripped in several places due to the miles of walking he had done in them, were at the foot of the desk's chair, while Gildshine, sheathed in its green sheath, was leaning against the desk itself.

Where am I? Keo thought, rubbing his eyes and yawning. *How did I get here?*

The last thing Keo remembered before falling unconscious was killing the demon and then losing consciousness because of Gildshine's ability. He was surprised that the Captain Knight and his men had not killed him in his defenseless state, but maybe they had instead taken Keo and his friends prisoner so they could find out who they were and what they were doing in the Old Kingdom.

That can't be right, though, Keo thought, glancing at Gildshine on the other side of the room. *Who allows a prisoner to keep his weapon or gives him a nice place to sleep? Either the*

Knights of the Old Kingdom aren't very good at keeping prisoners or I'm not actually a prisoner at all.

Good morning, Keo, said a familiar feminine voice in Keo's head suddenly. *I see that you are awake.*

Keo looked around, but as usual, he did not see his invisible friend. "Jola? Is that you?"

Yes, it is, said Jola. *I see you have recovered from using Gildshine's ability.*

"Yes, but I have so many questions," said Keo. He sat up, rubbing the back of his head as he looked around the room again. "Where am I? Where is everyone else? How long have I been out?"

I'm not good at explaining things, Jola said. *I'll get Dlaine and let him know you're awake. But I can tell you that you've been out for about a day, although a lot has happened in that day that Dlaine can tell you about.*

With that, Jola's voice went silent and Keo knew better than to try to contact her when she no longer wanted to talk, mostly because he had no idea how to speak telepathically as Jola did. So he just sat there in the bed for a couple of minutes before the door to his room opened and Dlaine poked his head in.

"Hey, Keo," said Dlaine as he entered, closing the door behind him as he did so. "How do you feel? Jola told me you were awake and were confused about what's happened since you were knocked out."

"I feel fine, though hungry and thirsty," said Keo, waving off Dlaine's question. "But that can wait. I need to know what happened after I killed the demon. Is Maryal safe?"

"She is," Dlaine said, nodding. "All four of us are, in fact.

Right now, Maryal is enjoying some breakfast that the Knights made for us. It's some kind of fluffy bread with butter, eggs, and jelly. Not sure what it is, but it's great and you should really have some when you get up."

"I don't care what we're having for breakfast," said Keo, folding his arms and scowling. "Why are the Knights feeding us breakfast, anyway? I thought that they wanted to kill us because we're 'spies.'"

Dlaine shook his head. "Not anymore. That Captain Knight guy—his name is Fariak, by the way—was grateful for our help in killing the demon. So he allowed us to come and stay the night in the Knights' outpost here in the mountains as a reward for our help."

"You mean he's not going to arrest or kill us?" said Keo.

"Probably not," said Dlaine. "He especially had a ton of respect for you. In fact, the guy actually carried you all the way here himself after you lost consciousness and he gave his men strict orders not to bother you while you rested."

"Strange," said Keo, rubbing the back of his neck, which felt a little stiff after lying in the same position for so long. "I guess he must really like me now or something."

"I heard that the Knights of the Old Kingdom can be extremely grateful to anyone who saves their lives or the lives of their men," said Dlaine. "The Knights of the Old Kingdom, as I understand it, view each other as brothers, so if you save one of them, it's the same as rescuing one of their family members. That's probably why he respects you now."

"Well, regardless of his motives, I'm just glad that we're all okay," said Keo. "Have you told him much about who we are and what we're doing?"

"Only the basics," said Dlaine. "You know, the demons are rising again, we're on the run from the Magical Council, trying to find King Riuno's son, and so on. They don't think we're spies anymore when I told them that the Magical Council has branded us traitors and put a bounty on our heads for trying to kill Nesma."

"Well, I guess that's okay, seeing as they let us stay here," said Keo with a sigh. He stretched his limbs and threw the blankets off of his legs. "Anyway, I'm going to get some breakfast. Once we do that, we can say good bye to the Knights and head for Tain."

Dlaine nodded, but then said, "About that … Fariak said that he wanted to talk with you before we left."

Keo frowned. "About what?"

"About those golden flames that appeared on Gildshine earlier," Dlaine said. "You know, the flames you apparently decided to keep a secret from me, Maryal, and Jola for some reason."

Dlaine sounded annoyed, even a little angry, while Keo sheepishly rubbed the back of his head and said, "Well, I *was* going to tell you guys about it, but only after I understood it, which I don't."

"Uh huh," said Dlaine, who sounded rather skeptical. "Just when were you planning to tell us that you can do that? I've never seen anything like it before. Nor have Maryal or Jola."

"Like I said, I don't really understand them," said Keo as he swung his legs over the side of his bed. "They first appeared when I was fighting that Plague demon back in the Citadel. It's what I used to kill him, but I don't understand where they came from and why. That's one of the reasons I wanted to go to the Old Kingdom in the first place, because I thought someone here might be able to tell me what these powers are and why I have them."

"Okay," said Dlaine, folding his arms across his chest. "And you didn't tell us about them immediately because—?"

"Because I didn't think you needed to know about them," said Keo. "Remember our original deal? How neither of us would share anything with each other that the other didn't need to know? You know, like how you still haven't told me much, if anything, about your past. I'm just invoking that clause in our agreement."

Dlaine suddenly stiffened. "Well, that's different because my past isn't relevant to our journey, whereas knowing that you can somehow conjure golden flames on your sword, even though you're not a Magician, is."

"Well, now you know," said Keo as he stood up from his bed. "Just give me a moment to get ready. I want to hear what Fariak wants to talk with me about, especially if it has to do with those golden flames."

A couple of minutes later, Keo and Dlaine stood in the dining area of the Knight's outpost. It was a large room with a long table with enough seats for six or seven people, but at the moment only Maryal, Fariak, and one other Knight were sitting around it. Maryal looked up from her breakfast of venison and bread and waved when she saw Keo and Dlaine enter, while the two Knights stood up as if Keo and Dlaine were royalty.

Keo had no trouble recognizing Fariak due to his bulk. But now the Knight was not wearing his helmet and visor, which was on the table next to his empty plate. Fariak's face was large and he had a short gray beard that looked well taken care of.

The other Knight was a much younger man—even younger than Keo by the look of his young face—but Keo did not know his name. He just noted that the man had blond hair and a few scars across his face, which somewhat ruined his youthful appearance.

"Keo of the Sword!" said Fariak, waving at him. His tone was a lot friendlier now in sharp contrast to his original hostile tone. "Glad to see that you're up and walking about. Are you hungry? We have plenty of food for breakfast if so."

Keo's stomach growled and he nodded. "Yes. I'm very hungry."

"Good to hear," said Fariak. He looked at the younger Knight. "Rez, please go and prepare a plate for our guest."

"No, that's fine," said Keo. "I can get it my—"

"No, I insist," said Fariak. He gestured at an empty spot on the bench that Maryal sat on. "You are our guest, and in the Old Kingdom, guests in our homes are always treated with as much respect as royalty. Just take a seat here. It is no inconvenience to us."

Keo, feeling uncomfortable at what he considered to be an imposition on the Knights' politeness, nonetheless took a seat at the table next to Maryal, who seemed to be enjoying her own breakfast a great deal. Rez, the younger Knight, walked over to the back of the room, where a large bowl of bread and venison stood, along with a jug of some kind of juice, which had a strong enough smell that Keo could smell it even from where he sat.

While Rez prepared Keo's breakfast, Keo looked at Fariak and said, "Thanks for allowing us to stay here and have breakfast with you and your men. That is surprisingly generous of you."

"It is nothing," said Fariak, waving off Keo's gratitude. "Your actions against that demon—" and Fariak said the word 'demon' with some hesitation, like he still wasn't sure about it, "—was deeply appreciated. Had you not slain it, it likely would have slaughtered all of my men, rather than just the two it killed. This is the least I can do for you."

Then Fariak leaned forward, looking a little sheepish. "I apologize for accusing you of being spies. Your friends told me your story and I now understand your situation much better. It is simply that I am one of the border patrols of the Old Kingdom and so we must be ever-vigilant against spies from the Magicians, who often try to sneak over the border to undermine us from within."

"I understand," said Keo, glancing at Rez, who was now walking back to the table with a large plate of bread and venison in his hands. "But where are the rest of your men? I thought you had at least five, not counting the two that the demon killed."

"They are out patrolling the Pass to make sure that no one is trying to sneak through the border," said Fariak. "They also went out to give my men who were killed by the demon a proper burial and to ensure that there are no other demons in the area."

"I'm sorry about your dead men," said Keo as Rez placed the plate in front of him and walked around the table back to his own seat next to Fariak. "I didn't intend for them to die like that."

"It is nothing," said Fariak, though there was a sadness in his voice that the Captain Knight failed to hide. "Every one of us Knights of the Old Kingdom know that we might die in our line of duty. They at least died fighting protecting their Kingdom from a demon, which is better than dying any other way. I don't hold it against you."

"All right," said Keo as he picked up a piece of venison and ate it. It tasted great, better than the increasingly stale bread and bacon that he and the others had had to subsist on during their journey to the Old Kingdom. "Anyway, Dlaine told me that you wanted to talk with me about something?"

"Yes, indeed," said Fariak. He rubbed his hands together, which seemed like a nervous habit. "Those golden flames that appeared on your sword ..."

"Yeah, those were amazing," said Maryal, looking up from her breakfast again to look at Keo. "I've never even heard of that. Are you sure you're not a Magician?"

"I'm not," said Keo. "I don't even know what those flames are or where they came from."

"But I do," said Fariak. "Or think I do, anyway, but I am extremely confident that they are what I think they are."

Keo, Maryal, and Dlaine looked at Fariak in surprise.

"You know what those golden flames are?" said Keo. He leaned forward over his plate of hot food, looking at Fariak intently. "Then tell me. I'm listening."

"Very well," said Fariak. "Now, I assume you travelers know who the Good King is, correct?"

"Of course," said Keo, nodding. "Everyone does. The Good King was the first King of Lamaira, who sealed the demons away a thousand years ago and then founded the Kingdom of Lamaira."

"Exactly," said Fariak. "The Good King was more than a mere mortal, however. He was said to be greater even than the greatest Magicians and was the slayer of the vile King Yeornas of the

Dracones."

"Yeah, we know that," said Dlaine, resting his chin on his fist as he looked at Fariak. "Are you going to get to the point or not?"

"I am, Dlaine of the Fist, I am," said Fariak. "I am sorry for taking my time. It is just that, whenever I think of the Good King and his mighty deeds, I can barely contain myself and feel an unstoppable urge to talk about his great accomplishments. Forgive me for the tangent."

"Please go on," said Keo, before Dlaine—who looked less than impressed with Fariak's apology—could say respond. "The golden flames. What do you think they are?"

"Ah, yes," said Fariak. "Do you know what one of the signs of the Good King's greatness was? How the people knew that he would save them from the demons all those centuries ago?"

"No," said Keo, shaking his head. "What was it?"

"Legend says that the Good King's sword could burst into golden flames on his command," said Fariak. He pointed at Gildshine. "Just like your sword can."

Keo, Dlaine, and Maryal looked at Gildshine, but then Keo looked at Fariak again and said, "Is that true?"

"It is," said Fariak, nodding eagerly. "All of the main legends about the Good King mention it. It is one of his most distinctive features in the stories of old, for his sword, Shadowbane, always burst into flame during the most crucial battles against the demons."

"What do you think my own sword's golden flames mean, then?" said Keo, resting his hand on Gildshine's hilt.

"I do not know for sure," said Fariak. He hesitated, and then said, "But I think that it is a sign that *you* are somehow related to the Good King, that you may, in fact, be the Kingdom's salvation."

Keo blinked. "The Kingdom's salvation? What do you mean?"

"You mean you have never heard?" said Fariak. He frowned. "But of course, I forget that you three are from South Lamaira, where your stories and legends differ from ours. Allow me to inform you of the prophecy that was handed down to those of us living in the Old Kingdom when King Riuno died. Rez?"

Keo looked at Rez. The younger Knight, who seemed quite reserved in comparison to the boisterous Fariak, simply said, "Shortly after King Riuno died, his seer—a woman known as the Old One—uttered a prophecy foretelling the return of King Riuno's son to the throne. The prophecy describes a young man arising from the wilderness, wielding a sword that can burst into golden flame, to reunite the Kingdom of Lamaira to defend it from evil, though it did not specify when."

Fariak nodded. "The entirety of the Old Kingdom is based around that prophecy. It is what has led us to try to keep everything the way it was before King Riuno's death, so that when the Rightful Heir returns to claim the throne, he will be able to use it to restore Lamaira to its original glory."

"So …" Maryal looked at Keo, uncertainty in her blue eyes. "Does that mean that Keo is the Rightful Heir to the throne?"

"Maybe," said Fariak. "I don't know for sure. I am but a humble Knight and not a very well educated one at that, but I know the prophecy by heart and you are the first person I know of who fits the prophecy's description of the Rightful Heir to a tee."

"Our Keo, the son of King Riuno and heir to the throne of the Kingdom of Lamaira?" said Dlaine in disbelief. He looked at

Keo. "No offense, Keo. I just can't see you wearing a crown and waving a scepter around without accidentally hitting a foreign delegate in the face and starting a war with some foreign country accidentally."

Keo rolled his eyes, but said to Fariak, "I'm not sure I'm your man. I'm just the apprentice of a swordsman who lives in the middle of nowhere. I'm not special."

"Are you sure?" Fariak said. "From what you've told me, you are a young man from the wilderness who wields a sword of golden flame and is trying to reunite the three major factions that control what was once the Kingdom of Lamaira to defend it against evil. That fits the description of the Rightful Heir almost perfectly."

"But I'm not a king or royalty at all," said Keo. "Granted, I don't know who my real parents are, but I doubt they were anyone of note. They were killed by bandits shortly after I was born and they left me nothing, which would make no sense if they were royalty."

"Why do you seem so eager to disqualify yourself?" said Fariak, tilting his head in confusion. "Why would you not jump at the opportunity to become the King of Lamaira?"

"Because I don't care about that," said Keo, folding his arms over his chest. "I only care about stopping the demons and saving everyone. Someone else can rule, if they want."

Fariak looked very disappointed by that, but then he shook his head and said, "Well, I might be wrong, anyway. But there is only one way to know for sure."

"And what is that way?" said Keo.

"Go to Tain and speak with the Keepers of the Old Kingdom,"

said Fariak. "Tain is not too far from here, just a couple days' journey on foot, so you should be able to make it there very quickly if you don't delay or run into any obstacles along the way."

"Who are these 'Keepers of the Old Kingdom' you speak of?" said Keo. "I've never heard of 'em."

"I have," said Dlaine. "They're the leaders of the Old Kingdom, right?"

"Correct," said Fariak. "After King Riuno's tragic death twenty-three years ago, some of his advisers, generals, and loyalists took control of the Old Kingdom in an effort to preserve it for the Rightful Heir's arrival. They are wise and fair rulers and have led us well for these two decades."

"How can the Keepers tell if I am related to King Riuno or not?" said Keo.

"I do not know the exact process they will use to determine that, but it is common knowledge among the citizens of the Old Kingdom that the Keepers can do it," said Fariak.

"Okay, but why would the Keepers grant me an audience?" said Keo. "They don't know me, so they have no reason to speak with me."

"Good point," said Fariak. He looked at Rez. "Rez, please get me a sheet of parchment and a quill and ink pot."

As wordlessly as always, Rez nodded, stood up, and left the dining room, but only for a brief moment. In another second, he was back, with all of the things that Fariak had requested. He placed them on the table in front of Fariak and quickly and quietly took his seat as Fariak dipped the tip of the quill in the ink pot and started scribbling quickly.

"What are you doing?" said Keo, watching Fariak with interest; he could not write himself, but he always enjoyed watching other people do it.

"Writing a letter of introduction that you should give to General Knight Sir Abohji in Tain," said Fariak without looking up from his writing. "If you give it to him, he will take you to the Keepers. He knows me, so when he sees that this letter is from me, he will know he can trust you."

"Well, that solves that little problem of ours," said Dlaine. "And we can even tell the Keepers about the demons while we're there. So we can kill two birds with one stone."

"Indeed," said Fariak as he finished writing the letter. He placed the quill down, folded the letter, stamped it with his seal, and then pushed it across the table to Keo. "Please take good care of it. And do not break the seal. If you do, Sir Abohji will not read it."

Keo took the folded letter and looked at the seal on it. The seal resembled the head of a dragon breathing fire, with a sword behind its head. It was a detailed seal, despite being so small, so Keo put it in his bag carefully to avoid damaging it.

"Thanks," said Keo, looking at Fariak again. "I don't know how we can ever repay you for your kindness."

"It is fine," said Fariak, waving off Keo's thanks like it was nothing. "You can repay me by stopping the demons and restoring the Kingdom of Lamaira to its original glory, whether or not you are the Rightful Heir that we have been awaiting for so long."

Keo nodded, but before he could say anything else, the floor of the dining room shook. It was only for a moment, but Keo was certain that he had felt it.

"What was that?" said Keo. He looked at the others. "Did anyone else just feel the floor shake?"

"We did," said Fariak, who was now looking around. "But that doesn't make any sense, because the border mountains don't have earthquakes or tremors."

"Then what was—" said Keo before he was interrupted by the doors to the dining room blowing open, like they had been blown open by a bomb. A huge smoke cloud funneled through the open doorways, obscuring whoever had caused that explosion.

"What in the name of the Good King—?" said Fariak as he and everyone else stood up, everyone reaching for their weapons as they stared at the smoke-filled doorway. "Who goes there? Identify yourself or face the wrath of the Knights of the Old Kingdom!"

A second later, a tall, gangly man stepped out of the smoke. He wore the black robes of a Magician and carried no weapons that Keo could see, but that was hardly the most interesting or noteworthy part of the man. What Keo really focused on was the man's face.

Or rather, the steel mask that obscured the man's features. It had two eye holes, revealing mad green eyes that darted around the room like a Low Woods lion searching for prey. There was no hole for the mouth or the nose, though there were a series of vents near the mouth, probably to allow the strange-looking man to breathe. The mask covered his entire head, making it impossible to tell what color his hair was or if he even had any at all, although Keo decided that they had far more important things to worry about at the moment than the masked stranger's hair style.

Then the masked stranger's green eyes focused on Keo. He

lifted one finger and pointed at him, and when he spoke, his voice was somewhat muffled through his mask.

"Keo of the Sword," said the masked stranger, his voice full of manic glee. "There you are. You are a tricky one to find, but as always, the Tracker never fails to find—and soon, kill—his target."

Chapter Four

THE TRACKER?" SAID KEO in confusion. He looked at Dlaine and Maryal. "Do you know who this guy is?"

Keo was surprised to see that both Dlaine and Maryal were as pale as ghosts. They didn't even seem to hear his question, so petrified with fear they were. Indeed, if Keo hadn't known any better, he would have said that they had both died right there on the spot.

Finally, however, Dlaine said, in a shaky voice, "He's Eliam of the Tracking, also known as Eliam the Tracker, so-named because he can track down anyone no matter where they go. And he is one of South Lamaira's worst criminals."

"How bad is he?" said Keo.

"He slaughtered an entire village full of innocent people about a year ago," said Dlaine. He shuddered. "I visited the place about a week after he did his dirty deeds. So many dead children, destroyed homes … three hundred people dead."

"So you are familiar with my work?" said Eliam, his muffled voice as mad as his eyes. "How wonderful. Many of the greatest artists of the age did not get recognition for their work 'til long after their deaths, but I, it appears, shall be recognized and remembered for my work much sooner."

"But I don't understand," said Maryal, who was literally shaking with fear now. "He shouldn't be here. He was arrested about a week before we went to Capitika. He was supposed to be tried and then executed for his crimes."

Eliam put his hands on his chest. "You are correct, traitor, that I was supposed to be executed. But Magician Nesma herself intervened in my trial, telling the court to give me over to her to perform a mission for her that, if successful, will result in me being pardoned for my crimes. Can you guess what that mission is?"

Keo gulped. "Kill me?"

"Exactly," said Eliam, nodding. "You are smarter than you look, boy. Yes, Magician Nesma was very clear that I must kill the 'murderer' known as Keo of the Sword. Now I have no idea who you killed, young man, nor do I care, because if this will allow me to avoid meeting the executioner's blade, then I will be more than happy to kill you and drag your body—or what's left of it, anyway —back to Capitika as proof of my success."

Nesma's truly lost it if she's depending on violent criminals like this guy to kill me, Keo thought, but aloud he said, "How did you track us down?"

Eliam, however, wagged a finger at Keo. "No, no, no. We Magicians don't reveal our secrets, least of all the secrets of my unique tracking ability. But, as an artist of explosions and chaos, I will accept it as a compliment, because only true artists are asked questions about their methods."

"What about my men?" said Fariak. He drew his broadsword. "I had a couple of my brothers set up outside to protect the guard tower. What did you do with them?"

Eliam tapped the metal chin of his mask. "They got in the way, so I blew them up. Hardly an elegant solution, I know, but even we artists must occasionally sacrifice elegance to practicality when our very freedoms are on the line."

Fariak's broadsword shook in his hands. "You monster. I will kill you in the names of my brothers you killed!"

"Sorry, old man, but I'm not here for you," said Eliam. He nodded at Keo. "All I need is Keo, although I was told to get his two friends if I could as well, because Nesma said she'd give me a thousand lems for each of his friends I brought in. And truthfully, I could use the money once I'm free, even though we artists do not crave money nearly as much as some."

"How dare you speak so contemptuously of me," said Fariak. "But it doesn't matter, because Rez and I will avenge our fallen brothers just the same."

"What?" said Keo, glancing over his shoulder at them. "You shouldn't. We can take him, but you guys—"

"We will fight," Fariak cut him off. "You four must escape to Tain while we hold off this monster. There is a back door you can leave from, so you do not need to bypass Eliam."

"But—"

"It is imperative that you go to Tain and meet with the Keepers," said Fariak. "Because if you truly are the Rightful Heir, then we cannot risk your life by allowing you to fight him."

Keo bit his lower lip, but then nodded and said, "All right. We'll head out now. Good luck."

"Hold on," said Eliam in annoyance. "When did I say that I was going to let you leave? I have spent the better part of a month following you through the wilderness and I, for one, am not going to let all of that work go to waste by allowing you to escape at the last moment."

Eliam raised his hands, no doubt to cast a spell, but then Rez drew a couple of boomerangs from his belt and hurled them both at Eliam. The boomerangs struck Eliam's hands, causing him to curse in pain as he jerked his hands back to his body.

The boomerangs flew back into Rez's hands, while Keo took advantage of that moment to run to the door on the opposite side of the room. With Dlaine and Maryal following him, Keo burst through the door even as he heard Fariak and Rez charge toward Eliam, who was now cursing furiously through his thick steel mask.

As Keo, Dlaine, and Maryal ran down the staircase, Keo said, "All right, guys. Once we get out, we're just going to run straight east, in the direction of Tain, and we don't stop until nightfall. Okay?"

"But what about the Knights?" said Maryal, glancing over her shoulder as another explosion sounded from the dining room, though it was somewhat muted by the doors. "Is there any way we can help them?"

"No," said Keo, shaking his head. "You heard Fariak. They are going to hold Eliam back while we escape."

"And what if Eliam kills them and tracks us down again?" said Dlaine.

"I don't even want to think about it," said Keo. "But if we must, we can fight."

They reached the back door quickly and Keo wrenched it open, allowing all four of them to spill out. They emerged into the morning sun, which shone brightly, in stark contrast to the fear and terror that filled Keo's heart. There was a path leading back onto the Pass, so they ran toward it.

Even as they ran, however, a louder-than-usual explosion caused them to skid to a stop and look back at the guard tower. The roof had exploded, sending chunks of flaming wood flying everywhere, and before their startled eyes, the entire building collapsed on itself with an even louder *boom*.

"Fariak! Rez!" Keo shouted, despite himself. "No!"

"Come on, Keo," said Dlaine, pushing him along. "Keep going. No guarantee that Eliam died, so we just got to keep going so he can't catch us. We can worry about Fariak and Rez later."

Despite his desire to go back to the guard tower and see if Fariak and Rez had survived, Keo nodded and soon they were running down the Cloudway Pass, not looking back at the burning, destroyed remains of the guard tower that they had escaped from.

They ran for a couple of hours until the guard tower and the smoke rising from it were lost from view behind the peaks of the mountains. Exhaustion forced them to run much more slowly than usual, but they still walked as quickly as they could, despite the rocky and uneven path they took. Keo expected Eliam to come chasing them any second, but no one chased them as they ran east, which was the general direction in which the city of Tain lay.

By late evening, when the sun was going behind the mountains and everything was becoming dark, Keo, Dlaine, and Maryal (and probably Jola, too, but Keo could not see or hear her, so he did not know how she felt) were forced to make camp in an empty but shallow cave they found. It was well off the main path, which meant that it was unlikely that anyone would stumble upon them, but Keo knew that if Eliam was still alive, he would probably not have any trouble tracking them down regardless of where they went.

Sitting around a fire that Dlaine had made from some of the wood he carried in his pack, Keo leaned against the cavern wall, panting as he popped open his flask and drank from it. The cold water felt good on his dry throat, but he stopped drinking quickly in order to avoid using it up too quickly.

Then, lowering his flask, Keo looked at Dlaine and Maryal. Dlaine looked even more exhausted than Keo, probably due to his age. He looked like he wanted to sleep, but his eyes remained open and kept darting to the opening, though it was too dark to see very much outside, and besides, Jola was probably keeping watch as she always did, so Keo did not see any reason to worry about anything that might be out there.

As for Maryal, she looked even worse than Dlaine, probably because she was not as used to physically demanding outdoors tasks like he was. She was just lying on the cave floor, panting hard, drinking from her own flask. Her face was still pale, despite how hard they had run, perhaps because of her fear of Eliam.

"So ..." said Keo in between pants. "I guess we're safe for now. I doubt Eliam survived the guard tower collapsing on itself like that."

"Don't ... don't count on it," said Dlaine, wiping sweat off of his face. "Eliam's a madman, but he's also a tricky bastard. He once survived a cave-in that trapped him several feet underground and no one is sure how."

"But the building outright collapsed on him," said Keo. "No one could survive that."

"Logically, yes, it should have killed him, but logic doesn't always apply to Eliam," said Dlaine. "The best I am willing to hope for is that Eliam got stuck underneath a particularly heavy support beam or something and so can't chase us, but I doubt even that will hold him long."

Keo shuddered. "I just can't believe that Nesma would send that madman after me. I know she hates me because she thinks I murdered an 'angel,' but I would never have guessed that she would have sent one of South Lamaira's worst criminals after me."

"Agreed," said Dlaine, nodding. "I've never even heard of the Magical Council doing this sort of thing before. Makes me wonder just how badly that demon messed with your friend's head."

"He had a year in which to do it," said Keo grimly. "When I spoke with Nesma, she seemed like a completely different person. Do any of the old stories talk about demons corrupting and manipulating humans?"

Dlaine shook his head. "None that I know of, but I'm no storyteller, so what do I know? All I know is that this just makes it more urgent than ever that we find King Riuno's son."

"You mean … the Rightful Heir?" said Maryal as she sat up. She looked at Keo. "Didn't Fariak say that *Keo* is the Rightful Heir?"

"It was just a theory of his," said Keo, rolling his eyes. "Just because I match the description of the guy in the prophecy doesn't mean I'm actually him."

"Yeah, but you yourself said that you never knew your parents," Maryal pointed out. "Could it be possible that your parents were King Riuno and his wife?"

"No," said Keo flatly. "My master, Tiram, told me that he found me abandoned in the woods when I was less than a year old. The Low Woods are a long way away from Tain, the old capital of the Kingdom of Lamaira, where Riuno and his wife would have lived. If I was royalty, I wouldn't have been anywhere near the Low Woods."

"Good point," said Maryal. She sighed and looked out into the darkness outside. "Maybe it isn't your destiny to ascend to the throne and become the King of Lamaira. But we won't know for sure until we meet these Keepers that Fariak told us about."

"Right," said Keo. "I just don't expect them to tell me anything except that I'm an ordinary swordsman, no different from any other, with a destiny no more special than anyone else's."

Then Maryal looked at Keo again, a curious look in her eyes. "Except for those golden flames on your sword. How do you explain that?"

"I don't," said Keo with a shrug. "But I don't really accept Fariak's explanation for it, either."

"But it's the only explanation we have at the moment," said Dlaine. He folded his hands behind his head. "Despite my joke earlier, I actually think it would be pretty nice to have a king as my friend. Maybe you could even give me my own small domain to rule over. I'd call it Dlaine Land or something like that."

Keo again rolled his eyes, but then suddenly yawned. Stretching his limbs, Keo said, "I'm done talking. We ran all day today, so I think we need to rest. But first thing in the morning, we head out for Tain, all right?"

When Dlaine and Maryal voiced agreement, Keo curled up

into a ball on the floor of the cave, in front of the warm fire, and closed his eyes, with Gildshine lying on the floor by his side.

But despite what Keo had just said, he found it hard not to think about what it would be like if he actually was the Rightful Heir spoken of in the prophecy. He had to admit that it was very eerie how closely he fit the description of the Rightful Heir as written in the prophecy.

If I was the Rightful Heir, then I *could stop the demons all by myself,* Keo thought. *I would just need to reunite the Kingdom, but I'm already trying to do that. I really don't want to rule, but maybe ruling the Kingdom of Lamaira wouldn't be such a bad thing. Maybe I would be a good king. Maybe it is my destiny after all.*

It was those thoughts that accompanied Keo as he drifted slowly into sleep. He even dreamed about sitting on a throne giving orders to his subjects, leading armies against the forces of the demons. And he found that he enjoyed the dreams quite a bit.

Chapter Five

IN THE MORNING, KEO awoke to discover that Eliam had apparently not tracked them down and murdered them in the middle of the night. Jola did not report seeing Eliam or anyone else outside of their cave, which, in Keo's opinion, was proof enough that the Tracker had indeed met his inglorious end back there at the guard tower. Dlaine still opined that Eliam was probably just badly injured and so could not chase after them as quickly as he normally could, but that he would sooner or later catch up with them despite their best efforts to lose him.

But as they spent the rest of the day traveling down the mountains, they did not run into anyone else, nor did they see any sign of Eliam following them. Even so, Keo kept his hand on Gildshine's hilt, keeping his eyes and ears open for any potential dangers or enemies along the path.

When they reached the foot of the mountains, they camped again, this time using their tents for shelter, because the foot of the mountains had no caves to hide in or trees to sleep under. In fact, the Old Kingdom was, as far as Keo could see, very flat country, with wide-open fields and roads that stretched on for as far as the eye could see, which was very different from South Lamaira's forests.

In any case, Keo and his friends traveled along the rough dirt road that led from the mountain straight into the flat lands. They made good time, covering vast distances each day, because the flatness of the land made it easy to walk quickly without getting too tired. They did not see anyone else along the path, although occasionally they passed by decayed houses and barns that apparently once belonged to farmers, though no one used them now.

It was only a few days later that the city of Tain appeared on the horizon. At first, it looked like a couple of tall lines reaching toward the sky, but as they drew closer, Keo saw more and more detail of the city itself. It had tall, gray walls, spiral towers with red roofs, and even what appeared to be a massive castle in the center, although from a distance it was impossible to see the castle in any great detail. Even so, there was no doubt that their journey was nearly at an end; in fact, the sight of the city spurred them to walk even faster along the road in order to reach it more quickly.

"Wow," said Keo as they walked, his eyes fixed on the city in the distance. "That didn't take us very long at all. And we didn't run into too many obstacles along the way, either."

"Yeah," said Maryal, nodding, a smile on her face. "I kept expecting a demon or something to pop out of the ground and try to eat us. But it looks like the rest of our journey is smooth sailing from here on out."

"Hey, I'm not complaining," said Dlaine, though he looked over his shoulder as if he expected to see Eliam following them again. "And maybe I was wrong. I guess Eliam really *is* dead. Otherwise, he would have already caught up with us by now."

Keo nodded. He could only think about meeting with the Keepers of the Old Kingdom and informing them of the demons' return. He wasn't sure whether they would believe him or not, but if he turned out to be the Rightful Heir spoken of in the prophecy, then they probably would. But if he didn't turn out to be the Rightful Heir … well, then that meant that Keo would need to figure out another way to convince them about the demons' return. How he would do that, exactly, Keo was not sure, but he was certain that he would find a way. Maybe they even had a Magician who could read weapons like Nesma and thus would be able to confirm the existence and return of the demons.

But as they approached the city's walls, Keo saw someone running down the road toward them. It was a young man of about eighteen, who appeared to be a messenger of some sort if the bag full of letters at his side was a clue.

Keo, Dlaine, and Maryal stopped to watch the gangly youth run toward them at full speed, causing Keo to raise his hand and say, "Hello there, messenger. Where are you—"

The messenger zipped past Keo, Dlaine, and Maryal without even looking at them. In fact, he ran by so fast that for a moment Keo thought that his eyes must have been playing tricks on him, but then he realized that his eyes were working fine and he turned around to see the messenger running up the road the way they had came.

"Hey!" Keo shouted. "Where are you going? We want to talk!"

But the messenger apparently ignored Keo, or maybe had not heard him, because he kept running like the wind. That made Keo think that they would never see him again, but then Dlaine snapped his fingers, a common signal he used to communicate with Jola, and in the next instant the messenger fell flat on his face onto the dirt road. The messenger tried to get up, but he was dragged back down the road toward them, which Keo figured was Jola's doing, because Maryal didn't look like she was using any of her spells to capture the messenger.

"Hey!" the messenger protested as he was dragged closer and closer to Keo and the others. "What is this sorcery? Let me go!"

But Jola did not let go of the messenger until he was right in front of Keo and the others, at which point the messenger's feet became separated from each other and the messenger himself jumped to his feet. He glared at Keo and the others, which would have been a lot more frightening if he was not such a skinny youth.

"Who the hell do you people think you are?" the messenger demanded. He rubbed his ankles and his back. "Manhandling me like that … why, this is unheard of. I should report you to the Knights of the Old Kingdom for this assault."

"My friend here wanted to know where you were going," said Dlaine, gesturing at Keo. "And also if you could tell us where General Knight Sir Abohji is, because we need to meet with him right away."

The messenger sighed impatiently. He pointed at the castle rising from the center of the city. "General Knight Sir Abohji is at the Old Castle, where the Keepers are, as most everyone else in the city is, due to today's momentous occasion."

"Momentous occasion?" said Dlaine. He frowned. "Is today some kind of holiday or something?"

"No, but I imagine it will be in the future," said the messenger. "Anyway, I must be off. I have absolutely urgent news to share with the rest of the Old Kingdom and I cannot waste any more time talking with ruffians like you about such inane things."

The messenger turned to leave, but then Dlaine caught the collar of the messenger's shirt and said, "Hold on. What's happened today that's so important that you have to tell the entire Old Kingdom about it?"

The messenger sighed impatiently again, but then looked at Keo and the others. And when he spoke, he sounded far happier and full of hope, in stark contrast to his earlier impatience.

"The prophecy handed down to us ages ago by the Old One has been fulfilled," said the messenger. He pointed at Tain again, at the large castle rising from within its city walls. "The long lost son of King Riuno—the *shelmai*, the Rightful Heir—has returned to claim the Throne and restore the Old Kingdom to its original glory at long last. Praise be to the Good King!"

Before Keo or the others could ask him to elaborate, the messenger shrugged Dlaine's hand off of his collar and dashed up the road again. Soon, he was out of sight, heading to the farthest reaches of the Old Kingdom to spread this news.

Keo looked at Dlaine and Maryal. "Did he just say what I think he said?"

"That King Riuno's long lost son has returned?" said Dlaine. "Yeah, I heard that, too."

"As did I," said Maryal. Her shoulders slumped. "I guess that means you aren't the Rightful Heir after all, Keo."

Keo nodded, but he tried to hide his own disappointment. "It appears so, but it does seem strange how he just managed to show up right when we went looking for him. Seems like far too much of a coincidence to me."

"It's destiny," Maryal said, rubbing her hands together eagerly.

"Destiny must want us to find King Riuno's son and tell him about the demons' return so he can reunite the Kingdom, just as he is prophesied to do. It makes sense."

"That might be true, but I have a lot of questions that that messenger kid left unanswered," said Dlaine. He looked at the city of Tain. "It seems almost too good to be true, but hey, maybe it's destiny like you said. Guess we won't know for sure until we enter the city and get a chance to speak with the guy himself."

"All right," said Keo, nodding again. "But I think we should be careful about who we tell about the demons when we get there. You never know who might be listening or what other people might do with that information if they had it."

"Right," said Dlaine. "I was just about to say that. Anyway, let's go. Don't want to be late for our date with the King's son, after all."

Upon arriving at the city gates, Keo saw that the gates had images engraved upon their surface. They showed scenes of some warrior, wielding a flaming sword, fighting against giant flying creatures that looked like strange dragon/demon hybrids. Keo guessed that the warrior on the gates was the Good King, because he knew of no other figure in legend who wielded a flaming sword, and he guessed that the dragon/demon monsters the Good King fought were demons.

But Keo paid little attention to that because he was more interested in entering the city and meeting the long-lost son of King Riuno rather than whatever the engraved images might show. He, Dlaine, Maryal, and Jola simply marched up to the gates, where the guards—a couple of Knights wearing old-fashioned armor, similar to what Fariak and the border Knights had worn—searched their belongings. According to the gatekeepers, this was the standard procedure for every visitor to Tain, because they wanted to make sure that travelers from out of the city were not coming to cause any trouble or break any laws. The gatekeepers showed some hesitation to letting Maryal in for some reason, but when they looked through her belongings and found nothing to suggest she was dangerous, they let her and the other inside.

Upon stepping through the gates, Keo was reminded of Capitika. Like Capitika, Tain had many tall buildings, but they all seemed older than Capitika's buildings. That did not mean that they looked bad, however. Most of the buildings looked magnificent and grand, including one building with a couple of statues of King Riuno standing at the entrance. Tain felt like it had stood for many centuries and that it would continue to stand for many more, which made sense, because Dlaine had told Keo that the old legends said that the Good King had founded Tain a thousand years ago, which was why it had been the capital of the Kingdom of Lamaira prior to King Riuno's death.

But Keo did not focus too much on the buildings. Instead, he looked around at its many streets and frowned. "Which way is it to the Old Castle?"

"Not sure," said Dlaine, scratching his chin as he, too, looked around. "I've never been here before. Maybe we should have asked the gatekeepers for directions before we entered the city."

At that moment, two young children—a boy and a girl, both probably about ten—dashed past them suddenly, but Keo called out, "Hey! Can you help us?"

The boy and the girl skid to a stop and looked over their shoulders at Keo and the others. They appeared to be siblings, based on the fact that their hair color and noses were almost exactly alike, and their clothing was even similar, too; dirty-looking shirts and pants that had patched holes.

"Yes, mister?" said the young boy. "What do you need?"

Keo was surprised at how easily the young boy asked him that question, because Keo was a stranger to the boy. He supposed that the Tainians were friendlier to strangers than the people of New Ora had been.

Nonetheless, Keo said, "We want to go to the Old Castle. Can you give us directions to it? We're not from around here and don't know our way around the city."

"Of course," said the young boy. He pointed in the direction that he and the young girl had been running in. "Just go up this street, turn right in a couple of blocks, and then—"

"Jos," said the young girl suddenly, grabbing the boy's arm. "Stop talking to them. Momma said we're not supposed to talk to strangers."

The young boy looked at the young girl—who apparently was in fact his sister—in annoyance. "I know that, but Momma ain't here and these people seem nice, so why shouldn't I talk to 'em?"

The boy's sister pointed at Maryal. "Because that lady is a Magician! She's wearing robes just like the ones in Daddy's pictures. And you know what Momma always said about Magicians."

Jos, the young boy, suddenly gulped. He stared at Maryal in fear before turning and running up the street, with his sister at his side, until they turned a corner and vanished from view.

Maryal folded her arms over her chest. "What was *that* all about? How does me being a Magician somehow make me inherently untrustworthy?"

"No, but I understand their distrust of you," said Dlaine. "Remember, the Restorationists are at war with the Magicians. Those kids have probably grown up hearing about how many West Lamairans the Magicians have killed in war, maybe including members of their own family. No wonder they ran when they realized what you are."

"But I wouldn't harm a fly," Maryal protested.

"I know, but they don't know that," said Dlaine. He scratched his chin. "It might be wise for you to ditch the robes, at least until we leave the city. We're lucky we just ran into a couple of scared kids. If we had run into some war veterans, well, I doubt we'd still be standing here having this conversation."

Maryal looked down at her robes. "Get rid of my robes? But these are what all Magicians wear."

"True, but if that will just make people think we're spies from South Lamaira, then you should take 'em off for now," said Dlaine. "Unless, of course, you think it is our destiny to get lynched by a mob of angry Restorationists before we can tell the Keepers about the demons, that is."

Maryal sighed, but started to remove her robes just the same. Soon she was wearing nothing except for her green tunic and pants and her robes were safely folded and stored inside her travel bag. She looked very small and skinny without her robes on, not to mention vulnerable, but Keo had to admit that if he had not known that Maryal was a Magician, he would not have been able to guess that she was one now.

"There," said Maryal. She looked at Dlaine in annoyance. "Happy?"

"Hey, don't get annoyed at me," said Dlaine, holding up his hands. "It's the Restorationists who don't feel butterflies in their stomach whenever they think about Magicians, not me. Well, okay, I don't, either, but I, at least, don't have a murderous hatred of the Magicians."

"Except for when you tried to kill Nesma," Keo pointed out.

"That was different," said Dlaine with a scowl. "The Magical Council is corrupt and needs to be overthrown. That doesn't mean I have any actual, special hatred for Magicians or anything like that."

Keo nodded, but he still hadn't entirely forgiven Dlaine for trying to assassinate Nesma. Yes, he understood Dlaine's dislike of the Magical Council, and yes, he knew he should have hated Nesma for the many times that she had tried to kill him, but he still could not bring himself to hate her or wish she was dead, regardless of how she had treated him. He only allowed Dlaine to travel with them because Dlaine's age and experience were a big help in their journeys. Besides, Dlaine had claimed that the Rebel Leader had given him the okay to travel with Keo, because Dlaine and Jola were not needed in South Lamaira at the moment and helping Keo would eventually lead to the destruction of the Magical Council anyway.

But Keo stopped thinking about that when he heard the sound of trumpets blaring from somewhere in the city. It sounded like it was coming from the Old Castle, prompting Keo to say, "We can talk about this later. It sounds like something important is about to happen, like a festival or celebration, so let's get to the Old Castle as quickly as possible."

"First, we need directions," said Dlaine. "Let's ask around."

It didn't take them long to find an elderly man who was happy to give them directions to the Old Castle. Following those directions, Keo, Dlaine, Jola, and Maryal made their way through Tain's streets, which seemed empty, probably because everyone was at the Old Castle, as the messenger outside the city had said. Of the few people they did see, no one looked at them funny, which meant that they did not suspect Keo and the others of being foreigners. Maryal, however, still looked uncomfortable about walking around without her robes on, but she did not draw any unnecessary attention to them, at least.

As they walked, Keo could not help but notice how different Tain was from Capitika. Its white, grand buildings, statues of King Riuno and old streets reminded Keo of the ruins of the city of Castarious near the Silver Falls back in South Lamaira. The main difference between Tain and Castarious, however, was that Tain was in far better condition than Castarious, no doubt due to the fact that Tain was still inhabited while Castarious was not.

As they drew closer to the Old Castle, the sounds of trumpets, drums, and other instruments playing became louder and louder, until soon Keo and the others found themselves standing behind a large crowd of people standing on the sides of the street. The crowd were apparently watching a parade of some sort going by, but Keo did not see anything at first except for a marching band marching through the streets on the other side of the crowd, several dozen men and women playing a variety of instruments, many of which Keo could not identify.

Curious about what this was all about, Keo walked up to one

of the spectators and asked, raising his voice to be heard above the music and cheering of the crowds, "What is going on here? Is this a parade?"

The spectator—a man with a handle-bar mustache—looked at Keo, a joyous smile on his face. "Haven't you heard? King Riuno's long-lost son, the *shelmai*, has returned! He is about to walk down these streets so that we commoners may see him ourselves! But," the man added, a sly look on his face, "I saw the King's son before he went to the Keepers and had them confirm his identity. Thought he was just another traveler, I did, and I even sold him some bread. Had I known then what I do now ... I would have simply given him the bread for free."

"Uh, right," said Keo. He looked over the heads of the cheering crowd, but still did not see the King's long-lost son. "What is King Riuno's son's name?"

"He calls himself Easan," said the man, who briefly looked back to the front of the crowd, probably to make sure that Easan was not walking by just yet. "But it doesn't really matter what his name is. He is the *shelmai*, the Rightful Heir, and soon the Kingdom of Lamaira will rise again, with him sitting on the Throne, as whole and strong as it was before King Riuno's tragic death!"

Keo nodded, but it was more out of politeness than agreement. "But, not to sound skeptical, how do we know that Easan is indeed the *shelmai*, the Rightful Heir?"

"The Keepers confirmed it," said the man, rubbing his hands together excitedly. "Easan—excuse me, *King* Easan, because that's what he really is or soon will be—went to the Keepers and they, through their own methods, confirmed his identity. It is a miracle, but it is true."

"When did Easan get here?" said Keo. "Sorry if I'm asking a lot of questions, but my friends and I just got here, so we don't know very much about everything that's happened recently."

"Easan arrived about a week ago," said the man. "But we didn't know that he was the Rightful Heir until just yesterday. Right now, we are waiting for him to come down the street to the Old Castle, a tradition that every new King of Lamaira used to do when they were of age to rule, a tradition that has now been revived. Great joy!"

Keo glanced at Dlaine and Maryal in surprise before looking back at the man. "So Easan will be crowned King of Lamaira today?"

"Not today, no," said the man, shaking his head. "This is just a ceremony to let everyone see him and know who he is. To let everyone know that our shattered Kingdom will be restored, that the prophecy has been fulfilled, and that the wars that have claimed so many of our finest young men—including my only son—will finally be over and that a new age of peace will be upon us."

The man spoke highly emotionally, so emotionally that Keo almost believed the man's words himself. But Keo reined his emotions in, because he wanted to learn more about this Easan fellow before he came to any conclusions about him.

Then the man suddenly looked back to the front of the crowd and gasped. "He's coming."

"Who's coming?" said Keo. "Easan?"

"Yes," said the man with a sigh.

Keo turned to look at Dlaine and Maryal. "I'm going to the

front of the crowd to see him. Come on."

Without waiting for either of their responses, Keo turned and started pushing through the crowd, although no one seemed to notice him, probably because they were so focused on Easan's arrival that they wouldn't have noticed Keo even if he had been cutting them down using Gildshine. He reached the front of the crowd and stopped before the white ribbons that separated the crowds from the parade route just in time to see a single man walking down the street. The entire crowd—easily hundreds strong—went silent as the man walked down the street.

The man who walked down the street all by himself strode with a confident and kingly stride. With every step, he made it clear that he was an authority to be obeyed and listened to, yet that he was also a kindly man. There was a fire in his eyes that told Keo that this was a man who desired justice above all else. And in fact, the man's eyes were red, which added to their fiery appearance.

As for the man himself, he looked to be about the same size and age as Keo, perhaps slightly taller. His hair, however, was longer and pure black and he had a square jaw and an aquiline nose. He reminded Keo of something he had seen somewhere, and then it hit him: The man walking down the street—who had to be Easan, because there was no one else that he could be—looked similar to the fallen statue of King Riuno that he had seen back in Castarious about a month and a half ago.

At Easan's side, sheathed in a red scabbard, was a sword that looked similar in size and length to Gildshine. Its handle, however, was gold and black, which looked a lot fancier and nicer than Gildshine's old bandaged handle. And even though the sword was sheathed, Keo could tell that Easan knew how to use it well.

Every step of Easan's leather boots was audible in the silence from the crowd. Keo understood why they had all gone silent. There was something about Easan—the way he walked, the way he held himself, the way he paid little attention to the crowd—that commanded reverent silence from the watchers.

But then, like a king commanding his subjects, Easan raised a hand and waved it at the crowds of spectators on both sides of the streets. As if on cue, the entire crowd applauded and screamed his name. Men shouted praises to the *shelmai*, the Rightful Heir, while women wept at his handsome sight and shouted his name in the hopes that he'd notice them. Even Dlaine and Maryal looked impressed by Easan's control of the crowd, which Keo found hard to resist himself.

As Easan walked, people on both sides of the street reached out to him. Keo at first thought that these were a bunch of thieves trying to steal Easan's sword (which looked like the kind of weapon you could sell to a rich man for a good sum of money), but then he heard the peoples' requests that they shouted at Easan:

"*Shelmai*! Please heal my son with your touch!"

"Rightful Heir! Please remove this deformity from my arm!"

"King Easan! Please bring my son back from the war on the western border! I beg of you!"

That last request actually caused Easan to stop. He turned to look at the woman who had said that, causing Keo to realize that the middle-aged woman who had shouted that request was standing next to him, Dlaine, and Maryal. Easan's attention, however, was on the woman, who had covered her mouth with her hand like she was worried that she might have offended

Easan.

Easan raised his hand again, but this time, the crowd went silent. It was amazing how quickly the crowd became quiet, almost like Easan had pulled an invisible lever that only he could see.

Then Easan lowered his hand and, still looking at the woman, said, "Woman, it is not proper of you to call me 'King' Easan yet, because I have yet to be crowned with my father's crown."

Easan's voice was deep and rich, despite the fact that he was obviously no older than Keo. It was soothing and comforting, yet there was also a slight reprimand to it, like a parent gently rebuking a disobedient child.

"I … I am sorry, *shelmai*," said the woman, who was shaking now as if she feared punishment. "I meant no disrespect. I simply wish for my son to—"

"To return home to peace and safety," Easan finished for her. He looked around at the entire crowd of spectators, a grim expression on his face. "And I promise that, once I am crowned King, I will bring back every son to every mother in Tain and in the other cities and towns in the Old Kingdom. Once I restore the Kingdom of Lamaira, no mother shall ever be forced to watch as her children march off to become one more casualty in the endless wars that have engulfed this nation. This, I swear, as the *shelmai*, the son of King Riuno, and the Rightful Heir to the Throne of Lamaira!"

As Easan shouted that, he drew his sword from its sheath and raised its silver blade above his head. Without warning, the sword burst into magnificent golden flame, much grander and brighter than Keo's flames, its light bathing Easan in a golden glow, adding to his kingly appearance.

The crowd on both sides of the street suddenly burst into wild, uncontrollable applause and shouts of joy, startling Keo. Many of them shouted, "Blessed be the *shelmai*!" and "Praise be to the Rightful Heir!"

But Keo said nothing, because at that moment, Easan looked at him as if he suddenly noticed Keo standing there.

The two stared at each other directly in the eyes for what felt like eternity, though it was probably only a brief moment. Easan looked surprised, as if he had not expected to see Keo here.

But then Easan looked away and continued marching up the street, the golden flames on his blade going out as he sheathed his sword again. The crowd suddenly started chanting, "Bless the *shelmai*! Bless the *shelmai*!" over and over again, while the middle-aged mother who Easan had comforted simply looked relieved that the Rightful Heir had heard her request and had promised to honor it.

But Keo led Dlaine and Maryal out of the crowd, into the back streets, where it was quieter and where fewer people were. He turned to look at them both.

"What did you think of all that?" said Keo, looking from Dlaine to Maryal and back again.

"Easan certainly seemed kingly to me," said Maryal. She sighed. "And he's so handsome and kind, too."

"I'm just curious about his golden flames," said Dlaine, folding his arms over his chest and glancing in the direction from which the chants of the crowd came. "I wonder why you and he can do it when no one else can. It doesn't make sense."

"I agree," said Keo, nodding. "Do you guys think that we'll be able to trust Easan, though?"

"Why wouldn't we?" said Maryal, tilting her head to the side. "Easan seemed like an honest man to me. A bit pompous, maybe, but did you see how he comforted that woman about her son? I've never seen anyone in the Magical Council do that to any of the mothers in South Lamaira who lost their sons to war before."

"That's a good point," said Keo. "He certainly did seem to care about that woman's suffering. There's just something about him I don't like, though."

"Jealous?" Dlaine said with a smirk.

"Jealous? Of what?" said Keo, looking at Dlaine in confusion.

"Jealous that Easan's the Rightful Heir and you're not, of course," said Dlaine. "That should be pretty obvious."

Keo scowled. "I'm not jealous of him or anyone else. I've never wanted to be the King of Lamaira, so what do I have to be jealous of?"

Even as Keo said that, however, he could not help but wonder what it must have felt like to be loved and adored by so many people without even having done anything of note yet. But Keo was not going to admit that receiving that kind of praise and adoration from other people would be nice, nor would he admit that he did in fact feel the tiniest bit envious of Easan's position as the Rightful Heir. He saw no reason to do it.

"Because if *you* had been the Rightful Heir or the *shelmai* or whatever they're calling him, then *you* would have been the one marching through the streets comforting mothers whose sons were sent to war," Dlaine pointed out. "And most people like it when other people praise them like that."

Keo felt his neck getting hot with embarrassment, but he said, in the firmest voice he could, "I don't care one bit about any of that. Let Easan get all of the praise and glory. I was raised by a man who didn't give a damn about what other people thought and I am the same way. All I care about is doing the right thing even if no one knows I did it."

Dlaine, however, didn't look terribly convinced by Keo's pleading. "Sure, kid. Anyway, we need to find Abohji and deliver that letter to him, like Fariak told us. It's the only way we'll get an audience with the Keepers."

"Right," said Keo, who was glad that Dlaine had decided to change the subject. "The messenger said that Abohji is at the Old Castle, right? So let's head over there and give him the letter."

With that, Keo, Dlaine, and Maryal started walking through the streets toward the Old Castle, the top of which was visible over the roofs of the other buildings. Even as they walked, however, Keo could not help but listen to the cheers and chants of the crowds watching Easan, which made him feel far more annoyed—and jealous—than he would ever admit to anyone, even to himself.

Chapter Six

THE OLD CASTLE WAS huge, probably larger than even the Citadel back in Capitika. It had several turrets and towers, all made of a beautiful white stone that made the castle look quite regal. The largest tower rose from the center, its navy blue roof shaped like a stalagmite, while at least a dozen Knights patrolled its walls or stood in front of the gates that separated it from the rest of the city. Again, Keo was reminded of Castarious, because the Old Castle's design reminded him of the twin towers of the ruined city, although the castle looked far better kept than those towers had.

Without hesitation, Keo, Dlaine, and Maryal walked up to the front gates, which looked like the gates to the city, except smaller and without any special engravings on them. Two Knights with purple highlights on their armor (which Keo assumed was an indication of their ranking, though he wasn't sure) stood before the gates, their swords sheathed at their sides, although they looked more than ready to draw their weapons at any moment to fight off any threats to the Old Castle.

One thing Keo noticed about the Old Castle was Easan's absence, but then, he supposed that Easan had probably already entered the Old Castle by this point. In any case, Keo simply walked up to the guards, who immediately looked at Keo and his friends, though it was hard to tell what they were thinking because of the visors of their helmets covering their faces.

"Halt," said one of the Knights, his slightly muffled voice reminding Keo of Fariak. "Who approaches the Old Castle? And what is your business?"

Keo stopped and pointed at himself and the others. "Keo of the Sword, Dlaine of the Fist, and Maryal of the Wind do. As for our business, we wish to speak with General Knight Sir Abohji and the Keepers."

He did not introduce Jola because she was invisible and did not think they would believe him if he told them that she was invisible anyway.

The two Knights exchanged looks (likely puzzled, but their visors made it impossible to see their facial expressions) and then looked at Keo again.

"We were not told that Sir Abohji and the Keepers were expecting visitors today," said the first Knight. He sounded highly suspicious.

"That's because they're not," said Keo. He reached into his bag and fished out the letter that Fariak had given them. He held it out to the Knight. "This letter is from Sir Fariak, the Captain of the southern border patrol. He told us to give this to Sir Abohji."

The first Knight took the folded up letter and looked at it closely through the visor in his helmet. He seemed to be trying to determine if it was a fake or not, but then he nodded and said, "This is indeed the genuine seal of the Old Kingdom. And I recognize Sir Fariak's handwriting from our school days. I will get this to Sir Abohji right away." Then the Knight looked at Keo. "You three, stay here until I return with Sir Abohji's response."

Keo nodded and watched as the first Knight opened the gates

wide enough for him to slip through, but not wide enough for Keo to see what the Old Castle's courtyard looked like. The second Knight continued to watch them while they stood there waiting for his friend to return, but he did not say or do anything to indicate that he was planning to harm them. Likely the second Knight was watching them just to make sure that none of them were going to cause any problems, which made Keo slightly uncomfortable around him, even though neither Keo nor his friends were planning to cause any trouble.

A few minutes later, the first Knight emerged from behind the gate and said, in a far more respectful and less suspicious voice than before, "The General Knight and the Keepers will see you now, travelers. Please follow me."

Keo looked at Dlaine and Maryal with surprise. He had not expected them to be let into the Old Castle so easily. That almost made him suspicious, but then he realized that Fariak and Abohji were both Knights, which meant that they trusted each other's word above all else. If Fariak's letter to Abohji said that Abohji could trust them, then it was only logical that Abohji would invite them in.

So Keo, Dlaine, and Maryal followed the Knight into the open courtyard of the Old Castle. The courtyard was full of servants running to and fro doing various tasks. A couple of male servants were repairing a crack in the walls, while some of the female servants were cleaning up what looked like horse droppings. No one looked up at them as they passed, probably because they were all so engrossed in their work that they had no time to pay attention to the new visitors who were following the Knight around.

The Knight led Keo, Dlaine, and Maryal across the courtyard, up the front steps, and through the front door of the Old Castle. Upon entering the lobby, the first thing Keo noticed were the two large statues of King Riuno standing either side of the doors. The statues were about ten feet tall each, their carved faces looking down on Keo and the others with grim expressions. They looked almost lifelike, especially their mouths, which told Keo that they must have been designed by a master sculpter.

The lobby itself had pristine floors, with white columns along regular ten feet intervals from the door to the other end of the lobby, which appeared to go to the back of the Castle. A single massive staircase in the center of the lobby went all the way up to a door at the very top, while several small staircases along the walls of the lobby appeared to lead into the smaller towers and turrets that Keo had seen outside. The lobby smelled like lemons, much better than the smell of horse manure outside, although Keo did not see anything that might explain where the scent was coming from.

"Welcome to the Old Castle," said the Knight, spreading his arms wide to indicate the lobby. "It was once of the castle of King Riuno before his death, and it was the castle of his father, and the castle of his father's father, going all the way back to the Good King himself."

Keo gaped at the size of the lobby. "This is amazing. I've never been inside a building this huge before, or this old."

"Few have, seeing as only the Keepers, their servants, and their guests are ever allowed in here," said the Knight. "But enough talking. General Abohji and the Keepers are awaiting you in the main tower. Follow me."

The Knight resumed walking across the red carpeting that led to the massive staircase in the center, and Keo and the others followed as usual. They followed the Knight up the tall staircase, toward the door at the very top of the steps. Keo suddenly wondered where Jola was before deciding that she was probably following them as silently and invisibly as always, otherwise she would have contacted them at some point to let them know if she was elsewhere.

When they reached the top of the stairs, the Knight pushed open the door and stepped inside. Keo hesitated briefly—it occurred to him that Easan might be in there and he was not sure that he wanted to speak with the Rightful Heir just yet—but only for a moment. Then he entered and looked around at the room he had entered, while Dlaine and Maryal followed after him.

They had entered a large throne room, parts of the floor covered in the same red carpeting down below in the lobby. Statues and paintings of various figures that Keo did not recognize stood along the walls, which Keo assumed were probably statues and paintings of the past kings of Lamaira. He did not know that for sure, of course, but it seemed logical to him, given how obsessed the inhabitants of the Old Kingdom were with the past and how regal the statues and paintings looked. Even so, that did not make the lifelike statues and paintings look any less magnificent; if anything, Keo found himself in awe of the sheer detail of the statues and paintings. The paintings in particular looked almost like actual pictures of the royalty they depicted and did not appear to be faded in the slightest.

At the end of the other end of the room stood seven thrones, six normal-sized in height, with the seventh twice as large as the individual thrones. The six normal-sized thrones were set on either side of the larger throne, which was empty, in contrast to the smaller thrones, which had people sitting on them. But Keo did not get a good look at the people sitting on the thrones until he followed the Knight over to them, at which point Keo saw that they were a bunch of old men and women.

Half of the seated elders were male, the other half female. They wore robes, but they were not Magician robes. Instead, these robes were far more elaborate and stylized, with gemstones embedded in the cufflinks and collars, meant more for style than practicality, he guessed. Each one of the elders had the seal of the Old Kingdom sewn into the chest and each elder also had their own staff, though their staffs were topped with different colored stones, ranging from red to blue to green to black to brown to white.

All in all, they were a highly regal and important-looking group of people. Yet their own grandness was nothing in comparison to the larger throne in the center, which appeared to have been carved out of crystal and gold, with two carved dragon heads on the armrests and a high back that resembled dragon wings.

Standing just off to the side was another Knight with red accents on his armor, but rather than wear his helmet on his head, he held it under his arm. This Knight looked different from all of the other inhabitants of the Old Kingdom that Keo had seen so far. His hair, for one, was red, and his eyes were slanted. As a result of his different appearance, it was hard for Keo to peg the man's age, but guessed that he was probably older than Keo himself.

When the red-haired man saw them approach, he immediately went over to greet them. As he did so, the Knight who had led them to the throne room said, "Greetings, General Knight Sir Abohji. These are the guests from Sir Fariak's letter, the ones who want to speak with the Keepers."

The red-haired man—obviously Abohji—nodded as he approached, though his eyes were on Keo and his friends rather than on his fellow Knight. "I guessed as much, brother, but thank you for confirming that suspicion for me. You may return to your duties now."

The Knight bowed deeply and then turned around and left, walking around Keo and the others very quickly. He was gone in only a few seconds, thus leaving Keo and his friends with Abohji and the six elders.

Abohji smiled and held out a hand. "Welcome, travelers from the south. I am General Knight Sir Abohji, the General of the Armies of the Old Kingdom. And you three are Keo, Dlaine, and Maryal, yes?" He pointed at each of them in turn as he said that.

Keo blinked in surprise, but shook Abohji's hand anyway. "Uh, yes. How'd you figure out who we all are?"

"Brother Fariak's letter described each of you briefly," said Abohji as he let go of Keo's hand. "It was therefore very easy for me to deduce each of your identities. I've solved far more complex mysteries than that with even less evidence." He looked around. "I don't see Jola, but the letter mentioned that she is invisible, so I assume that she is here even though I cannot see her at the moment."

That was when Keo noticed Abohji's accent. Master Tiram had once told Keo that the various peoples of the three factions did not have extreme differences in accents due to the fact that everyone had been part of the Kingdom of Lamaira in the past, but Abohji's accent—while by no means thick—sounded nothing like any accent Keo had heard so far on his travels. Abohji's words were clearly enunciated, leaving little room for error, which made Keo wonder whether Abohji was not speaking his first language.

Whatever the case, Keo said, "Very impressive." Then he looked over Abohji's shoulder and said, "And they are—?"

Abohji's smile vanished, replaced by an angry scowl. "'And they are'? Listen, foreigner, that is not how you address the Keepers of the Old Kingdom. Had it not been for their wisdom and guidance, the Old Kingdom would have vanished decades ago and Lamaira would be in even worse shape than it is now, so show some respect."

Keo actually backed up at Abohji's sharp tone, even though the Knight had not done a thing to indicate he was going to harm Keo. "Sorry. I didn't know."

Abohji sighed, though it seemed like he was more annoyed at himself than at Keo. "No, no. I apologize. My own temper got the best of me. I should not have shouted at you. That was unnecessary on my part. But you still should treat the Keepers with respect."

"Of course," said Keo, nodding, although he now watched Abohji more warily, because he did not want to accidentally set his temper off again.

"Anyway," said Abohji. He straightened his stance. "Allow me to introduce you to the Keepers of the Old Kingdom." Abohji stepped aside and, after briefly bowing at the Keepers, said,

"Keepers of the Old Kingdom, these are the travelers Sir Fariak's letter spoke of, the ones who claim that the demons of old are rising again. They are Keo of the Sword, Dlaine of the Fist, and Maryal of the Wind. And their invisible friend Jola, who is likely somewhere nearby, though where exactly, I do not know."

The Keepers stared at Keo and his friends with eyes that were hard to read. They appeared to be sizing up Keo and the others and Keo noticed more than a few of them note Gildshine sheathed at his side. It made Keo feel a bit uncomfortable, but he tried not to look guilty of anything so he would not arouse any unnecessary suspicion.

"You four are from the south?" said one of the Keepers, an old man with a long gray beard.

"Yes," said Keo, nodding. "I assume Sir Abohji told you about Sir Fariak's letter and its contents."

"That he did," said the first Keeper, who Keo guessed was the leader of the group. "Sir Fariak's letter claimed that a demon had appeared on the border between the Old Kingdom and South Lamaira, but you travelers helped the border Knights kill it with your magic sword."

The Keeper did not mention Gildshine's blade bursting into golden flames, which made Keo think that Fariak must not have mentioned it in the letter. Or maybe, because of Easan's confirmation as the *shelmai*, the Keeper had already written off Keo as a possible candidate for the Rightful Heir.

Regardless, Keo said, "That's right. But it's not the only demon we've fought on our journey. We've fought and killed four others before we came here."

"*Four* other demons?" said another Keeper, a woman with

hair as white as snow. She looked at her fellow Keepers in shock. "Impossible. The old legends say that the demons were sealed away for good by the Good King. How, then, could you have fought five demons so recently?"

Keo gave a brief but detailed explanation of everything that he and his friends knew about the demons, starting with his fight with the demon in the Low Woods and ending with his battle with Plague of Wrath in Capitika. The Keepers and Abohji listened to his story, some with horrified expressions, others with troubled faces, but not a single one of them interrupted or uttered a word until Keo finished speaking.

Then the first Keeper, the man with the long gray beard, stroked his beard in worry. "If your story is true—and I see no reason it should not, because you must be an honest man if Sir Fariak trusts you—then this is sobering news indeed. The legends of old describe the great slaughter that the demons wrought on humanity in their heyday and, if the demons rise again, then we may see similar chaos soon if we do not stop it."

"Agreed, Aster," said the female Keeper from before. "But if you think about it, not all is lost. We still have five and a half months before the demons rise again, but even better, we have the *shelmai*, the Rightful Heir, Easan, who can ascend to the Throne of the King and restore the seal to its original might."

The Keeper gestured at the large throne in the middle of the other thrones, which Keo now finally understood to be the throne for the next King of Lamaira. Yet Easan was nowhere to be seen, either sitting upon it or standing near it.

"A good point, Seria," said Aster, nodding. "Yes, I almost forgot about Easan. We were supposed to crown him King of

Lamaira today, in fact. His coronation was planned for later in the afternoon, but perhaps we can push it back a little earlier, if his coronation is what will help to save all of Lamaira from the demons."

A pang of jealousy shot through Keo when he heard Aster speak so well of Easan, but he ignored it. "I think we will also need to reunite the entire Kingdom, too."

"Ah, that should not be a problem, I think, with Easan on the Throne," said Aster. He glanced at the Throne. "Easan is a skillful negotiator and orator. He should have no trouble appealing to the loyalists in the other two factions who, like us, have longed for the return of the *shelmai*, who is prophesied to reunite the entire Kingdom of Lamaira upon his ascension to the Throne."

"Do you wish for me to retrieve the Rightful Heir, Your Wiseness?" said Abohji. "He is currently resting in his room from the excitement of the parade."

"Yes, yes, right away," said Aster. He gestured toward the exit. "I want him to know about the demons and to take the Throne so we can begin our preparations for the demons' arrival. The Old Kingdom shall rise again."

Although Keo was still annoyed at how the Keepers treated Easan, he was nonetheless relieved at how quickly the Keepers had believed him. He was now convinced that maybe they would be able to save Lamaira from the demons after all. The biggest obstacle he could see now was reuniting the Kingdom, but he was certain that the Magicians and Divinians would be willing to reunite under Easan after they learned of the threat that the demons posed to them all, even with the Magical Council's resistance.

As for Abohji, he nodded and started walking toward the exit. But just before he reached the door, there was a sudden rumbling in the room that made Keo and everyone else, including the Keepers, look around in surprise.

"What was that rumbling?" said Maryal, rubbing her hands together anxiously. "Does Tain usually have earthquakes?"

"No," said Aster, shaking his head. "I have no idea what it could be. But I doubt it is any good."

At that moment, Keo saw something move out of the top corner of the Throne and looked up, but saw nothing except for the shadows cast by the light of the chandelier.

Then two large, bat-like wings expanded from the back of the Throne, causing Keo to point and shout, "Watch out!"

The words just left his mouth when something with large wings shot out from behind the Throne and soared toward him and the others. Keo and his friends scattered as the large creature flew past them, its wings nearly clipping the back of Keo's head. The Keepers gasped in surprise and fear, while Abohji turned and drew his own sword, watching as the creature clung to the ceiling above.

And when Keo looked up at it, he saw that it was a large, demonic-looking bat with the same blood-red eyes that all demons had. And it was looking at him.

Chapter Seven

WHAT IN THE GOOD King's name is that thing?" said Aster, staring at the giant bat that was glaring down at them from the ceiling. "In all my years, I have never seen anything like that before."

"It's a demon," said Keo as he unsheathed Gildshine and held it before him. "I've never seen this one in particular before, but I recognize the eyes, because all demons have them."

"A demon?" said Seria. She clutched her chest and looked up at the bat demon again. "That is an actual *demon*? Like the ones from the legends?"

"Yes," said Keo, nodding. "And if we don't kill it, it will kill us."

"Keepers!" said Abohji from his position near the door. "I will help defend you from the demon. I—"

"No," said Aster, shaking his head. He pointed at the door. "You must go and get Easan and anyone else you can find. Tell him that a demon has somehow sneaked into the Throne Room and that we need his aid right away."

"But—"

"Go!" Aster shouted. He gestured at Keo and the others. "They can protect us until Easan gets here, seeing as they have fought demons before and know how to fight them."

Abohji looked reluctant to leave the Keepers behind with the demon bat, but he nodded anyway and was out of the Throne Room in an instant.

The demon did not appear to notice Abohji leaving. Instead, it let out a loud screech that made Keo and the others cringe before it swooped down toward them at a frightening speed.

Keo slashed at the demon with Gildshine, but the demon moved out of the way just in the nick of time, causing Gildshine to miss. But then Maryal blasted it with a burst of air, which actually knocked the demon out of the air and sent it crashing to the floor, where it rolled a couple of times before coming to a stop at the feet of a statue of some ancient Lamairan king that Keo did not recognize.

Taking advantage of the demon's dazed state, Keo ran over to it and tried to bring Gildshine down on its body. But the demon covered its body with one of its wings, causing Gildshine to bounce harmlessly off its wing, and then the demon snapped at Keo, but he jumped backwards out of its reach before it could hurt him. He slammed Gildshine into the demon's face, but that just annoyed the demon more than anything, causing it to slap him away with its other wing.

Getting hit by the demon's wing was like getting punched by a giant. The blow sent Keo flying and he hit the marble floor hard, temporarily stunned from the impact of the fall. He recovered quickly enough to raise his head just in time to see the demon fly towards Maryal and Dlaine, who were near the Keepers trying to keep them safe from the demon.

Maryal tried blasting it out of the air again with another burst of wind, but the demon avoided that attack and slashed at her with its claws. The blow hit her in the head, causing her to collapse immediately, although she looked more unconscious than dead, thankfully.

Dlaine, on the other hand, avoided its claws, but ended up getting smacked in the face by its wing. That knocked him flat off his feet and must have hit him harder than it looked, because he did not get up again.

The demon turned to face the Keepers, who still sat petrified in their thrones, but then a blast of fire that came seemingly from nowhere—no, from Jola—struck the demon in the back. It shrieked in pain and surprise before whirling around to find out who had attacked it, before receiving another blast of fire to the face, making it shriek again, though this time it sounded more angry than in pain.

Keo scrambled to his feet (even though every bone in his body hurt from the previous blow he had received) in order to help Jola, but then the demon lunged forward and hit something he couldn't see. Keo heard Jola's small body go rolling across the floor, but as always, he could not see her, although he figured that she was probably out of the fight for now, because that demon appeared to have hit her at least as hard as it hit Dlaine and Maryal.

That left Keo standing all on his own, which the demon also seemed to realize, because it now looked at him with an almost giddy facial expression, if such an inhuman face could be said to look giddy.

Have to end this fight quickly, Keo thought. *Should I try Gildshine's ability or should I try to access the golden flames again?*

Keo had no time to mentally debate with himself about the

merits of either power, because at that moment the demon lunged toward him with a shriek that nearly left him deaf. Keo had just enough time to raise Gildshine up before the demon landed before him and tried to bite him, but Keo held back its teeth with Gildshine, although just barely, because the demon was pushing back hard against him with surprising strength. Even worse, Keo could not concentrate long enough to focus on using either ability, because all of his focus was on keeping the demon from pushing him down and tearing him apart with its fangs and claws.

Then, without warning, a flame—a golden flame—shot over Keo's head and struck the demon in the forehead. The demon suddenly stopped pressing against Keo and staggered backwards awkwardly across the floor, shrieking again in pain as its forehead burned. It slapped its wings against its burning forehead, trying to put out the fire on its forehead, although it did not seem to be having much success with that.

Confused, Keo had no idea what happened before he heard a familiar voice behind him say, "Looks like I got here just in the nick of time."

Easan strode up to Keo's side, looking as cool and unconcerned as he had appeared back in the parade. At his side was his own sword, which was now burning with the golden flames of the Rightful Heir. His eyes, however, were on the demon that was now looking at them both with hatred.

"The *shelmai!*" Aster shouted from his throne behind the demon in an exuberant. "You have come to save us!"

"Abohji came to my room and explained the situation," said Easan, brushing aside some of his long hair from his face. "I didn't believe him at first, seeing as the old tales say that the demons were sealed away by my ancestor, but I see that my skepticism was unwarranted." He looked at Keo, although it was with some disgust in his eyes. "And who are you?"

"Keo of the Sword," said Keo, panting. He felt annoyed at Easan's disgusted tone, but he said nothing about it. "One of the travelers from the south who told the Keepers about the demons."

"Ah," said Easan, stroking his chin. "Yes, Abohji did mention that there were some travelers from the south who were protecting the Keepers. I was expecting … something a little bit more impressive than a kid with an ancient sword."

Keo scowled. "You don't look much older than me yourself, *shelmai*."

Easan rolled his eyes. "It was just a joke. But then, I've always believed that you southerners aren't very good at laughing at yourselves. Makes you rather arrogant, in my opinion."

Keo was about to respond, but then the demon growled again, instantly drawing both of their attention to it. The demon had succeeded in putting out the golden fire on its head and looked ready to attack them again.

"Never mind," said Easan, raising his own sword before him. "We can talk about your lack of a sense of humor later. Right now, why don't we kill this demon together?"

"All right," said Keo, although he now liked Easan less than before. "Demons can only be killed by magic, so we'll need those golden flames of yours to kill it."

"I wouldn't do it any other way," said Easan. Then he looked at Keo, still frowning. "But you might want to think about staying out of the way. My fighting style is a bit … wild, I suppose you'd say, and you don't seem like the type smart enough to avoid getting hit accidentally by my swinging blade."

"I can look after myself, thanks," said Keo. "I don't need an arrogant easterner like you telling me what—"

Keo was interrupted by the demon shrieking and flying toward them again. Keo and Easan separated, allowing the demon to fly between them, but as it passed Easan's sword burst into golden flames and he slashed at the demon. His sword nicked the demon's wing, causing it to crash into the floor again with a shriek of pain, while Easan walked after it, his sword still on fire.

As for Keo, he was focusing on accessing the fire deep within him, the one that would allow him to use his own golden flames. Unfortunately, the fire did not seem to be there, but he focused on it anyway because he did not want to use Gildshine's ability and get exhausted if it failed.

Thus, Keo watched as Easan slashed at the demon, forcing the demon to retreat to avoid being harmed by his fire. Easan was a very good swordsman; his slashes were quick and always on target and he left no openings for the demon to take advantage of. He forced the demon back with confidence, showing absolutely no fear in the face of the spitting and growling monster that was before him. He almost seemed bored, even, as if the demon wasn't putting up much of a fight.

But then Easan tried to stab it. Unfortunately for him, he was clearly not very good at stabbing, because his attack missed and left an opening for the demon. The demon slapped him in the face with its wing, knocking Easan's sword out of his hands, causing its golden flames to sputter as it flew away out of his reach. Easan himself was knocked back onto his behind, but he had enough sense left in him to back up from the demon, which now advanced on him with a look of triumph on its bat-like features. It appeared that the demon was going to kill Easan ... unless Keo saved him.

Without even thinking about it, Keo ran to save Easan. As he ran, he suddenly felt the fire within him burn hotly, but he didn't think about why. He just ran at the demon as Gildshine burst into golden flames, just like Easan's sword.

The demon, however, was too close to Easan to notice Keo's approach. It reared its head back and lunged for Easan's face with its fangs bared and its mouth wide open. Easan could only look away, but then Keo finally reached Easan and the demon and—with Gildshine's golden flames sparking everywhere—stabbed Gildshine directly into the demon's open mouth.

The demon choked as Gildshine stabbed and burned through its head. It violently pulled back, yanking its head off of Gildshine, but that was the demon's very last action. It then fell onto the floor, twitched once, and stopped, black blood oozing from its mouth before its body turned into dust, which then sank into the floor out of sight.

Panting, Keo lowered Gildshine and looked down at Easan. "You okay?"

But Easan did not look like he was capable of speaking anymore. With his mouth hanging open, he was staring at the golden flames wrapped around Gildshine, which burned as brightly and warmly as ever.

Then Keo heard several gasps from the back of the room and looked over his shoulder to see all six of the Keepers staring at Keo in pure astonishment. Like Easan, they were staring at Gildshine as if they had never seen such a sword before.

That was when Keo realized why everyone was staring at Gildshine.

"By the Good King's name," said Aster, his voice low and shocked. "It cannot be … a *second* Rightful Heir?"

Chapter Eight

A FEW MINUTES LATER, Keo—with Gildshine back to normal and sheathed at his side—stood in front of the Keepers, right next to Easan, whose arms were crossed over his chest and whose expression told Keo that he was upset at this recent turn of events. Dlaine, Maryal and Jola were gone; although they had been conscious, the Keepers had still insisted that their doctors look over the three to ensure that they had not suffered any serious injuries that could turn fatal.

But the Keepers had demanded that Keo stay here, along with Easan. Keo knew exactly why they wanted him here, of course, but he wished he was with his friends, because he didn't like Easan and he did not want to talk with the Keepers about what he knew they wanted to talk with him about. He just felt uncomfortable about it, even though none of the Keepers showed any malice toward him.

The six Keepers, still seated in their thrones, looked even graver than they had when Keo had told them about the demons. Only Aster seemed even capable of speaking, but he was stroking his beard and appeared entirely lost in his thoughts, as if he was trying to make sense of what he and the other Keepers had just seen.

"Keo," said Aster suddenly, looking up at Keo with a questioning gaze. "You are not a Magician, correct?"

"Yes," said Keo, nodding. "I have no magical abilities of my own. My sword does, but I do not."

Aster stroked his beard again. "Oh, dear. That just makes things far more complicated. How can there be two Rightful Heirs?"

"I don't know," said Keo, shaking his head. "I haven't had these powers very long myself, so I don't know where they came from or why I have them."

"How can there be two *shelmai*, though?" said Seria. Her voice trembled slightly. "The prophecy states that there is only supposed to be *one* Rightful Heir. And all of our historical records state that King Riuno only had one son prior to his death. It makes no sense."

"Could the records be wrong?" said one of the Keepers, a bald, fat old man with large folds of skin. "I am not saying that I doubt the records, but perhaps King Riuno had two sons with separate mistresses."

"Impossible," said Aster. "We spent years ensuring that every detail of the records was accurate. I even remember the announcement of the birth of King Riuno's son on the day that it occurred. If he had had another, we would have known."

Keo glanced at Easan. Easan looked nothing like him, so Keo doubted they were even half-brothers, although if they were, he was not sure what to make of that. Keo had never known any member of his family before, so he was not sure how he was supposed to treat his half-brother, if Easan was indeed related to him at all.

Easan, for his part, didn't look at Keo. He seemed to be treating Keo like he was beneath his notice. Keo assumed that

Easan was just jealous that Keo might be the actual *shelmai*, which would have made him smile, but he did not, because he did not want the Keepers or Easan noticing his satisfaction.

"True," said the fat man, scratching his large belly. "But I don't see how else we can explain the obvious fact that we have two young men standing before us who match the description of the *shelmai* in the prophecy almost to a tee."

"Why is there any doubt about who the true *shelmai* is?" said Easan suddenly. "You did the tests. You know I carry Shadowbane, my father's sword. You know I am my father's son. I should be sitting on the Throne now wearing the crown of my father, not standing beside this southerner who clearly doesn't know anything about what it takes to be royalty."

"And you do?" said Keo. "Tell me, what kingdoms have *you* ruled recently? The Kingdom of your ego, maybe?"

Easan glared at Keo, but Aster said, "Enough bickering, you two. Easan, I understand your frustrations, but the fact is that we cannot simply crown you King of Lamaira when there is another young man who is equally qualified for the job standing right beside you. We want to be absolutely certain that we are placing the correct *shelmai* on the Throne, and right now none of us are quite certain about which one of you is supposed to sit there."

"Can't they share the Throne?" Seria suggested. "I know that the Kingdom of Lamaira has never had two kings at once, but—"

"No," said Aster. "From the time of the Good King until King Riuno's death, Lamaira has always only had one king at a time. If we had two kings, they would bicker and argue endlessly and may divide the Kingdom even more than it is now. There must be one King, and one King only, but I do not know which of these two young men is supposed to be that King and which one isn't."

"Hey, it's not that big of a deal," said Keo. "Easan can have the Throne, if he wants. I just want to—"

"Nay," said Aster. He pointed at Keo. "If you are indeed the true *shelmai*, then you *must* sit on the Throne no matter what. The prophecy and tradition demands it."

Although Keo looked disappointed, deep down, he was actually relieved that Aster had shot down his offer. Keo didn't really think of himself as kingly material, but he liked seeing Easan look so angry at him that he decided that he wouldn't mind if he became the King of Lamaira as long as it annoyed Easan.

"Keo, do you happen to know who your parents are?" said Seria. "Perhaps that will help us determine if you are the Rightful Heir or not."

"I was orphaned when I was only a few months old," said Keo with a shrug. "I never knew my parents and don't know who they are."

Seria grimaced and then looked at Easan. "And you?"

"The same as him," said Easan stiffly. "Orphaned at a young age, I never knew my parents. I came to Tain when I learned that my sword is the legendary Shadowbane, which belonged to the Lamairan Royal Family before it was lost in the chaos that engulfed Lamaira after my father's death. Thus, I knew it was my destiny to ascend to my father's Throne and restore Lamaira to its original glory among the nations, as both prophecy and tradition state should happen."

"This is still no good," said the fat man. He looked at the empty Throne ruefully. "And here I was thinking that today we might finally get to see the Throne filled after decades of emptiness."

"We might still be able to, Rura, though probably not today," said Aster. "We need to figure out a way to determine which of these two young men is destined to sit on that Throne first."

"How are we supposed to do that?" said Seria. "Both of them have equally legitimate claims to the Throne, but we can't have two Kings."

Aster stroked his beard again. "I am aware of that. But I think I may know a way we can determine the true heir to the Throne."

"And what is that?" said Rura.

"Recall, my fellow Keepers, what happened the last time there were two heirs to the Throne," said Aster. "It was some fifty years ago, at the end of the reign of King Murza, the father of King Riuno. Murza was about to retire from the Throne, but he had twin sons who had equal claims to the Throne: Riuno and his brother, Zamel."

"I recall that, yes," said Seria. "But I do not remember how they settled the dispute."

"They dueled for it," said Aster. "I recall it because I was a young man when it happened and they had set up the duel in a large arena for the people to watch. Although it was slightly more complicated than a simple duel, because an ancient law at the time stated that anytime there was a dispute for the Throne, the citizens of Tain were supposed to choose the successor by watching the duel and voting for who they thought fought best."

"Ah, yes," said Rura, nodding. "I remember that as well. If I recall correctly, the history books say Zamel defeated Riuno, but the citizens of Tain chose Riuno because they considered him more honorable and trustworthy than Zamel."

"What happened to Zamel after that?" said Keo.

"He lived as a minor noble in this very Castle until he disappeared after his brother's death," said Rura. "No one knows where he went, but I personally believe he was killed in the chaos that enveloped the entire Kingdom."

"Zamel's fate is irrelevant," said Aster. He looked at Keo and Easan in satisfaction. "The answer to our dilemma is obvious: We will set up a duel between you two, one that the Tainians will watch in order to determine who the next King of Lamaira should be."

Easan immediately reached for Shadowbane and looked at Keo. "Why don't we settle this here and now? Why do we have to do a big duel in front of everyone? That sounds like a waste of time to me."

"Because that is what the ancient laws written by the Good King state," said Aster in a firm voice. "And we must always abide by the ancient laws, for it is in these laws that we find peace and order. You must surely know that, Easan, if you are the *shelmai*."

That seemed to work, because Easan took his hand off of Shadowbane's handle and folded his arms across his chest again. "Very well, then. The ancient laws must be followed by everyone, including royalty such as myself."

"*Potential* royalty," Keo said. "Remember, you aren't King yet."

Easan glared at Keo again. "Neither are you, so why don't you save the jabs for the duel? Of course, we could spar right now if you want, but I really don't want to embarrass you in front of the Keepers, you understand."

Keo was tempted to accept Easan's offer and duel him there and then, but Aster said, "Cease your bickering at once. It does us no good and proves nothing except that you two act more like quarrelsome children than grown men."

"It's not my fault that Keo is not as witty as me," said Easan with a shrug. "I can only assume that the poor man grew up without a natural proclivity toward wit like I have. That is almost as bad as growing up poor, but at least a poor person can earn money to raise themselves up from their poverty, whereas as those who lack wit can never gain it through other means."

Keo glared at Easan, but rather than respond to that, he looked back at the Keepers and said, "When will the duel be ready?"

"We do not know," said Aster. "It has been half a century since the last duel for the Throne was held. We will need to consult the Archives and find out the rules and traditions surrounding it, although we will try to do it as quickly as possible in order to have a king on the Throne as soon as possible."

"What are we supposed to do in the meantime, then?" said Keo.

"We will give you and your friends rooms in the Old Castle," said Aster, "where you can stay until the day of the duel. If you wish, you can also train with the Knights or walk around Tain and familiarize yourself with our magnificent and ancient city."

"Okay," said Keo. "I want to go check on my friends and see how they're doing anyway." He looked at Easan. "Easan, what are you going to—"

Easan was already walking away to the Throne Room's exit, without even having said anything. And then he was gone, slamming the door shut behind him so hard that the chandelier hanging from the ceiling actually shook slightly, though it thankfully did not fall.

Keo looked back at the Keepers awkwardly. "Um … I guess he's not very happy about this duel."

"That is not surprising," said Aster. "After all, wouldn't you feel the same if, after thinking you were going to become the next King of Lamaira, someone who might be your half-brother turned up and threw your own parentage into doubt?"

"I guess I would," said Keo. "Anyway, I will leave and let you guys research about the duel. Let us know what you find as soon as you can."

"Certainly," said Aster with a nod. "One of our servants will show you to your guest room, because the Old Castle is a very large building and is easy to get lost in if you are not familiar with its layout. And once we find out more about the duel, we will contact you and Easan shortly."

"Thanks," said Keo.

With that, Keo turned and walked toward the exit, wondering how good a fighter Easan was and whether he would be able to beat him in a duel. Not that Keo really wanted to duel him, but he understood now that there was no way they could prepare for the demons' invasion without a king to lead the Kingdom. And that king was going to be either himself or Easan.

I just hope that the duel doesn't take us very long, at least, Keo thought. *We have only five and a half months until the demons return. And time is running out.*

Chapter Nine

KEO SAT IN A chair in Dlaine's room, reclining on its comfortable, if archaic, seat. He looked at Dlaine, who was lying on the bed, and then at Maryal, who was sitting in another chair in the other corner of the room. They—along with Jola, who was still invisible and seemed to be lying on a couch on the left side of the bed—had been listening to Keo as he explained what the Keepers had decided to do and what they were going to do about Keo and Easan. He had finished explaining the situation to them a couple of minutes ago, but neither had said a word, probably because they were still processing what he had said. Both of them looked okay, despite the blows they had taken during the fight with the demon, which made Keo feel relieved, because he had worried that they might have taken wounds they would take a while to recover from.

"A duel, eh?" said Dlaine. He rubbed his forehead in thought. He looked rather comfortable in his bed and unlikely to move or get up from his current position. "And then a vote afterward by the people to determine the winner. Never heard of that before."

"It's an old custom, apparently," said Keo with a shrug. "The last time it happened was about fifty years ago, when Riuno and his brother fought for the Throne and Riuno won."

"Well, I hope you win this one, Keo," said Maryal with a smile. "I believe it is your destiny to defeat Easan and win over the hearts and minds of the people of Tain. Then you can get to work on uniting the three factions against the demons."

Keo nodded, but then frowned. "But I don't know the first thing about ruling a Kingdom, much less reuniting three factions that have been at war with each other for years. Especially if Nesma is still a part of the Magical Council. I doubt she would listen to me or let the other Council members listen to me, even if I am the Rightful Heir."

"You have a point," said Maryal with a shrug. "But regardless, I think that destiny is on your side, because why else would destiny have allowed you to come here if not to lead you to the Throne and save the Kingdom?"

Keo folded his arms over his chest. "Maybe you're right. Maybe it is my destiny to ascend to the Throne and reunite the Kingdom. But first, I need to focus on beating Easan and getting the people to like me."

"Was Easan a good fighter?" said Dlaine, propping his head up on the large fluffy pillow on his bed. "I didn't get to see him fight."

"I think he was," said Keo, nodding. "He was actually winning for a while there, but the demon managed to disarm him and would have killed him if I hadn't intervened. In a straight one-on-one fight, I think Easan would be a challenging opponent for sure."

"Can he really summon golden flames like you?" said Maryal, leaning forward interestedly.

"Yes," said Keo. His shoulders slumped. "And he can do it more easily than me. The sword he wields is called Shadowbanc, which was the sword used by the Good King and passed down through the Good King's descendents over the centuries. I think he's had more practice controlling his golden flames than I have."

"That gives him an advantage over you for sure," said Dlaine. He pointed at Gildshine, which leaned in its sheath against the side of Keo's chair. "What you need to do is practice summoning your own golden flames so you can use them against him in your duel. It could also help you win the crowd, because if the people see that you can use golden flames just as well as Easan, that will make it easier for them to accept that you are the Rightful Heir or the *shelmai* or whatever they're calling you now."

"Agreed, but it's not easy to summon those golden flames," said Keo. He sighed. "It takes a lot of concentration and effort and doesn't always work even then."

"Which is why I said you need to practice it," said Dlaine, rolling his eyes. "Spend as much time as you can practicing it until you can summon those golden flames as easily as breathing. Then, when you fight Easan, you'll have a better chance of defeating him."

"Right," said Keo. "Got it. I'll ask the Knights if they have some place I can train, preferably somewhere in private where Easan can't see me."

"Smart kid," said Dlaine. He stroked his chin and seemed to be thinking about something else. "What about that demon from earlier, though?"

"What about it?" said Keo. "It was here, it attacked us, I killed it. The demons have been trying to kill us even before I tried to stop them. What's there to wonder about?"

"It just seems awfully convenient that a demon would appear out of nowhere like that and attack the Keepers right in the middle of their throne room," said Dlaine. "How did it get in there without us noticing? Why did it choose that moment to attack? Why not attack the Keepers when we weren't around? If its goal was to kill the Keepers, then it picked a rotten time to do it."

"The demons hate us more than the Keepers," said Keo. "I think the demons see us as a bigger threat than the Keepers, because we've killed several of their fellow demons already and are actively trying to stop them from rising again. So it makes sense that they would wait until we were in there to attack us."

"I'm still not sure," said Dlaine. "If the demon killed the Keepers, that would have thrown the Old Kingdom into chaos, which would have made it harder for us to reunite the Kingdom. And there was no reason for it to wait for us there if it wanted to kill us. It could just as easily have waited until we got our rooms here and then killed us when we least expected it."

"I think you're over-thinking this," said Keo, "although I admit it is kind of strange how that demon attacked us *just* when we got there. I wonder if it was following us or not."

"Maybe it was, maybe it wasn't," said Dlaine. "All I know is that we can't let our guard down around these demons. They're very crafty and have already shown they can plan long term without us even realizing it."

"Are you saying that we should investigate the demon's appearance here?" said Keo. "That will be kind of hard because the demon is dead and it didn't leave any clues behind."

"I didn't say we should investigate it, only that I think that it was far too convenient that this demon showed up like this," said Dlaine. "I think that someone in the Old Castle might have let it in. I don't know who or why, but I bet they let it in to kill us or the

Keepers or both."

"Should I go and tell the Keepers that you suspect someone in the Old Castle might have let the demon in?" said Keo, glancing at the door. "Because if your theory is true, then the Keepers need to know about it so they can have someone look around the Castle for any clues to the identity of the traitor."

"You can if you want, but I'm not sure if you should," said Dlaine with a shrug. "It is just a theory, after all. It's entirely possible that the demon just sneaked in on its own without any help from the inside, which would be easy for it to do because no one would be looking for it. But I think it far more likely that someone on the inside let it in, whoever it is."

"I'll mention your theory to the Keepers next time I see them," said Keo. "Even if it's not true, it would be smart for us to keep an eye out for any suspicious activity. That demon might have an ally that might try to avenge its death, so we'll need to make sure that other demons can't get in to harm us or anyone else in the Castle."

"Excellent idea," said Dlaine. He yawned. "Having a hard time keeping my eyes open, so I think I'll just take a nap for now."

"Okay," said Keo. He stood up from his chair. "I'm going to find out where I can train for the duel and also see more of the city. Tain seems like an interesting place and I imagine we'll be here for a while, so I'm going to familiarize myself with the place."

Maryal stood up, an excited gleam in her eyes. "Oh, can I come with you? I also want to see Tain, but more importantly, I want to help you lay the foundations for your successful victory against Easan."

Keo looked at Maryal in confusion. "Are you going to help me train?"

"Nope," said Maryal, shaking her head. "I'm afraid that I'm more familiar with magical duels than sword duels, and I don't know anything about your golden flames, so I can't help you there, either."

"Then how are you going to help me defeat Easan?" said Keo. "Just stand on the sidelines and cheer me on while I train or something?"

"I'll do more than that," said Maryal with a smile. She jerked a thumb at her chest. "I'll be your political adviser."

Keo shared a mystified look with Dlaine before looking back at Maryal. "Political adviser? I'm not getting into politics."

"Yes, you are," said Maryal. "Remember what you told us? The citizens of Tain will vote on you or Easan, regardless of the duel's outcome. Therefore, you need to work on introducing yourself to the people and letting everyone know how wonderful and amazing you are. And I am going to help."

"What experience do you have with politics?" said Keo.

"I worked with Magician Erawa of Torgan," said Maryal. "Helped get her the position because she was a friend of mine. It's not quite the same thing as getting people to like you, seeing as the Magical Council is the final authority on which Magician is assigned to which town, but I'm confident that the general principles behind winning the favor of the Council will work in winning the favor of the Tainians."

"If you say so," said Keo. "But I'd really rather find some place to train first, and then try to convince the people to like me later."

"All right," said Maryal. She tapped her chin in thought. "It will be an uphill battle either way, though, because the Tainers already love Easan, but maybe that's made Easan complacent or maybe his support has already peaked. If so—"

"I said we can talk about this later," Keo cut her off. "Okay? I just don't want to worry about this yet, especially since we don't even have a date for the duel just yet."

Maryal frowned. "Fine. But I'm still going to be thinking about everything we can do to increase your odds of being picked by the people to ascend to the Throne."

"That's fine," said Keo. "Anyway, let's get going. If we can find a place to train before dark, that would be great."

Chapter Ten

ON THEIR WAY OUT of the Old Castle, Keo informed Abohji—whose office was located on the ground floor of the Castle—about Dlaine's suspicion about a possible traitor within the Castle who might have let the demon in earlier. Abohji thanked them for sharing their theory with him and said that he would have a couple of his Knights start asking around for anyone who might have seen or heard something strange prior to the demon's attack. He also said he would share this theory with the Keepers, just in case any of them knew anything that could help, as unlikely as that was.

When Keo mentioned that he was looking for a place to train as well, Abohji gave Keo directions to the Knights' training grounds, which he gave Keo permission to use due to his possible status as royalty.

According to Abohji, the training grounds were only a couple of streets away from the Old Castle, but he did not let them walk there on their own. Instead, Abohji ordered one of his Knights to take Keo and Maryal to the training grounds in a horse-drawn carriage, because Abohji had heard that Keo might be the Rightful Heir and so believed it only appropriate that Keo should have transportation to the training grounds, rather than having him walk there like a peasant.

Keo tried to protest that this was unnecessary, but Abohji

insisted that Keo and Maryal take the carriage and would not take no for an answer. So Keo reluctantly climbed into the carriage, with Maryal following much less reluctantly, because she said she was getting tired of walking everywhere and liked the idea of taking a carriage to reach their destination.

One short trip later, they were walking into a large, dome-shaped building only a few streets away from the Old Castle. According to the Knight who had taken them there, the training grounds had been built close to the Old Castle so that the Knights training there would not be far away from the Castle in case it came under attack.

But Keo forgot all about that as he and Maryal stepped through the doors and into the training grounds itself. The interior was huge and wide-open, making it almost feel like they were still standing outside, even though the roof and walls were quite visible. Keo and Maryal stood at the top of the stands that was apparently where other Knights sat when they were not training, because Keo spotted a couple of helmet-less Knights sitting in the stands either chatting with each other or resting in between practice sessions.

On the opposite side of the training grounds hung five massive banners down the walls. These banners showed the symbol of the Old Kingdom, though each banner was in a different color: red, blue, green, yellow, and purple. Keo did not know why they were hanging there, but then again, there was a lot that Keo did not understand about the Old Kingdom.

Down in the training grounds themselves, a dozen or so Knights were practicing their techniques. The air was full of the sounds of swords clanging against other swords or against metal shields, the *twang* of arrows as archers fired at targets, and the neighing of horses as a couple of Knights on the far left side of the training grounds practice jousting. It was hot in here and smelled like sweat and dirt, but Keo did not mind that, because it reminded him of how he smelled after doing an intense practice session with Master Tiram back home that seemed like a lifetime ago now.

Maryal, on the other hand, pinched her nose and said, "Okay, we found the training grounds. Can we leave?"

Keo shook his head. "Nope. I came here to train, remember? I'm going down to practice with Gildshine. You can sit here in the stands and watch if you want."

Maryal looked at Keo in annoyance, but he didn't care. He just ran down the steep steps to the field below, doing his best to avoid tripping over his own feet and falling and ignoring the questioning looks from the few Knights sitting in the stands watching their brothers practice. When he reached the dusty, firm earth of the grounds itself, he looked around to see where he could practice, but he was so unused to the Knights' training grounds that he did not know where to start until he heard someone shout, "Hey! Who are you?"

Keo looked to his right. A Knight, with purple highlights on his armor, was walking toward Keo, though his sword was thankfully not drawn. The Knight carried his helmet under his arm, revealing his short, pitch-black hair and horribly scarred face. His face looked like it had been mauled by a bear, which made Keo wonder how that had happened.

Keo turned to face the Knight and said, "I'm Keo of the Sword. I'm not from around here, nor am I a new recruit or a

Knight or anything, but Sir Abohji—"

"Your name is Keo?" said the Knight, stopping several feet from Keo, a questioning look on his scarred face. "The *other* Rightful Heir? The one who is not Easan?"

Keo blinked. "Yes, that's me. How do you know that?"

"News travels fast among the Brotherhood," said the Knight, gesturing at his fellow Knights, all of whom were too busy practicing to pay attention to Keo. He looked Keo over critically. "Hmm. Not as kingly as Easan or King Riuno."

Keo scowled. "Are you just going to stand there and make snide comments about my appearance or are you going to introduce yourself?"

"Oh, right," said the Knight. He jerked a thumb at his chest. "My name is Sir Simil and I am a Purple Order Knight."

Simil said that with pride, as if being a 'Purple Order Knight' was some great accomplishment that few ever succeeded in doing. Keo, however, didn't see what was so great about it, although it seemed to explain the purple highlights on his armor.

"Uh, good for you," said Keo. "And I'm … well, nothing special. I was raised by a master swordsman in the Low Woods for most of my life before I struck out on my own to stop the demons from returning."

Simil's eyes widened. He looked both ways and then leaned in closer to Keo, as if to ensure no one would eavesdrop on their conversation. "You mean the demons really *are* coming back? And you and Easan *did* kill one in the Throne Room today?"

Keo nodded, but said, "Actually, I was the one who killed it. Easan didn't really help and I actually saved his life, but yes, the demons are real and will rise again unless we get a new King of

Lamaira fast."

Simil swore under his breath and then said aloud, "Damn it. Now I owe Draps thirty lems."

Keo quirked an eyebrow. "What?"

"One of my brother Knights," said Simil. "You see, when news of the return of the demons first filtered down from Sir Abohji, we thought it was just a rumor. I bet my friend, Draps, thirty lems that the demons didn't really exist, but now it looks like I'm going to have to pay up the next time I see him." Simil sighed. "My luck sucks sometimes."

"Well, sorry to hear that," said Keo. "Anyway, you mentioned that you are a Purple Order Knight. What does that mean? I've never heard of it."

"You haven't?" said Simil. "Oh, right. You are not from around here. Yes, well, see those banners hanging from the ceiling over there?"

Simil pointed at the large banners that Keo had noticed earlier, which looked even bigger now that Keo was closer to them. He could tell that they were each three times as large as he was, which amazed him because he had never seen banners that big before.

"Those banners represent the five Orders in the Brotherhood of the Knights of the Old Kingdom," said Simil. He pointed at each one in turn as he said their names. "Red stands for the Red Order, Blue for Blue Order, Green for Green Order, and so on."

"But what are the five Orders?" said Keo. "I don't understand."

"To put it simply, think of the Orders as different ranks in the army," said Simil. "Red Order is the highest—and hardest—to get into, while Purple Order is the lowest and easiest to get into. Not to discount the Purple Order, of course, because getting into any Order is always hard," Simil added hastily, as if to make sure that Keo did not think he was putting down his own accomplishment.

"How do you get into the different Orders?" said Keo.

"You have to be assigned to an Order by Sir Abohji or one of the other Generals by performing a mighty deed," said Simil. "There are no hard and fast guidelines that explain how you get into the different Orders, but generally, the more difficult or daring tasks you complete, the higher you are ranked. For example, I got into the Purple Order by being part of the unit that beat back an invading force of Divinians from the west."

"Is everyone in one of the Orders?" said Keo.

"Not everyone, no," said Simil, shaking his head. "The Purple Order is the biggest, since it's the easiest to get into, with one hundred Knights in it, but the Red Order is the hardest to get into. It has only two Knights in it."

"Just two?" said Keo. "What did they do to get there?"

"Sir Abohji is one of them," said Simil. "He got there after foiling an assassination attempt on the Keepers two years ago. As for the other one, Sir Nilo, he won the Battle of the West Border that dramatically expanded the Old Kingdom's territory east into the Divinians' country a couple years back."

"I've met Sir Abohji, but where is Sir Nilo?" said Keo, looking around at the training grounds, but not seeing any Knights with red highlights on their armor.

"Sir Nilo is commanding the western forces against the Divinians," said Simil. "Trust me when I say that he's probably the best Knight operating today. He's a living legend. I met him once, last year when he was visiting for Fall Day, though we didn't talk much because he was busy celebrating the holiday with his family."

Simil spoke of this Sir Nilo person with nothing but respect in his voice. Keo decided that he would find a way to meet this Sir Nilo at some point, perhaps after the duel if he won. Sir Nilo sounded like he could be a useful ally against the demons, if only for his military prowess.

"Anyway, what are you doing here in the training grounds?" said Simil.

Keo patted the handle of Gildshine, which was still sheathed at his side. "I'm going to get some training and practice in for my duel with Easan, of course."

"You are going to duel Easan?" said Simil. "Why?"

Keo realized just then that no one outside of the Keepers, Easan, Keo's friends, and Keo himself were aware of the duel that Easan and Keo would duel to determine who the true *shelmai* was. As far as he knew, the Keepers had not yet announced the duel to the rest of Tain, so he said, "The Keepers will explain later, but Easan and I are going to duel to determine who will get to become the next King of Lamaira."

Simil scratched his chin, an interested look on his face. "Really? When will this duel take place?"

"I don't know yet," said Keo. "The Keepers are still researching it in the Archives, but I decided to take advantage of this time to get some training in and practice summoning my golden flames."

"Hold on," said Simil. He glanced at Gildshine and then back at Keo's face. "You're telling me you can summon golden flames on your sword, just like the prophecy says that the Rightful Heir is supposed to be able to do?"

"Of course," said Keo, "though I don't yet have complete control over it, which is why I came here to train."

"Can I help?" said Simil, whose sudden interest made Keo look at him strangely. "I mean, I don't know how I can help train you, but I've never gotten a chance to see Easan's golden flames myself, so I think watching you do it is the next best thing."

Keo frowned, but nodded anyway. "Sure. I need someone to show me around this place, anyway, seeing as I just got here and don't know what the rules are."

"All right," said Simil. Then he suddenly looked up at the stands and said, "Hey, whose that woman up there?"

Keo looked up at the stands, too, and saw Maryal sitting near the top by herself. She waved when Keo saw her, but she still didn't look particularly happy about being here. The sleeves of her shirt were rolled up, probably due to the heat of the training grounds, and he could even tell that her nose was still wrinkled, even though she sat a good distance away from Keo.

"That's my friend, Maryal," said Keo, looking back at Simil. "She came with me because she wanted to see more of Tain."

Simil smirked at Keo. "Friend, huh? Granted, I normally don't have much of an interest in women from the south—their skin tends to be too pale for my tastes—but she's a looker, I'll give you that."

Keo blinked. "She's not my girlfriend, if that's what you're implying."

"She isn't?" said Simil in surprise. "Well, then you're leaving gold in the dragon's den, as we say in the Old Kingdom. Does she happen to be looking for any suitors?"

"I don't think so," said Keo. "As far as I know, she's single and doesn't have any interest in courting anyone right now."

Simil slicked back his hair, glanced at Maryal again, and then said, "Sounds like a challenge worthy of a Purple Order Knight."

Keo sighed in annoyance. "Listen, can we just get on with the training now? That's what I came here to—"

Keo was interrupted by a massive explosion from the top of the stands, causing him, Simil, and the other training Knights to look up at the stands in shock. The doors of the training grounds flew outwards, coming directly toward Keo and Simil and forcing the two to separate to avoid getting hit. The doors slammed into the ground hard, where they lay a smoking and twisted wreck.

Again looking up, Keo saw smoke billowing from the open doorway, but he was really looking for Maryal. He spotted her lying unconscious over the seats in front of her, perhaps knocked out by the blast, although she did not appear to be lethally injured from what he could see.

"What in the Good King's name was that?" said Simil, staring with horror at the twisted metal hunk lying on the ground.

That was when a figure stepped out of the smoke. The figure's right hand was held out, like he was pushing against some invisible force, while the helmet of a Knight was in his other hand, a helmet which contrasted sharply with his own featureless, dull metal mask.

Then the masked figure—who Keo recognized, with dread, as Eliam the Tracker—looked down at Keo, met his eyes, and said, in a muffle voiced that Keo could nonetheless hear even from a distance, "Ah, there you are. I've been looking all over for you, but I knew I'd find you eventually, because the Tracker never fails to find—and kill—his target."

Chapter Eleven

KEO DREW GILDSHINE FROM his sheath as Simil said, "Who is that?"

"Eliam the Tracker," said Keo. "A wanted criminal back where I come from, given the task of hunting and killing me by the Magical Council."

"I have never heard of him before," said Simil. He immediately slammed his helmet onto his head and drew his own sword from his sheath. "But if he's a wanted criminal who intends to murder you, then I will fight him like any other criminal."

"You'll need to be careful," said Keo, without looking at Simil. "Eliam is a powerful Magician. He can blow things up with his magic and has already killed several of your fellow Knights."

"He has?" said Simil in surprise. "Who?"

"Sir Fariak and the Knights under his command at Cloudway Pass," said Keo.

"Sir Fariak?" said Simil. His voice became full of anger. "Then that just gives me another reason to kill this monster!"

Before Keo could respond to that, Eliam spread his arms and said, "Happy to see me, Keo? I hope so, because I'm happy to see you, knowing that my freedom is not very far away now. Why don't we—"

One of the Knights in the stands yelled and ran up the stairs toward Eliam, his sword lowered and aimed toward Eliam's chest. Eliam, however, didn't move. He just stared in amusement as the Knight charged at him, before raising one hand and holding it out before him with the palm wide-open.

A flash of light emitted from Eliam's palm and the Knight's body exploded inside his armor, causing him to fall to the steps and go tumbling down them, trailing blood behind him. The other Knights in the training grounds gasped at the sight, while Eliam jumped off the top of the stands with superhuman agility.

He flew over Keo and Simil's heads and landed behind them, forcing them both to walk backwards out of his reach. Up close, Keo could see burn marks and scratches all over Eliam's mask, clothes, and hands, but the Magician didn't even seem slightly bothered by it. He just raised his hands, almost like he was going to surrender, but Keo knew better than to assume that.

The earth in front of Keo exploded, blinding him and Simil briefly. Keo, however, could hear Eliam running toward him and jumped to the side just as he felt Eliam's hand rush past him. Keo swung Gildshine at Eliam, but the Magician leaped into the air once again and landed several feet away from Keo and Simil.

"Almost got me there," said Eliam, his muffled voice nonetheless quite clear to Keo. "Too bad your aim is so bad that you couldn't even hit the broadside of a barn with it."

Keo stepped forward, but then heard the sounds of dozens of suits of armor and boots clanking against each other and looked to the left to see all of the Knights in the training grounds rushing to attack Eliam. The Knights had drawn all of their weapons, but Keo noticed Eliam aimed his hand at them, causing Keo to shout, "Watch out!"

But Keo was too late, because in the next second, an explosion occurred in the middle of the group of Knights, knocking down some and sending others flying. Keo could tell a few were dead, but it seemed like most of them had survived, although there was no way that any of them were going to be getting back up again to fight Eliam any time soon.

"Brothers!" Simil shouted. He glared at Eliam. "Vile Magician, how dare you assault so many of my fellow Knights! This is outrageous."

"Outrageous?" Eliam repeated. He gestured at the scattered and unconscious and dead Knights. "This is art. But then, they say that the best art causes offense, so I will take your outrage at my work as a compliment."

Simil obviously did not know what to say to that, but that did not stop him raising his sword and attempting to charge at Eliam. But Keo held up Gildshine in front of Simil's path and said, "Wait. He'll kill you if you attack him like that."

"Keo is correct," said Eliam. He raised his hand again, "Though his holding you back is the epitome of the 'kind, but pointless' gesture I've come to expect from others, because I will just kill you anyway."

Keo and Simil once again separated, but this time Eliam must have seen that coming, because he raised both hands and aimed them at the two as they ran. That was when Keo realized that Eliam was planning to blow them *both* up.

The ground underneath Keo exploded without warning, sending him flying several feet into the air. He crashed hard on his back, gasping in pain. His legs felt broken and his back felt like it had shattered upon impact, but Keo forced himself to get back up. As he did so, he looked at the area to see where Eliam was.

Simil lay on the ground dozens of feet away from him. He appeared unconscious, but thankfully not dead. His armor was blackened and dirty, probably due to the explosion that had gotten him, while Eliam was now turning to face Keo.

"Well, well," said Eliam, mad glee in his voice. "It looks like it is just you and me, at long last. So just stand still for a moment until I've scattered every last bit of your body all over this damn city."

Despite the pain, Keo charged toward Eliam, carrying Gildshine in both hands. Eliam raised both of his hands, but Keo rolled forward just as the ground exploded where he had been standing just moments before.

Rolling back to his feet, Keo swung Gildshine at Eliam, but the Tracker ducked. He reached out with both hands to grab Keo, but Keo jumped backwards out of his reach. Keo then tried to stab him, but Eliam dodged it fairly easily and pointed his open palm at Keo.

Alarmed, Keo jumped to the side just as the ground exploded again. More dirt flew into the air, some of it hitting Keo in the head, but Keo swung Gildshine at Eliam again. This time, he actually slashed Eliam's hand, causing Eliam to jerk it back and clutch his now-bleeding hand to his chest as he staggered backwards.

Seeing an opening, Keo moved in, slashing Gildshine again, but Eliam must not have been as badly injured as he appeared, because he dodged the attack as easily as ever. But he also kept outside of Gildshine's reach, which told Keo that he had the

Tracker on the ropes.

Smiling in triumph, Keo ran toward Eliam, ready to stab Gildshine straight into his heart. Eliam looked to the left and to the right, like he was trying to find a way to escape, but Keo knew that there was nowhere that Eliam could escape.

Then, when Keo was only a few feet from Eliam, the Tracker jerked out his other hand, aiming it at the ground under Keo's feet. Keo had just enough time to realize what Eliam was about to do before the ground literally exploded under his feet again.

Once more, Keo was flying through the air. He crashed on his back on the ground, the impact knocking the air from his lungs, but before he could get back up, Eliam was upon him and slammed his boot into Keo's chest. That blow made Keo gasp in pain, because he didn't have enough air to scream. He looked up at Eliam, whose murderous eyes were quite visible through his metal mask.

"You are an annoying little twit," said Eliam. He aimed his good hand at Keo's face. "It will be a pleasure to feel your blood splatter over my mask."

There was no way Keo could get up or fight back now, because he was too weak to even move. He just stared up at Eliam, hoping that his head exploding would not be too painful at least.

But then, without warning, Eliam suddenly started gasping in pain. He clutched his throat and staggered backwards, taking his foot off of Keo's chest. Keo raised his head, watching in surprise as Eliam apparently had trouble breathing, although why, he was not sure until he heard a voice in the stands shout, "Keo!"

Keo looked up and saw Maryal—having apparently regained

her consciousness—standing at the bottom of the stands. She held her hands out toward Eliam and Keo immediately understood that she had used her magical powers to take away Eliam's air, which explained why the Tracker was having such a hard time breathing.

"Get him!" Maryal shouted.

Keo nodded and rose back to his feet, although slowly due to the pain from the impact of the crash. He held Gildshine in both hands, but just as he did that, Eliam noticed Maryal and raised his good hand to blow her up.

But Eliam was much slower than normal, probably due to his lack of air, and it was that slowness that gave Keo the opportunity he needed. He charged at Eliam and slammed the flat of Gildshine directly into Eliam's masked head.

Eliam's mask must not have been as protective as it looked, because the second it connected with Eliam's head, there was a *clang* and Eliam collapsed immediately. He was still alive, but Keo could tell that the Tracker was not going to be getting up again anytime soon. Sighing, Keo planted Gildshine into the ground and leaned on it for support.

At that same moment, several Knights burst through the doorway at the top of the stands. They immediately spotted Keo standing over Eliam in the field and ran down the steps to go meet him.

"You!" the lead Knight—a member of the Green Order based on his armor's highlights—said as he and his fellow Knights approached Keo, apparently ignoring Maryal, who had sat back down in one of the seats in the stands, most likely to rest. "Identify yourself!"

"I'm … Keo of the Sword," said Keo, finding it hard to speak because of his exhaustion. He gestured at Eliam. "And I just saved several of your fellow Knights—and maybe your entire training grounds—from being blown into pieces."

Chapter Twelve

AFTER KEO EXPLAINED THE situation to them, the Knights hauled Eliam out of the training grounds. The lead Knight, who called himself Sir Horan, said that Eliam was going to be taken to a special dungeon deep beneath the Old Castle that had been designed to hold Magicians, although he did not explain how the dungeon would prevent Eliam from using his magic to escape. Yet Horan seemed confident that the Tracker was going to remain under lock and key until the Keepers decided what to do with him, so Keo didn't question that.

As well, the Knights had brought a Healer with them who treated Keo and Maryal's wounds, but who also had them sent back to the Old Castle once he learned that they were the Keepers' guests. He told them that they would have to rest until they were better and that until then they should remain in their beds in their rooms in the Castle, which was fine by Keo, because he was so exhausted and in pain from his battle with Eliam that he felt like he could sleep for a whole month and still be too tired to do anything else.

When they arrived at the Old Castle, Sir Abohji briefly asked Keo what happened, but Keo was too tired to do anything other than give him very brief, to-the-point answers. Abohji, however, did not seem bothered by that, probably because he intended to learn the full details from Sir Horan or one of the other Knights who had been there.

And, although both Keo and Maryal had taken some serious hits during their battle with Eliam, Keo was informed by the Castle's Healers that he was apparently going to be all right as long as he got bed rest and did not overexert himself for a while. He hadn't even broken any bones. And while Keo had known for a while that he was tougher than most people, he was still surprised to learn that he did not need as much healing as Maryal, despite having been thrown through the air twice during his fight with Eliam.

But Keo was also pleased, because he did not like having to rest in bed while the demons were still out there somewhere. True, he needed the rest and the demons' return was still several months away, but the fact was that Keo felt like a sitting duck in bed, where any demon could attack and kill him in his sleep without hesitation.

Evidently, however, the demons must have decided to leave Keo and the others alone, because a full week passed after Eliam's attack and neither Keo nor his friends were attacked by any demons. Nor did he hear about any demon sightings, even though Sir Abohji informed Keo that he had given orders to all Knights within the Old Castle and the city to keep an eye out for any suspicious demonic activity in the area. That made Keo feel a little better, but he was still very aware of his own vulnerability and found it hard to relax and rest like he was supposed to.

During his week of rest, Keo did not see Easan, although the Healer who came to check on him three times a day would occasionally tell Keo about what Easan was doing. Apparently

Easan had taken it upon himself to interrogate Eliam in order to find out what Eliam knew about the Magical Council, although the Healer did not know how successful Easan was. It seemed unlikely to Keo that Easan would have any success interrogating Eliam, who had seemed like the kind of person who would never break, but Easan had an iron will as well, so perhaps he was having more success than Keo knew.

Keo did not hear from the Keepers at all during the week. He was told that the Keepers were still researching the duel, as well as searching for any legends that might help them locate the demons' pit and figure out a likely spot where they would return. Keo did not understand what took the Keepers so long to do this, but then he was informed that the Archives contained literally thousands of old volumes, some ranging from the founding of the original Kingdom of Lamaira, and that many of the oldest books were written in Ancient Lamairan, an old dialect no one except for a handful of scholars spoke or read today. So Keo tried to be patient and wait for them to find out what they needed to know to ensure the duel would be done according to tradition, which was much harder than it seemed, though he managed it well enough.

At the end of the week, the Healer proclaimed that Keo was well enough to walk. Keo, happy to hear that, soon got out of his bed, dressed, and then went into the small dining room set aside for guests in the Old Castle. There Keo found Dlaine, Maryal, and Jola (although, as usual, she was invisible, the only hints of her existence being bits of the food from one of the plates vanishing every now and then) seated around a small wooden table with a white tablecloth. Everyone had an identical breakfast of eggs, jelly, toast, milk, coffee, and some other things Keo could not identify but which smelled delicious.

Taking a seat in the only vacant seat, Keo grabbed a fork and knife and said, "This looks great."

"It is," said Dlaine, who pausing with a piece of bacon halfway to his mouth. He looked at Keo with concern. "How do you feel?"

"Better than after my fight with Eliam last week," said Keo as he stabbed a piece of sausage and then tore off part of that sausage with his teeth, chewed it up, and swallowed. "Ah. Hits the spot."

"Well, you at least have to admit that I was right," said Dlaine as he returned his attention to his food.

"Right about what?" said Keo, looking at Dlaine in confusion.

"About Eliam surviving," said Dlaine. He looked at Keo with a smirk. "Remember? I said that Eliam probably survived the border tower falling on him. I was right."

"Did you wait all week just to brag about that to me?" said Keo in annoyance.

"Sort of, but I really want to know *how* he survived," said Dlaine. "Did he say?"

"Nope," said Keo, shaking his head. "Eliam didn't say much. He just walked in, took out the Knights, and immediately started trying to kill me. And he probably would have succeeded if not for Maryal here."

Keo looked at Maryal when he said that. She looked much better than she had during their fight with Eliam, although there were bags under her eyes like she had not slept well recently. She didn't even seem to be paying attention to their conversation, her eyes on her half-eaten breakfast, which she was playing with like she was distracted by something.

"Hey, Maryal, are you there?" said Keo. "Hello?"

Maryal suddenly looked at Keo. "What?"

"I was saying to Dlaine that the only reason I survived against Eliam was because of you," said Keo. "Weren't you listening?"

Maryal put her fork down. "No, I wasn't. I was thinking of something else."

"What were you thinking about?" said Keo, tilting his head to the side. "Your food?"

"No," said Maryal. "I was thinking about how you saved the Knights and how that's improved the public's perception of you."

"What do you mean?" said Keo.

Maryal sighed and rubbed her forehead. "Remember how you need to win the approval of the Tainians in order to win the Throne?"

"Yeah," said Keo, nodding. He took another bite out of his sausage and swallowed. "What of it?"

"Well, I was in the hallways of the Old Castle earlier and I overheard a couple of servants talking about you in glowing terms," said Maryal. "They were talking about how heroic it was of you to save the Knights from that 'mad Magician,' as they described Eliam. They seemed to think you were a hero, which you are, of course."

"Is that a good thing?" said Keo.

"Of course it's a good thing," said Maryal. "Think about it. Haven't you noticed how high the Knights of Lamaira are held in regard around here, even by the peasantry?"

"Nope," said Keo. "Haven't noticed a thing."

"Well, it's something I've noticed, anyway," said Maryal. "The people of Tain treat the Knights like heroes. Because you saved the lives of so many Knights and defeated a Magician who posed a real threat to the safety of the Tainians in general, I think that's improved the public's perception of you by quite a bit."

"Oh," said Keo. "Well, I wasn't intending to do that, but that's good, right?"

"It's great," said Maryal, rubbing her hands together eagerly. "It's even better because Easan has had far more time to win the approval of the public than you have, so this is a great first step in getting the Tainians on your side."

"Good to hear," said Keo, nodding as he ate some toast. "Speaking of Easan, I heard he was interrogating Eliam. Has he been up to anything else?"

"Not that I know of," said Maryal. "During the few times I've seen him, he's been storming around the Castle looking quite furious. I think he's angry that you stopped Eliam and he didn't, and also that you saved him from the demon."

"He's angry I saved his life?" said Keo. "That's ridiculous."

"Easan is very prideful, in case you hadn't noticed," said Maryal. "I think he was so used to being treated like the Rightful Heir that he doesn't know how to handle the fact that he might not be so special anymore. He's probably worried that he might not get the Throne, which he sees as his birthright, now that you are around and have cast some doubt upon his own parentage."

Keo shrugged. "I guess that's his problem, not mine. Still, I wonder if I should try talking with him or not. Even if only one of us can have the Throne, that doesn't mean we have to be enemies or hate each other. Maybe we could even work together to figure out how that demon got into the Castle."

"Easan would never sit down and have a reasonable conversation with you, so I don't see any point in doing it," said Maryal. "If you ask me, what you need to do is go out into the streets of Tain today and do some campaigning. Let everyone see the Hero of the Knights of the Old Kingdom."

"Is that what you're calling me now?" said Keo. "The Hero of the Knights of the Old Kingdom?"

"It's what I've heard some Knights call you," said Maryal. "But you can just shorten it to 'the Hero,' which I think is less of a mouthful. How does Keo the Hero sound?"

"Better than the alternative," said Keo. "But I still don't want to go walking around introducing myself as Keo the Hero. Just seems kind of arrogant."

"That's what you have *me* for," said Maryal, pointing at herself. "You don't even really need to say anything. I can talk to people for you. I'm good at that, so you don't need to worry your little head about anything."

Keo was doubtful about that, but before he could voice these doubts, the door to their dining room opened and a male servant poked his head through. "Keo of the Sword?"

"Yes?" said Keo, looking at the male servant. "What do you need?"

"The Keepers require your presence in the Archives," said the male servant. "They wish to speak with you and Easan down there."

Keo exchanged looks with Dlaine and Maryal before putting down his fork and knife and standing up. "Well, I guess I can't leave them waiting, then."

"Very well," sad the male servant. "Just follow me, sir, and we should reach the Archives in no time."

The male servant led Keo down a set of stairs that went deep into the earth. The stairs were wide enough so that Keo would not feel claustrophobic, but Keo nonetheless tasted a change in the air quality the further down they went. It went from the fresh and clean air of the main floors to an ancient, earthy, even slightly smoky, taste, not to mention it became darker and darker as well, although the male servant carried a bright torch with him to alleviate the darkness somewhat.

While the air and steps were much drier, Keo was reminded nonetheless of the secret entrance that he and the others had used to enter Capitika a month ago. He half-expected to see the frog demon come barreling up the steps toward them at any moment, even though the frog demon was dead. As a result, Keo kept his hand on the hilt of Gildshine as they walked deeper and deeper into the Archives.

Eventually, they reached a doorway at the bottom of the steps, an old-looking wooden door that had a heavy iron lock, which the male servant opened with an equally heavy-looking key on his ring. When he unlocked and opened the door, he entered first, following by Keo, who was amazed at what he saw on the other side.

They had emerged onto a platform high above a large room full of hundreds of large shelves that rose high from the floor below and stretched well into the distance. Each bookshelf carried hundreds of books on its shelves, ranging from books that looked almost new to ones that looked so old that they would fall apart if you looked at them the wrong way. Keo had seen few books during his youth—mostly just a handful from the bookseller in New Ora, who often sold books from other far-off lands to the wealthy in that town—but this was easily the most books he had ever seen in one location before. In fact, Keo had never even known that there were this many books in the world, so he just stood there for a moment staring at all of the shelves with his mouth hanging open.

"It is quite impressive, isn't it?" said the male servant, causing Keo to look at him. "I never get tired of seeing this whenever I have to come down here, usually to retrieve a specific volume for one of the Keepers."

"When I was told there were literally thousands of books down here, I thought it was an exaggeration," said Keo. "But this … this is real."

"Indeed, but our journey isn't over yet," said the male servant. He gestured to a set of stairs leading down to the ground floor, where the bookshelves stood. "Please follow me. The Keepers do not have much tolerance for lateness."

Keo nodded, and soon was following the male servant down the stone steps to the ground floor below. As they walked, Keo looked at the massive, numerous shelves, which looked big enough to crush him if they were to fall on him. He wondered who had built these and how, but decided not to ask this servant that question, mostly because he doubted the servant knew the answer to that question himself.

When they reached the ground floor, the shelves seemed even taller. As Keo followed the male servant between the massive shelves, he could not help but feel a sense of awe. Keo was normally not one to care about books, but there was something different about these books. Maybe it was due to their age or how many books were here, but as Keo walked between the large shelves, he felt like he had to be a lot more quiet than he usually was.

Soon, they arrived at a large, bookshelf-less space in the center of a group of shelves, which was also where a table with several tall stacks of books was located. The Keepers, all six of them, stood around the table, as did Easan, who as usual had his arms crossed over his chest. He scowled when he saw Keo and Keo returned the scowl, but said nothing because he knew that the Keepers would not tolerate any bickering between them.

"Keo," said Aster, waving at Keo from his spot on the other side of the table. "It is great to see you. We are glad that you wasted no time in getting here, though we apologize for interrupting your breakfast."

"No, it's all right," said Keo. "I got enough to eat."

"Very well," said Aster. He nodded at the male servant who had led Keo here. "You may leave and return to your regular duties."

The male servant bowed in affirmation, then stood up and walked away, leaving Keo, Easan, and the Keepers alone in the Archives.

Keo glanced at Easan and said, "Why is *he* here? I thought you just wanted to talk to me."

"We wanted to talk to both of you because you are both in the running to get the Throne, of course," said Aster. "Or will be soon, anyway. We wanted to share with your our findings on the duel that will determine who will become the next King of Lamaira."

"Finally," said Easan with a sigh. "I thought you Keepers would never stop researching about it. What did you learn?"

"We learned quite a bit," said Aster. "For example, we've discovered that it has not been practiced exactly the same way over the centuries. At one point, for example, there were three different heirs to the Throne, who fought a three-way duel that was rather bloody and ended with the winner going on to become one of the most bloodthirsty Kings that Lamaira has ever seen. But there is enough similarities between the duels to let us discern a basic pattern in them."

"And what is that basic pattern?" said Easan. "We are listening."

"The pattern is thus," said Aster. "First, the quarreling heirs must both be able to lay a strong claim to the Throne, whether through proving blood relation to the last King or some other means. For example, if King Riuno had left a will stating the identity of the next heir, then that would give one of the heirs a legitimate claim to the Throne."

"What is our strong claim to the Throne?" said Easan. "Our golden flames?"

"More or less," said Aster. "The fact that both of you fit the description of the *shelmai* exactly means that you both have equally strong claims to the Throne. But we want to make sure that you two are indeed blood-related to Riuno, so we must ask for a drop of blood from each of you."

Keo held his hand against his chest and Easan stepped back.

"A drop of blood?" said Keo. "What do you mean?"

"A literal drop of blood, of course," said Aster. He nodded at Seria, who held up a golden goblet with some kind of clear liquid in it that didn't appear to be water. "We must put a drop of blood into this goblet to ensure that you both are indeed related to the late King."

"How will putting some of our blood into that goblet prove anything?" asked Easan, who seemed just as skeptical of the goblet as Keo was.

"This goblet—which is called the Blood Goblet—is a magical artifact that has been in the Lamairan Royal Family for generations," said Aster, nodding at the Goblet. "It was crafted by the Good King himself, using ancient magic that even we Keepers do not know, shortly after he founded the Kingdom of Lamaira. He designed it to help his people in determining whether competing successors for the Throne were in fact related to him."

"How does it tell you if someone is related to him?" said Keo.

"Simple," said Aster. He held up his index finger on his right hand. "By putting a drop of your blood into the Goblet, the liquid in the Goblet will change color. If it turns blue, then that will prove that you are indeed related to King Riuno; if it turns red, however, then you are not related to the King or to any other member of the old Royal Family."

"Oh," said Keo. "That's simple."

"Very," said Aster. "Now, Easan, you may do it first, since you arrived in Tain before Keo did."

Easan—who didn't look thrilled at the idea of having to cut his own finger—nonetheless walked over to the Goblet, which Seria placed on the table near a stack of books. When Easan reached the Goblet, he raised his finger over it and allowed Seria to take a knife and cut it very slightly.

One tiny droplet of blood leaked out of the cut, which fell

from Easan's index finger into the Goblet below. When the drop fell into the Goblet, the Goblet's clear liquid turned a brilliant bright blue, like the sky on a sunny day, before returning to its original clearness, while Easan pulled his hand away from the Goblet and wrapped a tiny bandage around his finger that Seria gave him. Easan then stepped back, looking quite pleased with the color that the liquid had turned when his blood touched it.

"All right," said Aster. He looked at Keo. "Keo, please go over to the Goblet and let Seria cut your finger. It will be a very shallow cut, so you won't have to worry about dealing with any unnecessary pain or scars."

Keo bit his lower lip, because he didn't like getting cut, but he nodded and walked over to the Goblet. He passed Easan, whose glare he could feel on his back, and raised his hand over the Goblet when he reached it.

Like with Easan, Seria took Keo's finger and cut it with the knife. As Aster had promised, the cut was shallow and didn't even hurt all that much, but Keo still had to stop himself from flinching when he saw a drop of his blood leak out of his finger and fall into the Goblet below.

When Keo's blood drop touched the Goblet's clear liquid, it turned purple for a brief moment—causing Keo's hear to jump and Seria to look at her fellow Keepers in surprise—before it turned just as blue as it had with Easan's blood. A second later, the blueness faded and the Goblet's liquid was clear again.

Wrapping the bandage that Seria had handed to him around his finger, Keo said, "What … what does *purple* mean?"

"I don't know," said Aster. He sounded like he was genuinely at a loss. "It is supposed to be blue or red. I have never seen or even heard of purple before."

"But it turned blue anyway," Seria pointed out. "So perhaps it isn't worth worrying about. The Goblet is old, after all, so maybe its magic is getting weaker or maybe Keo's drop was not as large as Easan's, which would have made it harder for the Goblet to recognize."

"Possibly, but this worries me nonetheless," said Aster. "We will have to do some more research in the Archives about this, in case any past Keepers have written anything about this. All I know is that I do not like these kinds of surprises, even if the Goblet has ultimately decided that Keo is indeed related to King Riuno."

"So does that mean we're still going to do the duel?" said Keo, glancing at Easan, who looked disappointed that Keo had passed the test.

"Yes," said Aster, nodding. "Of course. You are both verified heirs to the Throne, but we can have only one King. Do not worry about the purple color of the Goblet's water. We will look into it ourselves later."

Keo doubted he would be able to stop worrying about this, but he nodded anyway and said, "All right. Now can you tell us what you learned about the duel?"

"Certainly," said Aster. "Firstly, we have already decided upon a date for the duel. It is set for one week from today, in the Grand Arena, where all such duels and competitions take place."

"A week?" said Keo. "That doesn't seem like enough time to get ready."

"Tradition dictates that the Throne must not be vacant for a long time if there are any known heirs to the Throne," said Aster.

"And Lamaira has already gone two decades without a proper King to sit on the Throne. We simply wish to get this out of the way as soon as possible so we can reunite the Kingdom and stop the coming demonic invasion, as the *shelmai* is prophesied to do."

"A week is plenty of time to prepare, if you ask me," said Easan with a chuckle. "Unless Keo the Hero decides that he would rather forfeit the match ahead of time and let me have the Throne. I will, of course, accept such a deal if offered to me, because the Kingdom of Lamaira should not go even one more day without a proper King to rule it."

Keo glared at Easan. "I'm not going to give up just yet. I was just thinking that the citizens of Tain might need more time to decide who they want to support. That's all."

"The Tainians have been looking forward to the duel ever since they heard of it," said Easan. "Many are just happy that the *shelmai*—whether he is me or you—will take the Throne, regardless of how the Rightful Heir must be chosen to do it."

"Easan is correct," said Aster. "The people of Tain are tired of waiting. The only reason we have even put it off as far as we have already is because we need to prepare the Grand Arena and ensure that everyone in the city knows when and where the duel is supposed to take place."

"Is that all you needed to tell us?" said Keo. "Is there anything else we need to know before the duel?"

"A few things," said Aster. "First, you will need to be fitted with the Ceremonial Armor, an ancient suit of armor that is supposed to be worn by members of the Royal Family when they are going to participate in a ceremony. This duel is technically a ceremony, even if an unorthodox one, and so both of you will need to wear the Armor during the duel as per tradition."

"How can both of us wear the same suit of Armor at once?" said Keo, looking at Easan and trying to imagine what it would feel like to have to wear the same suit of Armor as him at the same time. It was a silly mental image.

"There are actually a few sets of Ceremonial Armor designed for exactly this sort of occasion," said Aster. "They are currently located in the castle vault, but we will be removing them shortly and will allow both of you to wear them during the duel."

"Oh," said Keo. "Okay. What else?"

"Secondly, we will have a pre-duel dinner on the night before the duel," said Aster. "According to tradition, the significance of this dinner is to give both participants a final meal before the duel itself. This is to give both participants a taste of what will be theirs if they win the duel, and thus give them more motivation to fight and win."

Keo liked the idea of a pre-duel dinner, while Easan looked like he thought the idea was utterly ridiculous.

"And thirdly and finally, both of you must visit the Good King's Tomb and show your respects to the Good King himself," Aster finished. "This does not guarantee you anything, although it does show that you are willing and ready to carry the mantle of the Good King as you lead the Old Kingdom back to its original glory."

"That's it?" said Keo. "That's all we have to do?"

"Yes," said Aster. "There are many other things you *could* do, of course, but these are the only absolute requirements that we could find in the Archives and you can do them in whatever order you wish."

"Very well, then," said Keo. "What should we do first?"

"Be fitted with the Ceremonial Armor," said Aster. He frowned. "Unfortunately, the Ceremonial Armor has not been removed from the castle vault since the death of King Riuno, so it will take our servants some time to find two sets of Armor for both of you."

"In the meantime, we suggest that you go to the Good King's Tomb and pay your respects to him there," Seria said. "The Tomb is located on the other side of the city, but it isn't difficult to find, although we can provide you both with servants who can show you how to get there if you wish."

"That's not necessary," said Easan. He turned to leave. "I already know where the Tomb is, though I haven't visited it before. But I think I'll go and do that, now that you have explained why we should."

"I don't know where it is," said Keo. "So I'll need someone to help me get there."

"Very well," said Aster. "We will arrange for one of our servants to take you there. We will then summon both of you back to the Old Castle when the Armor is ready."

"All right," said Keo. "Can I bring any of my friends with me?"

"Certainly," said Aster. "Bring whoever you like, but when you go and pay your respects to the Good King, you must enter *alone*. Do you understand?"

Aster put a lot of emphasis on the word *alone*, which told Keo that Aster was very serious about making sure that Keo understood this. Keo didn't really understand why it was that important, but he supposed it had something to do with tradition, so he decided not to question it.

So Keo nodded and said, "I understand."

"Good," said Aster. He pointed behind Keo and Easan. "Now both of you may go. It is not wise to delay paying your respects to your ancestor, because that is sometimes the difference between those who succeed and those who fail. Remember that."

Keo did not see any connection between paying respects to his ancestor and succeeding or failing, but as usual, he said nothing about it. He just turned and followed another servant (who Keo had not heard arrive) back the way they came. This time, Easan walked beside Keo, probably because they were both leaving in the same direction, but they did not look at or talk with each other the whole time they followed the servant up the stairs and out of the Archives. Keo did glance at Easan once, noting that Easan, as usual, seemed angry.

Angry that he isn't going to get the Throne without a fight, Keo thought with some satisfaction. *Angry that I am just as much a son of Riuno as he is, at least if that Goblet is to be believed.*

That reminded Keo of the purple color that the Goblet had turned when his blood had fallen into it. It didn't make any sense to him, especially when Aster had admitted that even the Keepers did not know what that meant. Even if it was just some sort of strange error on the Goblet's part, it made Keo wonder if he really was related to Riuno at all or if it was some kind of fluke.

Whether I am or am not related to him, I'll have to focus on winning the duel, Keo thought. *And maybe the Good King's Tomb will help me understand what that purple color meant.*

Chapter Thirteen

KEO, DLAINE, MARYAL, AND Jola stood outside of the Good King's Tomb. The Tomb was a massive, square building located on the other side of Tain, just as Aster had said. It looked old and withered, likely because it had stood for centuries and was where the Good King's corpse was said to have been laid to rest. Large statues of the Good King himself—who looked somewhat like King Riuno, except far more muscular and with a short beard—stood on either side of the entrance like gatekeepers protecting the city gates. The entrance was currently closed, but some of the Keepers' servants were busily moving aside the huge round stone disk that stood in front of its entrance and which kept people from entering it. It was slow-moving due to the size and weight of the disk, but the servants were working hard and would likely have it open very soon.

Keo looked around at the area surrounding the Tomb. A tall metal fence separated the Tomb from the rest of the city, while a small bed of crimson flowers surrounded the Tomb on all sides. A stone pathway led from the gate in the walls up to the Tomb's front steps and only entrance.

Because the Tomb's gates were usually kept closed, there was no one else standing in the courtyard of the Tomb with them, except for Easan, who had arrived via a different route to the Tomb than they had. Easan stood several feet away from Keo and the others, having only barely acknowledged their existence when they arrived here and showing zero interest in interacting with any of them after that. Keo thought it strange how Easan, despite his popularity with the people, apparently did not have his own group of friends to travel with him like how Keo did.

I wonder how he got to Tain all by himself, then, Keo thought. *Then again, he's a native of the Old Kingdom, unlike me. Maybe he lived in a nearby town and so didn't have to travel as far or through as much danger as I did.*

In any case, Keo was fine that Easan ignored them. He could barely stand the young man, even though he now knew beyond a shadow of a doubt that the two of them were related and probably half-brothers. Keo had never had any siblings, but he found that his feelings toward Easan had not changed a bit since seeing the Goblet's water change colors upon taking a drop of Easan's blood. If he could go the rest of his life without having to speak with Easan again, Keo would have done it.

But Maryal, for whatever reason, kept looking between Keo and Easan like she was confused about something. Yet she didn't say anything, which just added to Keo's annoyance.

"What?" said Keo. "Did I say something?"

"What?" said Maryal. "Oh, no. It's nothing you've said. I was just thinking about what you told us on the way here, about how you and Easan are verified sons of Riuno. I was just trying to see if there were any physical similarities between you two. Family resemblance and all that."

Keo glanced at Easan and then looked at Maryal again. "There are no physical similarities between us. We look completely different."

"I know," said Maryal, nodding. "It's what I've noticed, which doesn't make any sense if you two are brothers."

"What if they had different mothers?" said Dlaine, who looked bored, probably because he had not actually wanted to come with them to the Tomb and had only agreed to come because he didn't want to be alone in the Old Castle all day. "That'd make 'em half-brothers, and also explain why they look different."

"That's what I thought, too, but even half-siblings usually share some features with the parent they share," said Maryal. She stroked her chin. "But you two don't share anything at all. It's very strange."

"It probably doesn't mean anything," said Keo. "And I don't really see any reason to worry about it. Maybe it is strange we don't look alike, but it doesn't really matter in the long run."

"I guess you're right," said Maryal. "But it won't stop bothering me. Siblings are always destined to resemble each other, yet here we have you two who don't look much like each other and yet are still related. It's driving me up a wall."

"Then stop letting it bother you," said Keo. "But now that you mention it, what happened to King Riuno's wife? I keep hearing about how he died, but wasn't he married?"

"According to legend, he was," said Maryal. "From what I've learned, his wife died during the chaos after his death, though no one ever found her body. Some people think she just went into hiding, but no one has ever found any evidence to suggest that, so everyone just thinks she's dead."

"Ah," said Keo. "I see. Maybe the Keepers could tell us more about her later, after I pay my respects to my ancestor."

Dlaine opened his mouth, but whatever he was going to say, he did not get a chance to say it, because the huge stone disk in front of the Tomb was suddenly pushed to the side by the servants who had been struggling to dislodge it. The disk rolled to the side loudly, revealing a round, dark entrance that seemed to go down forever. The servants stumbled for a moment before catching themselves and standing to the side, out of the entrance's path, probably to allow Keo and Easan to enter.

Then Keo looked at Easan and said, "Do you want to go in first or should I?"

Keo expected Easan to arrogantly proclaim that he was going to go in first and pay his respects to the Good King, but then Easan actually took a step back and said, "No, no, you can go first, Keo. I will go in after you."

That took Keo by surprise, especially the fear in Easan's voice. While the Tomb did look kind of creepy, Keo did not think that it was *that* scary. Besides, it wasn't like there was anything dangerous down there, although Keo bet that it probably didn't smell very good.

Nonetheless, Keo nodded and said, "All right. I'll be in and out quickly, so you won't have to wait for the pleasure to pay your respects to our ancestor."

Easan glared at Keo, probably because he noticed Keo's sarcasm and did not appreciate it.

But Keo said nothing else to Easan. He simply told Dlaine, Maryal, and Jola to wait out here for him before walking up the steps of the Tomb, past the servants who were learning against the Tomb's disk-shaped door and panting from the effort of opening it, and then—after the briefest moment's hesitation—into the

Tomb itself.

The very first thing Keo noticed about the Tomb's interior was that it was pitch-black. It was almost impossible to see anything, even his own fingers in front of his face, after traveling only a few feet inside. And Keo did not have a torch with him to expel the darkness, although then he remembered his golden flames. Unsheathing Gildshine, Keo focused on summoning the golden flames, but as always, he did not feel the fire within him for a few minutes before the warmth in his spirit appeared and then the flames appeared on Gildshine again, except this time they were much weaker than usual and flickered often. Even so, it took a lot of Keo's concentration to keep them lit.

As Keo walked down the steps deeper and deeper into the Tomb itself, he looked around at the walls and ceiling, curious about what he might see. He saw painted pictures of what appeared to be depictions of the Good King's battles with the demons, because the paintings almost universally depicted a lone warrior, wielding a sword that looked very much like Gildshine, slashing away at frightening-looking monsters that surrounded him on all sides. The demons depicted on the walls looked far worse than any demon Keo had fought, making him feel glad that he had not been forced to deal with those kinds of demons himself.

The air down in the Tomb was stale and smelled of death, which only became stronger and stronger the further down Keo walked. He had to cover his mouth and nose at one point, but he still kept going. He told himself that he was only going to be down there for less than an hour and then leave quickly. Yet even that thought was barely enough to keep him walking down deeper and deeper into the Tomb.

But finally, after about a minute or so of walking, Keo emerged into a much larger room. He looked around to see what the room was like.

Unfortunately, the golden flames of Gildshine did not reveal much, because they were small and weak and the shadows of the Tomb were thick and deep. But Keo got a sense that the room he had walked into—which he assumed was where the body of the Good King had been laid to rest—was much larger than he could see, although that did not stop him from looking around at what little the flames *did* show.

From what Keo could see, the Good King's Tomb was not home to just the Good King's corpse, but also to the corpses of the other Kings of Lamaira who had succeeded him. He believed this because he passed several sealed stone coffins on his way to the Good King's coffin, many of which were inlaid with gold, rubies, silver, and other things. They also had inscriptions carved into them, but because Keo could not read, he did not know what they said, though he assumed that the inscriptions identified each deceased King laid to rest here.

There had to be hundreds of these coffins, because Keo passed by coffin after coffin without even seeing the Good King's coffin, which he figured was at the back of the room away from the others. And then there was the fact that there were probably hundreds more coffins hidden outside of Keo's view by the shadows, which helped Keo grasp just how old the Kingdom of Lamaira was. He had always known that the Kingdom had lasted one thousand years before the death of King Riuno, but it had always been abstract knowledge. Here, though, was physical proof of the Kingdom's age.

And I am a descendent of all of these Kings, Keo thought, looking at the coffins as he passed them. *But I hardly know any of their names or what they did. Maybe, if I win the duel, I'll take the time to study Lamairan history and find out more about these men and who they were and what they did.*

But then Keo caught himself. Why was he thinking about learning about these Kings just because he might win the duel? Keo wasn't even really interested in becoming the King of Lamaira … or at least he hadn't been, anyway. Yet now, walking through this massive Tomb and seeing with his own eyes just how many men had ruled Lamaira before him, Keo now imagined himself sitting on the Throne, reuniting Lamaira, and then being laid to rest with the rest of these Kings after he grew old and passed away. He had never thought much about his own passing, but now that he did, he thought he'd prefer to be buried among his ancestors rather than in the Low Woods, as much as he loved the old forest that he grew up in.

Will my coffin be as fancy as these ones? Keo thought, looking at the old coffins as he walked past them, his footsteps loud in the empty Tomb. *I wonder if any of these kings even got a say in how their coffins looked or if that was decided by their heirs after their deaths.*

After a few more minutes of walking, something huge loomed in the flickering light of Gildshine's golden flames. Curious, Keo increased the power and light of the flames as much as he could, which wasn't quite as much as he wanted, but he succeeded in making more light for him to see the massive structure before him.

It was a huge stone casket, although it looked different from all of the other ones that Keo had seen so far. Its design was ancient, with chipped corners and no rubies or gold or anything else embedded into it. It towered over every other coffin in the area, but even without being able to read the inscription of the podium before it, Keo understood that this was the casket of the Good King himself. It looked old enough.

Why is it so big, though? Keo thought. *The Good King wasn't that big when he was alive, was he? Or maybe it's just big to emphasize how important he is. That's probably it.*

Keo walked up to the podium in front of the massive casket and looked up at it. He stood there in silence for a few seconds, not sure what to say to his long-dead ancestor. Aster may have told him to 'pay his respects,' but Keo, for the life of him, was not sure what that meant. The inhabitants of the Old Kingdom always followed tradition, but apparently this time Keo had a lot of freedom in how he chose to pay his respects to his ancestor.

So Keo said, "Good King, I, Keo of the Sword and one of your descendents, am here to pay my respects to you. You can't hear me right now, but perhaps my words will somehow reach you in the afterlife. I ask only that your spirit grant me guidance and wisdom in dealing with the responsibilities of being the King of Lamaira, if I win the duel and the people of Tain choose me as their king."

Keo stood there in silence. He wasn't sure what else to say or do. The Good King's casket was silent. He expected to hear something—maybe the spirit of the Good King calling to thank him for paying his respects—but nothing happened for a good few minutes as Keo stood there.

I've paid my respects, Keo thought. *Time to go.*

With that, Keo turned to leave, but then he heard what sounded like a claw scraping against stone and he froze. He looked to the left and to the right, but did not see anything in the shadows or in the light of his flames. Yet he was certain that he had heard something with claws move nearby, even if he couldn't spot it or pinpoint its exact location in relation to his own.

Another demon, Keo thought, a sense of dread running up his spine. *Of course.*

Keo had expected to run into another demon at some point, and indeed, this was the perfect place for a demon to attack him. It was dark and huge, with plenty of places for a demon to hide, and Keo was all alone. True, Keo could defend himself with Gildshine, but the demons had already shown themselves to be cunning and intelligent foes. All this demon needed to do was sneak up on Keo and get him when he least expected it, which would be easy to do in this dark place.

Then Keo heard the scratching of a claw against stone again. This time, it sounded like it was coming from directly behind him, causing Keo to whirl around to face whatever was there, Gildshine in both hands.

But Keo saw nothing except for the Good King's casket. Then he heard movement above and looked up at the top of the casket.

Standing on top of the casket, its eyes reflecting the light of Gildshine's golden flames, was a large dragon looking down directly at Keo.

Chapter Fourteen

THE DRAGON'S CLAWS GRIPPED the lid of the casket. Its snout was long and smoky, while its scales and skin were as black as midnight, which made its massive body blend in well with the shadows of the Tomb, even with Keo's golden flames lighting the area. He could not see its wings, although he suspected that they were folded against its back.

Regardless, Keo stood there, frozen in fear, staring at it. He had never seen a dragon before. Master Tiram had told him legends about dragons, of course, but he had been told that dragons had not been seen in Lamaira for a hundred years. This one had to be a demon, because it was the only way to explain the presence of a dragon here in the Tomb. Granted, Keo had never seen a demon take on the form of a dragon, but he wouldn't put it past a demon to do something like that.

Yet the dragon did not seem to be looking at Keo with hostility the way a demon would. It simply stared at him with its huge, lantern-like eyes, but it was hard to guess what it was thinking because its face was so different from a human's.

But then Keo studied it a little bit more and realized that the dragon was looking at Keo with interest. He found himself understanding the interest in its eyes; in fact, he thought that the dragon seemed almost concerned about him, which was bizarre because Keo had certainly never met this particular dragon before, or any dragon at all for that matter, so there was no reason for this dragon to care about him.

Another thing Keo did not understand was why the dragon was here or how it even got down here at all. The Keepers had not mentioned that there was a dragon down here, awaiting the appearance of the Good King's descendents. Maybe it was another one of the Old Kingdom's strange traditions, but then, if it was, the Keepers surely would have mentioned it at some point.

Has it been down here this entire time? Keo thought, watching it carefully as the dragon's eyes swept over his form. *If so, then how has it survived? There isn't any food or water down here, unless it has been chewing on the bones of my ancestors, although I'm not sure how a dragon of that size could get much nutrition from bones as old as these.*

Although the dragon did not seem hostile, Keo was not going to take any chances. He considered running, but then he realized that the dragon could probably easily catch up with him, either by flying or running, and then snap him up like a rat.

But Keo wasn't sure he could fight the dragon all by himself. Master Tiram's tales about the dragons of old had said that one dragon was strong enough to destroy entire armies of humans. In fact, the story of Fronr the Dreaded had said that it took an army of a million of the mightiest men in Lamaira and nine other countries to stop him, and even then, half a million men died in the struggle and another quarter ended up suffering severe injuries, both physical and mental, for the rest of their lives.

Now Keo was not sure if the story of Fronr the Dreaded had any truth to it, because Master Tiram had treated it as nothing more than a silly story at the time, but Keo had no doubt that he was no match for this dragon. He could try calling for help, but he was so deep inside the Tomb at this point that he wasn't sure that anyone could even hear him. And even if they did hear his calls for help, would they be fast enough to get down here in time to save him? Or would they arrive just in time to see him get killed, and then die themselves when the dragon decided to kill them as well?

I'm all alone no matter how you look at it, Keo thought. *The question is, how do I survive long enough to get out of here?*

The answer, of course, was that Keo *wouldn't* survive. Keo didn't think of himself as a pessimist, but even he knew that he was outclassed in every way by this dragon. Nonetheless, if the dragon attacked, he would fight back with everything he had, if only because he would prefer to die fighting than to die like a coward.

But then the dragon opened its mouth. Keo, expecting the dragon to breathe fire, took a battle stance, even though he was well aware that there was nothing he could do to actually defend himself from the dragon's flames.

What Keo did not expect to happen, however, was for the dragon to speak. And not only did it speak, but it spoke in understandable Lamairan as well.

"Brave swordsman," said the dragon. Its voice was surprisingly human, yet with a hint of the dragon behind it. "You have already faced many challenges on your quest, but the worst still await you, especially as the demons' power and influence continues to grow and spread throughout the remains of Lamaira."

Keo was almost too shocked to respond, but then he shook his head and said, "Who are you? How do you know what I've been through? And where did you come from?"

"I cannot answer these questions, swordsman," said the dragon. It sounded sorrowful. "It is a great risk for me just to appear to you like this. But I had to do it, because I believe that you have the power to save Lamaira, whether or not you realize it."

"Power?" said Keo. He glanced at Gildshine's golden flames. "Do you mean these flames?"

"Your true power isn't even known to you yet," said the dragon, shaking its head. "But if you wish to know the true extent of your power, then you must travel to the Upper Mountains in the north, where your other people live."

Keo knew what the Upper Mountains were. They were a range of mountains north of Lamaira that were devoid of human inhabitants. No one knew exactly what lay in those Mountains, although Keo had heard stories describing mountain trolls and living rock monsters infesting the Mountains' highest peaks.

But Keo still said, "The Upper Mountains? My other people? What do you mean?"

"You will understand if you go there," said the dragon. "The demons you have faced thus far have been weak and ineffectual, but not all demons are weak. Some make even me tremble in their sheer might, though all pale in comparison to the might of their King."

"Who is their King?" said Keo. "The first demon I fought back in the Low Woods, he mentioned a King of Demons. Who is he?"

"That, too, I cannot answer," said the dragon, "but I can tell you this: If Lamaira is going to survive the demonic threat, then you must travel to the Upper Mountains and seek out aid from your other people there. If you fail in this task, then it will not matter if you successfully reunite the three factions, because the King of Demons will crush you under his might."

"What is this aid in the Upper Mountains?" said Keo. "Can you tell me anything about it?"

"Not yet," said the dragon, shaking its head. "But you must go to them anyway. And it *must* be you, because they will listen to no one else."

"But I have the duel with Easan in a week," Keo said. "And if I win the duel and become the King, then I will have no time to go to the Upper Mountains and seek aid there from the people you've told me about."

"You must still go, regardless of the outcome of your duel," said the dragon. "Even if you defeat Easan, you and Lamaira will still lack the power and strength necessary to stand against the demonic forces that grow in strength every day."

"Okay, but can you at least tell me where the demons are going to return?" said Keo. "That is something we still don't know."

"I can tell you that the demons will rise from the pit, where they were banished by the Good King ages ago," said the dragon. "As for the pit's location—"

The dragon suddenly stopped speaking. It raised its head, as if it saw something.

"Dragon?" said Keo. "What is it?"

Then Keo heard it. Footsteps in the shadows behind him, boots clicking against the ancient stone floor of the Tomb. It sounded like someone was coming, but Keo did not know who.

"I must go," said the dragon, its voice a mere whisper now. "But remember, Keo of the Sword: To defeat the demons, you must go to the Upper Mountains, no matter what happens next week."

With that, the dragon pulled back into the shadows outside of the light from Gildshine's flames. Keo stepped forward to ask it to come back, but before he could say anything, a familiar, sneering voice behind him said, "There you are."

Keo turned around just as Easan stepped into the circle of light created by Gildshine's flames. He folded his arms over his chest, looking unimpressed.

"What are you doing here?" said Keo. "I thought that we were going to take turns paying our respects to the Good King."

"You were taking too long," said Easan simply. "And so I came down to see if you had perhaps tripped on the steps and smashed your head open on the floor. Sadly, it looks like your balance isn't as bad as I thought."

Easan's mocking tone annoyed Keo, who said, "Well, for your information, I was just making sure to pay my respects to the Good King correctly. That's why I was taking so long down here, though thanks for coming to check on me. You're the last person I'd expect to do that."

"I wasn't concerned for your safety, if that's what you are thinking," said Easan. "I simply wish to get all of the formalities and traditions out of the way as quickly as possible so there is no delay for my inevitable rise to the Throne."

"Inevitable?" said Keo. "I didn't know you could see the future."

Easan scowled. He leaned forward, which made him seem more threatening. "Recall, brother, that the people of Tain love *me*. They see me as their true hope. Whether I win the duel or not, the people will choose me over you. I almost feel sorry for you, knowing your inevitable defeat, and if you wish to give up now —"

"No," Keo interrupted. "I'm not going to give up. The people may love you, but that doesn't mean they will always love you. I'm going to give it my all and won't give up until I actually lose to you in a fair fight."

Easan pulled back. He did not seem to know what to say to that, so he changed the subject and said, "I heard you speaking to someone, but I don't see anyone in here aside from us."

Keo considered telling Easan about the dragon, but then he realized that he didn't trust Easan with that kind of information. He still needed to think about it himself, after all.

So he said, "I was talking to the Good King, of course."

Easan raised an eyebrow. "He's dead."

"I know," said Keo. "But I wanted to let him know that his kingdom was going to be reunited again and to share with him some of my own fears and worries anyway. It was how I chose to pay my respects to him."

Easan looked skeptical, but then he shrugged and said, "All right. I don't particularly care about that. Why don't you just run along back to that old fart and your girlfriend and go back to the Castle? I want to pay my respects to the Good King by myself."

"Okay," said Keo. "I was just finishing up anyway. But do you need a light?"

Easan drew Shadowbane from its sheath and held it up.

Immediately, Shadowbane burst into brilliant golden flames that made Gildshine's own golden flames look puny in comparison. Shadowbane's flames illuminated far more of the Tomb than Keo's did, showing even more ancient coffins that stretched far out in every direction.

Easan smirked at Keo. "No. But do you?"

Keo didn't respond. He just glared at Easan and then walked around him back to the Tomb's entrance. As Keo walked away, he looked over his shoulder at Easan, who had walked up to the Good King's casket and was now kneeling before it, making himself look very humble indeed.

But Keo decided not to think about Easan anymore. He just kept walking, thinking about what the dragon had told him, and trying to make sense of it all. He decided to talk about it with Dlaine and Maryal. Perhaps they would be able to help him understand what the dragon had told him.

Chapter Fifteen

WHEN KEO EMERGED FROM the Good King's Tomb, he told Dlaine, Maryal, and Jola that he wanted to talk with them about something he had seen in the Tomb, but not at their current position. Because it was lunchtime, Keo and the others decided to find some place to eat and where Keo could tell them about what he'd seen in private.

One of the servants who had opened the Tomb recommended to them a bakery near the Tomb that, in the servant's own words, made "bread that tasted liked heaven."

So Keo and his friends went to the bakery, which was called Olom's Bakery, named after the owner of the bakery. Even before they stepped inside the bakery, Keo could smell the scent of fresh bread being baked, which instantly made his mouth salivate.

They walked up to the counter, which was currently unoccupied. That made Keo wonder where the owner was before a voice called out from the kitchen in the back, "Please wait one moment! I am coming to take your order!"

A second later, a man with a handlebar mustache stepped out from the kitchen and walked up to the counter. The man was wiping flour off of his hands with a rag and had a flour-covered apron covering his body, but there was something familiar about the man, like Keo had seen him somewhere before.

"Welcome to Olom's Bakery," said the man, flashing them a

brilliantly white smile. "My name is Olom and—"

Olom abruptly ceased speaking when his eyes fell on Keo. His jaw dropped, like he had just seen something that he could not believe.

"By the Good King's name," said Olom, shaking his head in an apparent attempt to regain his composure. "You are Keo the Hero, right? The second *shelmai*? The one who saved our brave Knights from that mad Magician?"

Keo nodded, although he felt a little embarrassed at Olom's exaggerated response. "Yes, I am."

"We met before," said Olom, rubbing his hands together eagerly. "Remember? It was at the parade last week, when you first arrived in Tain. I told you about Easan."

"Now that you mention it, I do recall talking to you," said Keo. "Anyway, we came here for lunch on the recommendation of one of the Old Castle's servants, so we're ready to buy whatever you have to offer."

Olom, however, didn't seem to be listening to Keo. He was now looking at his shoes and muttering under his breath, "What luck I have. First I fed the first *shelmai*, now I will feed the second. The Good King must be smiling upon my business."

Then Olom looked up at Keo and the others and gave them an even wider smile than before. "Yes, yes, of course I will serve you. In fact, I will even give you a fifty percent discount on all of the products in this bakery."

"Fifty percent?" said Keo. "That's awfully generous of you, Olom, but—"

"But we'll graciously accept your kind offer," Maryal said, interrupting Keo and flashing her own smile at Olom. "The *shelmai* always appreciates the generous offers of the people of Tain and will almost certainly remember them when he rises to the Throne."

"Wonderful," said Olom. Then he held up a pen and paper. "Just tell me what you want and I will make it and bring it out to you myself."

Keo wanted to say that they didn't really need the fifty percent discount, but Maryal had taken full control of the conversation now and she was the one who ordered for all of them. Not that Keo would have ordered, seeing as he wasn't familiar with the baked goods that Olom offered, but he wondered what Maryal was doing anyway.

After Maryal gave their order to Olom, the baker told them that he would have all of their food fresh from the oven in ten minutes. He showed them to a booth in one corner of the bakery (which apparently also acted as restaurant) and then vanished behind the kitchen. A moment later, the sounds of baked goods being prepared could be heard coming from the kitchen as Olom worked furiously to make their food for them in a timely manner.

Keo, who sat next to Dlaine and opposite Maryal, looked at her and asked, "Why'd you say that we accept the offer when you knew I was going to reject it?"

"Because it's never wise to turn down an offer like that in your situation," said Maryal, rolling her eyes. She gestured toward the kitchen. "You saw Olom. He thinks you're a hero. If you are going to win the hearts and minds of the people of Tain, then you need to show them that you appreciate and accept their offers. If this will help Olom become your supporter, then he might tell his friends and family, who might then also become your supporter or at least will rethink their allegiance to Easan."

"Oh," said Keo. "I didn't realize that."

"Few do," said Maryal. Then she patted Keo on the arm. "But that's why you have me. With my help, you won't even have to participate in the duel in order to win."

"I'm just glad we're getting such a steep discount," said Dlaine. He patted his pocket, which jingled with the money in it. "Did you see the price for a loaf of bread? Two hundred lems. We couldn't afford that even if we wanted to."

"Exactly," said Maryal. "Keo, winning the approval of the people of Tain is not going to be easy, but you have to do it if you're going to beat Easan and ascend to the Throne. It's basic politics."

"All right," said Keo, nodding. He rubbed his stomach. "You're right. I'm too hungry to argue the point anyway."

"Good," said Maryal, who looked quite pleased with herself for winning the argument. "Anyway, Keo, you said you wanted to tell us about what happened in the Tomb. Did you see something strange in there?"

Keo looked back to the kitchen, but all of the loud noises most likely meant that Olom couldn't hear anything they said. So he explained to Dlaine, Maryal, and Jola, as briefly and quietly as he could, about the dragon in the Tomb and what the dragon had told him.

By the time he finished, Dlaine and Maryal looked just as mystified as Keo felt. Jola was probably puzzled as well, but Keo could not see her, so he did not know how she looked. Nor did he hear her voice in his head, though that didn't matter because he knew that Dlaine and Maryal, at least, would respond to the story.

Dlaine drummed his fingers on the table, clearly lost in thought. "Well ... that's certainly a wild story if I ever heard one."

Maryal leaned across the table toward Keo, looking at him straight in the eye. "Was it *really* a dragon you saw? An actual, real-life dragon?"

"It was," said Keo, nodding. "I saw it with my own two eyes. It looked just like how the old legends described them."

"But where did it come from?" said Maryal. She pulled back, looking confused. "How did it even get in there without us seeing it?"

"I don't know," said Keo. "What makes that even weirder is that it wasn't some small baby dragon. It looked like a full-grown adult to me, big enough to chew me up and spit me out. But that's not as important as understanding what it had said to me."

"About having to go to the Upper Mountains?" said Maryal. "And how 'your other people' are there and how you need to go there to access your 'true power'?"

"Yeah, that," said Keo. "The dragon said that I would need to go to the Upper Mountains and get help there if we are to defeat the demons once and for all. But what is in the Upper Mountains?"

He looked at Dlaine and Maryal for answers.

But it was Jola, surprisingly enough, who answered telepathically. *The Dracones.*

"The Dracones?" said Keo. "The dragon people? Aren't they a myth?"

"So everyone says," said Dlaine, leaning back in his seat, but hardly looking relaxed. "But I see where Jola is going with this. The Dracones are said to live in the Upper Mountains, far away from civilization, but no one has actually seen any, so no one knows if they are actually there or not."

"Was that dragon telling me to go to the Dracones, then?" said Keo. "To a group of people that may not actually exist?"

"No idea," said Dlaine with a shrug. "I wasn't there, but hey, we didn't think dragons existed anymore, either, and yet you spoke to one not even an hour ago. Maybe the Dracones do exist after all."

"I'm just not sure that I should go there," said Keo. "The Upper Mountains are supposed to be hard to reach and even harder to climb. It might just be a huge waste of time, even though I think that dragon was genuinely trying to help me."

"But what if it isn't?" said Maryal. "We've had good luck so far in defeating the demons, but I am not sure that the rest of Lamaira is ready for them or could stand much of a chance against them in a battle. Maybe the Dracones will be able to help us … if they exist, of course."

"Even if the Dracones do exist, even if they are in the Upper Mountains, do we really need their help?" said Keo. "I just think that it makes a lot more sense to stay here in the Old Kingdom—whether or not I win the duel—than it does to go on a wild goose chase into lands that very few people have ever returned from alive."

"I agree," said Dlaine, nodding. "All of the old legends never describe the Dracones as being particularly kind toward humans anyway. Even though Dracones are supposed to be part-human themselves, a lot of the old legends set after the Good King founded the Kingdom of Lamaira describe dozens of wars between humans and Dracones. I doubt the modern Dracones are any more tolerant or kind than their ancestors."

"Exactly," said Keo. "So I don't see any reason to worry about this. I just thought I'd tell you guys about it so we'd all know and to see what you guys thought."

"I agree we shouldn't be going abroad in search of a people who may or may not exist," said Maryal, "but I can't help but wonder why that dragon showed itself to you. Wasn't it about to tell you where the demons were going to rise from?"

"It was, but then Easan came in and the dragon fled because it didn't want anyone else seeing it," said Keo, folding his arms across his chest and scowling. "Stupid Easan."

"What makes that frustrating is that no one knows where the demons were sealed away," said Maryal, glancing toward the kitchen, although Olom still did not appear to be finished making their lunch just yet. "All of the stories I know say that the Good King sealed the demons away in the 'pit,' but the stories never mention where its located. Magicians have been arguing about its exact location for centuries now and there's still no consensus on where this 'pit' is located."

"Do you think the Keepers might know?" said Dlaine. "They are pretty knowledgeable about all of the old stories and legends. They might be able to tell us where the demons were sealed away."

"I hope so, but I'm not optimistic about that," said Keo. "The Keepers didn't seem to know where the demons were sealed when I spoke with them, but maybe there's an old book somewhere in the Archives that says where they are. The Archives are a big place, after all, and there are literally thousands of old books down there, so there's got to be at least *one* book that holds the information we need to know."

"We'll have to ask the Keepers about that when we go back to the Old Castle later," said Maryal. "I'm sure they'll be able to find *something* for us, even if it's just a clue to point us in the right direction for further research."

"Let's hope so," said Keo. "Because if we are going to stop the demons, we'll need to know where they are going to rise again. Otherwise, it won't matter if we succeed in reuniting the Kingdom, because the demons will still have an important edge on us."

At that moment, Olom stepped out of the kitchen, carrying a large tray with their food on it. The baker walked over to their table with the tray in both hands, saying, "I deeply apologize for my lateness—I ran into a few problems getting everything together—but here is your order, just as you asked."

Keo smiled when he smelled the food, which smelled absolutely better than anything Keo had ever smelled before in his life, but before Olom could place the tray on the table, there was a sudden scream in the streets outside. Keo immediately looked out the window and saw a woman in the streets who was being assaulted by a couple of thuggish-looking men. The woman wore an expensive-looking purple robe and appeared to be quite wealthy, but none of that mattered because one of the men had grabbed her while the other was trying to wrest something from her hands that was too small for Keo to see but which he knew must have belonged to her.

Without even thinking about it, Keo stood up and dashed from the table to go save the woman, ignoring the surprised calls from the others to come back. He burst out of the bakery and ran over to the thugs, who did not notice Keo approaching until Keo grabbed the man trying to steal the thing from the woman and threw him to the street as hard as he could.

The thug hit the street hard and lay there, stunned, while Keo turned his attention to the second thug, who still held the woman in his grasp. But he was now staring at Keo in surprise and confusion, rather than rage and anger.

"Who the heck are you?" said the thug in a rough and gravelly voice.

Before Keo could answer, the woman who was being held by the thug slammed her foot down on the thug's boot as hard as she could. The thug let out a yell of surprise and let go of her, allowing the woman to run away out of his reach. She stopped next to Keo, while the first thug got back up to his feet and faced Keo.

"Thanks," said the woman, who Keo could now see was holding a box to her chest. "I didn't think anyone would come to save me."

"No problem, but it's not over yet," said Keo, looking at the two thugs, who had both recovered from the attacks on them and were now advancing on him and the woman with their hands balled into fists.

"Who do you think you are?" said the first thug with a sneer. His eyes glanced at Gildshine, sheathed safely by Keo's side. "A Knight?"

Keo shook his head and drew Gildshine. "No. I'm just a guy who doesn't like seeing thugs like you harming innocent women."

"Oh, now you're acting all tough like you could take us on," said the first thug. He punched his fist into his other hand. "We'll just walk over you, take that what woman has, and be on our way."

"You'll have to knock me down on the street before you can walk over me," Keo said. "And I'm not easy to knock down."

"Did you seriously just say something *that* cheesy?" said the first thug in astonishment. He shook his head. "Doesn't matter. Get him!"

The two thugs ran toward Keo, while Keo pushed the woman back behind him to keep her out of the fight. She did not object in the slightest.

Then Keo dashed toward the two thugs and met them halfway. The first thug threw a punch at Keo, which he dodged, but the second thug kicked him. That actually connected, hitting Keo in the knee and bringing him down onto the street, but he quickly kicked out the legs of the first thug and brought him down to the street as well. The second thug, however, was still standing and raised his boot to bring it down on Keo's head, but at the last second, Dlaine appeared and punched the second thug in the face.

The second thug staggered backwards from the blow while Keo and the first thug rose back to their feet. Rather than go in for the kill, the first thug stepped backwards, looking at both Keo and Dlaine with a new uncertainty in his eyes that told Keo that he was not so sure he could win now.

Looking at Dlaine, Keo said, "What are you doing here? I thought you were back in the bakery."

Dlaine grinned. "What? And let you have all the fun? I've been itching for a fight anyway. Let's show these two how we fight back in the south."

Keo smiled back and nodded, then turned his attention to the thugs. They had both recovered from the previous blows dealt to them, but they did not appear eager to engage either Keo or Dlaine in a fight again.

Nonetheless, the first thug said, in a sneering tone, "What's this? Got your grandpa to help? I'm more worried he'll throw out his back fighting us than actually beating us."

"But he can hit hard, Kal," said the second thug, rubbing the side of his face where Dlaine had punched him. "Almost knocked me out completely. He ain't no ordinary grandpa, that's for sure."

"Grandpa?" Dlaine repeated. He laughed. "Can your grandpa do this?"

Dlaine ran at the two thugs with his fists lowered. The first thug, the one called Kal, tried to throw a punch at Dlaine, but Dlaine dodged it easily and responded with a punch of his own. Kal fell flat on his back on the street, while his friend drew a knife from his pocket and tried to stab Dlaine, but Dlaine grabbed the second thug's wrist and twisted it, forcing the second thug to drop his knife onto the street.

Before the knife even hit the pavement, Dlaine slammed his fist into the jaw of the second thug. The second thug immediately collapsed onto the street, and a second later his knife fell onto it as well.

"There," said Dlaine, dusting off his hands with a satisfied smirk on his face. "That's what you get for not respecting your elders."

Keo had forgotten just how good a fighter Dlaine actually was, so when he saw that both of the thugs were down already, he at first thought that his eyes must have been playing tricks on him. But when he blinked and looked again, he saw that the thugs were indeed down for the count.

Then, without warning, Kal's eyes opened. He immediately pulled a knife out of his breast pocket and jumped to his feet. Dlaine's back was to Kal, so he did not see the knife that was coming for his back.

But there was no time to warn him. Keo drew Gildshine from its sheath and, as he did so, golden flames erupted along its blade without another thought from him. He pointed Gildshine at the thug and fire leaped out from Gildshine's tip, flew past Dlaine's shoulder, and burned Kal's knife hand, forcing Kal to drop the knife and cry out in pain as he clutched his wrist.

Dlaine—who must have heard Kal's cry of pain—whirled around and socked Kal in the face without hesitation. And like his friend, Kal was knocked down to the street, but this time, he appeared to be unconscious for good.

Dlaine lowered his fists, while Keo lowered Gildshine, which was no longer burning with its golden flames anymore. Dlaine looked at Keo and said, "Thanks for the save."

"No problem," said Keo, giving Dlaine the thumbs up. Then he looked at the rich lady behind him and said, "Ma'am, are you hurt?"

The rich lady seemed to have lost the ability to speak, because she was staring at Keo in pure shock with her mouth hanging open. It was like she had just seen a ghost, although Keo was not sure what she was so surprised about.

Then Keo heard movement and looked around to see that their fight in the streets had not gone unnoticed. Random civilians were standing nearby, staring at Keo, Dlaine, and the unconscious thugs in surprise. Some people were even watching from the safety of their homes, poking their heads out the windows of nearby buildings to see the fight.

It occurred to Keo that the entire fight must have been watched by all of these people. While none of them looked angry with Keo or Dlaine, he wondered nonetheless if they had done something wrong. He doubted there were laws in Tain against saving civilians from thugs like what Keo and Dlaine did just now, but he still worried that the people might be angry with Dlaine and him for some reason.

Then the rich woman said, "Those golden flames ... are you Keo the Hero? The other *shelmai* I've heard so much about?"

Keo nodded. "Yes, that's me. And you are?"

The rich woman brushed back her hair and said, "Why, I'm Hesera, the most famous actress in the entire Old Kingdom. And you just saved my life. I must thank you for it."

"You're welcome," said Keo. He looked around at all of the people still staring at them. "Why is everyone still staring at us?"

Hesera opened her mouth to say something, but at that moment Keo heard the clanking of armored feet and looked down the street to see five Knights running toward them. When the Knights reached Keo, Dlaine, and Hesera, four of them immediately went over to check on the unconscious thugs, while the other one—who was probably the captain of this group of Knights—walked up to Keo and Hesera, though with his visor covering his face, it was impossible to tell what he looked like.

"What happened here?" said the lead Knight, his voice somewhat tinny through the visor. "We received reports from witnesses that there was an assault and attempted robbery on someone here."

Before Keo could explain, Hesera grabbed Keo's arm and pulled herself right up to his side. "I was just walking down the street, Sir Knight, when I was attacked by those ruffians. But then this fine young man—Keo the Hero, in case you didn't recognize him—and his friend saved me. Neither Keo nor his friend have done anything wrong or committed any crimes. Of that, I can assure you."

Keo wished Hesera was not so close to him, but he doubted he could push her away without looking like a jerk. So he just nodded and said, "That's exactly what happened, Sir Knight, but if you need more details, we can provide them."

"No, no, that won't be necessary," said the Knight, shaking his head. "I recognize those two thugs. Kal and Saze are already wanted for robbery and several other crimes. We'll be hauling them to jail, but if we have any questions, we'll be sure to contact you. You are staying at the Old Castle, correct?"

Keo nodded. "Right."

Then the Knight suddenly bowed. "It was an honor to meet you, Keo the Hero. I wish you luck in your duel with Easan next week."

With that, the Knight stood upright and walked away to join his fellow Knights, already barking at them to take the thugs to jail. Keo watched the Knight go, puzzled at his behavior, before he heard Maryal shout, "Keo!"

Looking over his shoulder, Keo saw Maryal rapidly approaching, with a piece of bread in her hand that looked like the freshly-baked stuff that Olom had made for them. She bit off a chunk of the bread and swallowed it quickly before she came to a stop before him.

"Keo, I'm so glad you and Dlaine are all right," said Maryal. "I would have come and helped you myself, but I was just so hungry and Olom's bread smelled so good."

"It's all right," said Keo, glancing at Dlaine, who was also approaching them. "They weren't that hard, not in comparison to the demons and Eliam, at any rate."

"Who is this?" said Hesera, who Keo remembered was still holding onto his arm. She sounded disgusted—and more than a little jealous—as she looked Maryal up and down.

"I'm Maryal, Keo's friend," said Maryal, who had a noticeably icy tone to her words as well. "And thanks for introducing yourself, by the way."

"Oh, excuse me, I thought *everyone* knew who I was already," said Hesera. "I'm Hesera, the most famous stage actress in the Old Kingdom."

Maryal's expression went from icy and even jealous to interested in a flash. "The most famous stage actress in the Old Kingdom? Does that mean you have a lot of fans and admirers?"

Hesera again brushed back her hair, which seemed to be a habit of hers, and said, "Why, I have more than a few, yes. Even Aster of the Keepers counts himself as one of my fans."

Maryal rubbed her hands together eagerly. "Well, that's great to hear. Are you going to reward Keo with anything, per chance, for saving your life?"

"Maryal—" said Keo, but Hesera said, "Why, I was intending to give him a thousand lems for saving my life. Why do you ask?"

"We can do without the money," said Maryal. She leaned closer toward Hesera a little, her eyes gleaming with triumph and eagerness. "Can you instead endorse Keo for the Throne of the

Kingdom? Tell your fans and admirers how great a King he'd make? How he'd be better than Easan?"

Hesera looked a little taken aback by the request, but then nodded and said, "Certainly. While Easan is certainly a handsome fellow, he never saved *my* life, not like Keo did, that's for sure. I wouldn't mind if it Keo became the next King of Lamaira, not one bit."

"Excellent," said Maryal. Then she looked at Keo. "Keo, do you want to go back to the bakery now and get lunch?"

Keo suddenly realized just how hungry he was, especially after that fight, and said, "Sure. I'm starving." He looked down at Hesera, who still clung to his arm like glue. "Hesera, can you please let go of my arm now?"

Hesera let go of his arm and said, "All right. But before you go, I want to give you another, more immediate reward than a simple endorsement."

Hesera popped open the box in her hands and pulled out a long, fancy-looking necklace, which she immediately put around Keo's neck. Keo looked down at the golden part of the necklace and saw that it was some kind of locket with the symbol of the Old Kingdom engraved on it. He popped open the locket, only to see that there was a tiny mirror on the inside.

He looked at Hesera in confusion. "Uh, thanks for the gift."

"You're welcome, but it's not a mere gift," said Hesera. "I have another just like it that can allow us to communicate over short distances. This way, we can stay in contact even apart … if you know what I mean."

Hesera winked at Keo when she said that, which made Keo feel uncomfortable. Nonetheless, he closed the locket and stuff it down his shirt as he said, "Well, I'm sure it will prove useful at some point if I ever wish to contact you again."

"Oh, I just know it will," said Hesera. "Anyway, I must be off. Good luck against Easan."

With that, Hesera walked down the street, away from Keo, Maryal, and Dlaine, who had been standing there rather silently for the past few seconds.

"Well," said Dlaine, causing Keo to look at him. He was grinning. "Looks like you have a new admirer, Keo. And she's a looker, too."

"Shut up," said Keo. He rubbed his stomach. "I'm hungry. Let's go eat already. I don't want to go another second without food in my mouth."

"But don't you realize what just happened?" said Maryal, rubbing her hands together eagerly. "Or will I have to explain it to both of you?"

"I think you'll have to explain it, because I'm not sure what just happened," Keo said, glancing at the bakery longingly.

"You just received an endorsement from one of the most famous and popular people in the city," Maryal explained. "I don't know much about this Hesera lady, but if she's a popular stage actress, then she probably has a ton of fans who hang on her every word. That means that they'll start to support *you* once they hear her gushing about how great you are."

"And then they'll be more likely to vote for Keo in the duel with Easan," said Dlaine, who sounded like he had just come to that conclusion himself. He wagged a finger at Maryal in approval. "Maryal, you are certainly not the kind of woman to let these opportunities pass you by, huh?"

"Of course not," said Maryal. "As Keo's manager, it is my duty to keep an eye out for these sorts of opportunities. It's the only way to get ahead in politics."

"I see," said Keo. "Well, that's great. I hope it works out like you said."

"Of course it will," said Maryal. "Now, let's go and grab lunch and then return to the Old Castle. We still have a lot of work to do if we're going to ensure that you win your duel with Easan in the eyes of the crowd, whether or not you actually beat him."

Chapter Sixteen

MARYAL'S PREDICTION WAS RIGHT. When Hesera announced her approval of Keo to her fans at the end of her most recent stage production, Keo experienced a sudden upswing in popularity. Suddenly, whenever Keo went out of the Old Castle, random people on the street started walking up to him and talking to him. Some simply expressed gratitude for saving Hesera and also stopping Eliam the week before, while others voiced their support for him in the upcoming duel against Easan. The attention wasn't exactly unwanted, because most of it was positive, but Keo started getting annoyed at how he could no longer walk the streets of Tain without being mobbed by his fans. So he restricted most of his walking to the Castle itself, and on the few occasions he did go out into the rest of the city, he'd go with his friends or in the carriage provided for him by the Knights.

Even the servants in the Old Castle—particularly the servant girls—seemed to support him, though he understood that the Old Castle's servants were about evenly divided between him and Easan. Even so, Keo would never have guessed that by observing the ways that the servants treated him, such as giving him extra food at mealtimes, always promptly refilling his glass without him even asking them, and changing the sheets out on his bed every day and providing him with the cleanest and fresh clothes available. They even treated his friends nicely, though not as nicely as him.

As for Easan, he seemed moodier than ever these days, at least whenever Keo saw him. Most of the time, Easan spent time either in his room in the Old Castle's second highest tower (the highest tower was where the Keepers lived) or down in the dungeon where he continued to interrogate Eliam, who apparently still had not talked. Keo assumed that Easan was just unhappy at Keo's massive jump in support among the people and servants, even though Keo had not been in Tain nearly as long as Easan.

But Keo didn't see any reason to try to talk with Easan. As far as he was concerned, if Easan was going to let his own jealousy sabotage his own efforts to win the Throne, then that was Easan's problem, not his. That just made it easier for Keo to continue to garner support, to the point where Keo was now starting to believe that there was no way he could possibly lose to Easan, especially when he overheard a couple of servants mocking Easan's surliness behind Easan's back one time.

The only thing that made Keo feel uneasy was the dragon's words. He still had not seen any sign of the dragon after its appearance in the Good King's Tomb, nor had he heard any rumors or sightings of the dragon in or outside of the city. He did ask the Keepers to do some research into the location of the demons' pit, but he was told that that knowledge had been lost to time and there probably wasn't anything in the Archives about it. Still, the Keepers did say that they would start looking for clues to the location of the pit where the demons had been banished, although they did not sound confident they would actually find anything in the thousands of tomes that made up the Archives.

In any event, Keo stopped worrying about that when he and Easan had to try on the Ceremonial Armor. According to the Keepers, the Ceremonial Armor had been worn by the Good King during his original battle with the demons a thousand years ago. It was supposed to be magic armor that was incapable of being broken by normal means and could not rust, either. There were actually three such suits of Armor, but the knowledge for making more had been lost to history, which was why the three that they did have were always kept in the castle vault for safekeeping.

And indeed, the two sets of Ceremonial Armor—one for Keo, and one for Easan—looked as new as if they had just been forged yesterday, even though they were a thousand years old each. Keo's armor was golden, while Easan's was silver, but both looked identical otherwise, especially with their helmets, which were shaped somewhat like dragon heads. The Armor fit both of them well, although Keo, who was not used to wearing any sort of Armor, at first found it awkward to walk around in, but he eventually got the hang of it. The Armors were then placed back inside the vault, where they would await until the day of the duel itself, when Keo and Easan would wear their Armors to fight each other.

All in all, Keo thought that things were looking up. Eliam was locked away in the dungeons beneath the Castle, more and more citizens of Tain were supporting him, he and his friends never had to go without food or water, they had nice beds to sleep in every night, and destiny itself seemed to be going out of its way to ensure that Keo would sit on the Throne. Indeed, Keo was now beginning to think of the Throne as his birthright, which it technically was, but until recently he had never quite grasped the meaning of that idea. He even agreed with Maryal that destiny was favoring him, although Maryal still went out into the streets of Tain daily to drum up more support for him anyway.

Indeed, Keo was even starting to think that it didn't even matter that Nesma still hated him and wanted him dead. Once he returned to South Lamaira as King, he was certain that he would get Nesma to listen to him and realize the error of her ways once he showed her the truth about the demons.

It was on the night before the duel that Keo was walking up the long staircase to the Keepers' chamber. He was going there to participate in the pre-duel dinner that Aster had told him about a week ago. He would have brought his friends along, but the Keepers had said that only Easan, the Keepers, and he were allowed to participate in this dinner. That was fine by Keo, because he was under the impression that the dinner wasn't going to be very long anyway, so he wouldn't be away from the others for that long.

As Keo climbed the stairs, he glanced down at the hall below, where he saw at least a dozen Knights, in full battle gear, standing around like they were waiting for something. Keo had noticed an unusual amount of Knights present at the Castle today, starting with a handful of Knights in the morning to a full unit shortly after lunch. He didn't know why these Knights were here, but he supposed that they wanted to provide extra security in case another demon decided to attack tonight, even though there had been no demon sightings in the last few days.

As a matter of fact, Keo wondered why the demons had not even bothered to try to attack him or the others since a couple of weeks ago. True, the vast majority of the demons were still sealed away in the pit, and would be for quite some time, but the demons never seemed to have any trouble sending any of their own to attack him or his friends. This troubled him, because he wondered if the demons were plotting something in the background, although perhaps the demons were simply tired of getting killed by him and had decided to wait until a more opportune moment to attack.

In any case, I can't afford to let my guard down, Keo thought, glancing both ways, though he was alone on the staircase. *The demons have already shown that they will go in for the kill if they think they can get away with it. I need to keep my wits about me, no matter what.*

Now that Keo thought about it, Sir Abohji had not reported discovering who might have let that other demon into the Castle when Keo first arrived in Tain. Either that meant that Abohji was still investigating the attack or he had not found anything to report to Keo. Keo assumed that Sir Abohji would tell him if he found any clues, so he didn't worry about it too much.

Reaching the top of the staircase, Keo opened the door to the Throne Room and stepped inside. Closing the door behind him, Keo looked around at the Throne Room to see what was being served for dinner tonight, but froze at the scene before him.

The Keepers sat at the other end of the Throne Room in their own thrones, with the main Throne as empty and vacant as always. Easan stood to the left of the Keepers' thrones, his arms crossed over his chest, a smirk on his face that Keo didn't like at all.

They were not the only people in the room. Twelve Knights—lead by Sir Abohji—stood between Keo and the Keepers and

Easan. Aside from Sir Abohji, the Knights had blue highlights on their armor, which meant that they were members of the Blue Order. Recalling what Simil had told Keo about the various Orders within the Brotherhood, Keo realized that he was looking at several of the best Knights in the Old Kingdom, all gathered together here for reasons unknown to him.

"Hello, everyone," said Keo, though he did not step forward. "I'm here for the pre-duel dinner." He nodded at the Knights. "Are they here to protect us from a possible assassin? I don't remember being told we'd have twelve Knights here. I thought it was just going to be us."

Sir Abohji stepped forward. His visor was down, making it impossible to see his expression, but Keo doubted he was smiling.

"Keo of the Sword," said Sir Abohji, his tone grim through the visor of his helmet. "Please remove your sword from your belt and place it on the floor at your feet. Then hold your hands above your head and allow us to take you away quietly."

Keo tensed, but did not move to remove Gildshine from its sheath just yet. "You are asking me to disarm myself? Why?"

"Because you are under arrest," said Sir Abohji, "for crimes committed against the Keepers and the Old Kingdom in general."

Keo stared at Abohji in shock. He was temporarily too stunned to respond, his mind moving quickly as he tried to understand what he had just heard. He was certain that his ears were playing tricks on him, but to his knowledge his ears were in perfect functioning order, so there was no way that he had misheard Abohji's words.

So Keo said, "Sir Abohji, I don't understand. What crimes have I committed against the Keepers and the Old Kingdom?"

"Several," said Abohji. He pulled out a scroll from nowhere, unfurled it, and started reading. "You are wanted for murdering several Knights of the Old Kingdom, conspiring with a foreign criminal to kill several more, aiding a demon in an attempted assassination attempt on the lives of all six Keepers, bribing two wanted criminals to assault an innocent woman for publicity purposes, and faking your parentage with demonic magic in order to ascend to the Throne and become the ruler of the Old Kingdom and Lamaira in general."

Keo's jaw dropped. "What? I didn't do any of that. Who made these accusations against me? I demand to see him."

"I'm right here," said Easan, who had walked around the Knights and was now standing much closer to Keo, though still outside of Gildshine's reach. He smirked again. "I was the one who made these accusations against you, Keo the 'Hero,' or should I say, Keo the Imposter."

"Imposter?" said Keo. "What do you mean? I don't understand even half of these accusations. Ever since I came to the Old Kingdom, I've done nothing but try to help the people of Tain. I've done nothing wrong."

Easan raised an eyebrow skeptically. "Oh? You haven't? That's what the guilty always say, but your accomplices outright admitted their alliance with you when I interrogated them."

"My accomplices?" said Keo. "Who?"

"Eliam the Tracker and Kal and Saze," said Easan. "But perhaps I should explain to you exactly how I discovered your treachery and deception. It wasn't easy, but it was worth it, because no deceiver should ever sit on the Throne of my father and pretend to rule the Kingdom righteously."

"Rightful Heir, we would prefer to arrest the criminal first and then explain it to him later," said Sir Abohji. "Otherwise, he might escape."

"No, no, I want him to hear exactly how I did it so I can crush his castle-sized ego into little bits," said Easan, waving off Sir Abohji's concerns like they meant nothing. "Unless you wish to contradict the wishes of your future King, that is, Sir Abohji."

Sir Abohji said nothing to that, but Keo could tell that Abohji did not approve of what he saw as a waste of time. But Abohji clearly respected the authority of Easan, which was probably why he was not opposing him.

"Now," said Easan, looking at Keo again. "You may recall how you came to the Old Castle a couple of weeks ago, bringing with you news that our border patrol had been slaughtered by a criminal known as Eliam the Tracker. You even brought with you a letter, allegedly written by Sir Fariak himself, that claimed that you were to be trusted as if you were a Knight of the Old Kingdom yourself."

"That's exactly what happened," said Keo, nodding. "Ask Eliam. He's insane, but I'm sure he'll be more than happy to tell you how he destroyed the border patrol and killed everyone there."

"But I *did* ask Eliam and that's not what he told us," said Easan, shaking his head. "What I discovered, over the course of my interrogation of Eliam, was that he is actually a friend of yours. He claimed that he had come with you and your treacherous little friends to the Old Kingdom on the orders of the Magical Council, which are under the control of the demons. You were supposed to arrive in Tain, 'prove' that you were the *shelmai*, and then take the Throne and kill off the Keepers and place the Old Kingdom under the control of the Magical Council, thus considerably expanding their territory and power."

"Now that is the most ridiculous story I have ever heard in my life," said Keo. He looked at Abohji and the Knights. "Surely you must agree that this is stupid?"

"There is actually evidence to back up Easan's accusations," said Sir Abohji. "The day after you and Easan went to pay respects to the Good King's Tomb, the messenger we had sent to the border patrol returned. He reported finding a scene of absolute destruction and death, with the border tower collapsed on itself and nearly every member of the border patrol dead. He found only one survivor, Sir Rez, who, though dying, managed to tell the messenger that several southerners were coming to Tain and that one such southerner, Eliam the Tracker, had already attacked and destroyed the border patrol for reasons unknown."

"And as I said, Eliam has already admitted to working with you," said Easan. "It makes sense, really. No doubt Sir Fariak and his fellow border patrol Knights tried to stop you when you attempted to cross the border, but you used your vile magic to destroy them utterly and then came up with the idiotic story that Eliam was trying to kill you on the orders of the Magical Council."

"How do you explain the letter written by Sir Fariak, then?" said Keo. He tried to keep calm, but it was almost impossible to behave calmly in the face of such outrageous and false accusations. "It was even in his handwriting."

"You forged it," said Easan simply. "Eliam told me that he is a good forger as well as a tracker. You had Eliam forge the letter so that you could easily gain direct access to the Keepers. And it worked, too, which is a testament to the truth of Eliam's claims."

"But why do you believe the confession of a mad man like Eliam?" said Keo. "What proof does he have to back up his claims? He's insane and therefore untrustworthy."

"He seemed perfectly sane when I spoke with him," said Easan. "But nonetheless, it fits. I mean, it is suspicious, is it not, how you arrived in Tain not long after I did, came up with a story about the demons coming back, and then saved the Keepers from an attack by a demon on that very same day? It is too coincidental to be mere chance or even destiny."

"Are you implying that *I* summoned the demon that attacked us on our first day here?" said Keo. "Why would I do that?"

"To bolster your weak claims to the Throne," said Easan. "You knew that the Keepers would be much more suspect of your claims due to your status as a foreigner. What better way to prove your story than to have a demon attack at the very moment you are explaining it to them? And then you show off your golden flames at the last minute, to further 'prove' that you are the *shelmai* and to bypass the Keepers' suspicion of foreigners? It worked too well for a while there, but I will admit that it was quite clever."

"But I killed the demon," Keo pointed out. "You saw me kill it. I saved your life."

"You may have killed it, but that was all part of the plan as well," said Easan. "If you had not killed it, then it would have looked quite suspicious and likely would have ruined your perfect little plan. I suspect that that demon knew that it would likely have to die, but the old stories always described the demons as being willing to take one for the team if it meant advancing their true agenda, so that doesn't surprise me in the least."

"Yeah, but if my plan was so great, wouldn't it have been ruined by you?" said Keo. "After all, you got here before me and were considered the *shelmai* before I came along."

"Yes, my presence did throw your plans off, but you obviously did not out yourself just yet," said Easan. "First, you had Eliam attack the Knights' training grounds and then you and your Magician friend defeated him in order to win the approval of the Knights and, by extension, the approval of the people in general. And it really worked quite well, considering how popular you are among the Knights of the Old Kingdom."

"We didn't even know that Eliam was going to attack us there," said Keo. "We thought he was dead because he was inside the guard tower when it collapsed."

"Eliam did mention that you abandoned him to die after the tower fell on him, but that you also managed to trick him into helping you when he caught up with you again," said Easan. "Though he didn't seem too happy about being left to die, which is probably why he betrayed you."

"Oh, come on," said Keo, tossing his hands into the air. "This is ridiculous. Eliam is lying just to get me into trouble."

"But what about the two thugs, Kal and Saze, who had assaulted the actress Hesera?" said Easan. "They also admitted that you had paid them off to assault her in order to make you look like the hero and cement the favor of the citizens of Tain."

"I didn't even know those two existed until I saw them assaulting Hesera in the streets," said Keo. "For that matter, I had absolutely no idea who Hesera was until I met her on that day, either. How, then, could I have come up with a plan to put her life in danger and then rescue her if I didn't know who she was or how popular she was among the people?"

"You are lying," said Easan, pointing at Keo accusingly. "Besides, it is far too convenient, isn't it, that you managed to rescue the most famous and popular actress in all of the Old Kingdom right when you most needed a boost in popularity?"

"It still doesn't make any sense," said Keo. He looked at the Knights and the Keepers. "Are any of you listening? Don't you understand how crazy his theories sound? He doesn't even have any hard evidence to support it."

"He has confessions from three separate individuals," said Sir Abohji. "Plus, his logic is sound. We did not have a demon problem until you and your friends arrived. We will give you and your friends a trial later, but for now we must ask you to come with us."

Keo took a step back, resting his hand on Gildshine's hilt. "What about the duel?"

"There will be no duel," said Easan. He pointed at himself. "Instead, I, Easan, the true *shelmai*, will be crowned King of Lamaira tomorrow, while you will be sitting in the dungeons beneath the Old Castle where traitors like you deserve to be."

"But I'm just as much a *shelmai* as you are," said Keo. "Remember? The Goblet proved my parentage."

"Remember how the Goblet originally was purple before it turned blue?" said Easan. "Obviously, you must have used demonic magic to change its color, the same demonic magic that has allowed you to summon false golden flames around your sword. You are probably not really related to King Riuno at all."

Keo bit his lower lip. "What about my friends? They'll help me escape."

"No, they will not," said Sir Abohji, shaking his head. "I have already sent some of the men under me to arrest your friends as well. All four of you will be thrown behind bars until your trial."

"You really think you can arrest two Magicians?" said Keo skeptically. "Both Maryal and Jola are very skilled Magicians, you know."

"My men have fought Magicians before on the war front," said Sir Abohji. "They are already familiar with Magician fighting styles and strategies, so I doubt they will have much trouble arresting your friends. Again, I must ask you to remove your sword and place it on the ground at your feet where we can see it. Otherwise, we will be forced to arrest you."

"I suggest complying with Sir Abohji's orders, Keo," said Easan. He gestured at the eleven Knights standing behind Abohji. "These are Blue Order Knights, which, as you might imagine, means that they are not a bunch of rookies fresh from the Academy. I doubt they'll go gentle on you if you anger them."

Keo hated to admit it, but Easan was probably right. There was no way that Keo could defeat Sir Abohji and his Blue Order Knights all by himself, even if he used Gildshine's golden flames. Keo would have been willing to risk fighting them if he knew that Dlaine and the others were free, but he did not. And if Easan helped the Knights, then Keo would almost certainly go down for sure.

But neither was Keo going to give up and go with them quietly. He didn't know what kind of magic Easan was using to trick the Keepers and Knights into believing that the others and he were spies, but he had no intention of spending any time in the Old Castle's dungeons. Not when he knew that his friends and he were innocent.

So Keo threw open the door and dashed out, intending to make a mad dash for the castle gates. But as soon as he left the room, he found his way blocked by another dozen Knights.

And before he could fight back, one of the Knights slammed the flat of his blade in Keo's face and Keo lost all consciousness.

Chapter Seventeen

KEO'S HEAD HURT. IT felt like someone had slammed a thick steel pipe against his skull, although nothing felt broken as far as he could tell. Still, the pain was almost unbearable, although it did seem to be going down.

Regardless of whatever pain he was experiencing, Keo needed to find out where he was. He last remembered being knocked out by one of the Knights of the Old Kingdom, but he had no memories of what happened after that.

So Keo opened his eyes and found himself staring at a dark, grimy ceiling in a small cell. He was lying on an old, sagging cot that smelled of blood and dirt, while his arms and legs were chained together by thick, rusty shackles that were so tight Keo could barely feel his hands and feet.

Groaning, Keo sat up and looked around at his cell. In one corner was a bucket that seemed to be his chamber pot, although it smelled like it had not been washed in quite some time. Keo's stomach growled because he had not eaten in a while, but there was no food or water anywhere in his cell, aside from what looked like a moldy, mouse-eaten piece of bread in another corner.

Keo looked at the bars of his cell. There was a very dim light in the hallway of the dungeons that showed him that there was no one in the hallway outside his cell. Keo strained his ears to listen, but he heard nothing at all except for what sounded like a mouse running somewhere nearby, though that sound, too, faded eventually.

Then a slightly muffled voice from the cell opposite his said, "Good morning, Keo … or evening. It's impossible to keep track of time down here, so I don't even know what day it is, much less what the current time is, but I thought I'd greet you anyway, mostly because I'm a gentleman."

Keo looked at the cell across from his. It was dark in there, too dark to see who had spoken, but then a familiar figure stepped up to the bars of his cell and wrapped his fingers around the bars, his face—or rather, mask—visible in the light from the hall.

"Eliam," said Keo, scowling at the masked figure. "I didn't think I'd ever see you again."

"On the contrary, I thought for sure we'd run into each other again at some point, because I still have to kill you and then tell that girl that I did it so can I get my freedom," said Eliam. He looked around at his cell, clearly disappointed at his current situation. "But it looks like, in my attempt to gain my freedom, I just ended up in another jail. How ironic."

"Where are my friends?" said Keo. "Are they down here, too?"

"How should I know?" said Eliam with a shrug. "I saw a couple of Knights dragging you in here like a sack of potatoes. I didn't see anyone else with them, though I bet they have probably put your friends in another part of the dungeons to keep you separated so you don't figure out a way to escape together."

"You sure seem to understand how the Knights think despite not being one yourself," said Keo.

"Oh, an artist like myself must always be willing to put oneself in the shoes of those who think differently from you," said Eliam, tapping the side of his head with one finger. "That, and I have experience with prison guards, for I was once a prisoner myself."

Keo raised an eyebrow. "Really? I thought you hadn't been caught before."

Eliam chuckled. "That was *before* I became Eliam the Tracker, hated and feared by everyone in South Lamaira. At the time, I was a petty thief with my partner and love of my life, a beautiful woman named Missy who was always there for me. We were caught trying to steal from a Magician's Tower once and then thrown in separate cells on different ends of the prison by the guards. That way, we would not be able to conspire with each other about how to escape."

"What happened to Missy?" said Keo.

"She was beaten brutally by the prison guards when she attempted to escape on her own," said Eliam. His mask hid his expression, but Keo caught the anger in his voice quite well. Eliam's hands tightened around the bars of his cell. "She broke out of her cell, tried to save me, but I told her to go on without me and that I would save myself later. But Missy, the lovely and loyal and kindhearted woman that she was, insisted on trying to save me anyway. But when it became clear she could not, the guards had already caught up with her and beat her to death right in front of my eyes. Her blood actually flew onto my face and clothes."

Even though Keo still hated Eliam, he found himself disgusted by the thought of those guards beating Eliam's wife before his own eyes. "That's horrible. What happened after that?"

"That was when I first gained access to my magical powers," said Eliam. His tone changed from anger to satisfaction. "I blew off the heads of the guards who killed Missy, then blew a hole in the prison wall so I could escape, and then blew up the prison itself purely out of spite, killing the fifty prisoners and ten guards inside it at the time. Then I destroyed the entire town that the prison was in, including the Tower of the Magician who I had tried to steal from, but it was all worth it, because I know that Missy would have wanted it."

Keo blinked. Considering how insane Eliam was, he wasn't sure how much of this story to believe and how much to doubt, but he decided not to worry about it.

Instead, Keo said, "How much time has passed since I was dragged down here?"

Eliam shrugged. "As I said before, I've lost track of time down here because there are no clocks to consult and the sun and moon are hidden from view. But if I had to guess, I'd say it has only been a few hours since the Knights put you down here, though don't quote me on that."

A few hours, Keo thought. *That means there's still time to get out of here and stop Easan.*

Then Keo looked up at Eliam again and said, "Did you tell Easan that you were working for me? That I had hired you to attack the Knights' training grounds in order to make myself look like a hero to the people?"

Eliam threw back his head and laughed. His laughter sounded strange through his mask, echoing slightly, which made him sound even madder than he already was.

"It was a joke," said Eliam, after his laughter died down. "Just a simple joke. I told that man that I was working for you because I wanted to ruin your life."

"Why?" said Keo.

"Because I am currently unable to take it," said Eliam. He tapped the bars of his cell. "So I did the next best thing: Tell that man that I was some hired help meant to make you look better."

"You still don't have your freedom, though," said Keo. "So did it really work out all that well for you?"

"Maybe not," said Eliam with a shrug. "But truthfully, I am not looking for my freedom now. I intend to escape at some point, but right now I am more than happy to have you where I can see you. That way, when I escape, I will have little trouble killing you, just as Magician Nesma ordered me."

Keo scowled. "I don't think the Knights are ever going to let you escape. Though now that I think about it, why haven't you used your magic to blow a hole in the wall of your cell and escape?"

Eliam let out an angry sigh. "Because this cell is coated in a substance known as antimagi. Ever heard of it?"

Keo shook his head. "No, I haven't. What is it?"

"Antimagi is a special substance that negates the inborn powers of Magicians like myself," said Eliam. He rubbed his hand on the bars of his cell. "It's coarse and rough, but if you didn't know what it was, you wouldn't even know it was there."

"How is it made?" said Keo.

"I don't know, but I do know that the Magical Council banned it in South Lamaira after it was first created, allegedly because it is toxic," said Eliam. Then he lowered his voice to a whisper, like he was revealing a dark secret. "But between you and me, the

Magical Council has a massive reserve of it that they use to coat their own cells and prisons. It's how they keep Magicians like myself locked up, though they would never admit that particular fact to the public, of course. They keep it for themselves so no one can ever use it against them, such as the Rebels."

That didn't surprise Keo. He was well aware of the corruption and hypocrisy of the Magical Council at this point, so hearing that they used a substance that they banned the common folk from using wasn't a shocking revelation to him. But Keo did make note of this antimagi so he could look for some later. He figured it would be useful to have some on hand should he run into other hostile Magicians in the future.

"So we can't rely on your magic to escape, then," said Keo. "Do you know of any other way to escape?"

"If I did, Tain would be little more than a pretty pile of rocks, with your head balanced on top as the centerpiece of my masterpiece, and I would be heading back to South Lamaira to inform the Council of the success of my mission," said Eliam. He gestured at his cell. "As you can see, however, I am still stuck down here and unable to do anything except talk. And talk is useless for escaping."

Keo looked around his cell, trying to find anything he could use to escape, but his cell seemed to be locked tight. There were no holes for him to crawl through and the door to his cell had a huge iron lock on it that looked impossible to break unless you had superhuman strength. Or a key, but Keo did not have the keys to his cell or to Eliam's, so that was irrelevant.

Then Keo remembered something and looked down at his belt. Gildshine was missing. Not just Gildshine, but its sheath, too. It was completely gone.

He looked up at Eliam, who was still standing at the bars of his cell, and asked, "My sword. What happened to it?"

"I don't know," said Eliam with a shrug, "but if I had to hazard a guess, I would say that the Knights probably confiscated it from you. Where they took it after that, I don't know, seeing as I know very little about this castle, but I do know that they probably took your sword away from you to make sure you didn't use it to escape."

Keo groaned. Not only was he chained up underneath the castle, separated from his friends, he was also unarmed. Keo didn't see how things could possibly get worse, but he chose not to say that aloud, because he was aware that the best way to ensure the worsening of a situation was to voice your hope that it wouldn't.

Looks like I'm stuck here, Keo thought. *And I will stay stuck until the Keepers decide what to do with me. Knowing Easan, I bet he will convince them to execute me, though now that I think about it, does the Old Kingdom execute its criminals or does it just lock them up forever and let them slowly rot away?*

Either way, he was going to spend a long time down here. Even if they did eventually release him, it might be too late to stop the demons by then.

"Damn it," Keo said, stomping the floor of his cell in anger. "Damn Easan and his smug little face."

"I wouldn't say that aloud, if I were you," said Eliam. There was a tiny hint of fear in his voice.

"Why?" said Keo, looking up at Eliam in annoyance. "It's not like anyone can hear us down here. I think that makes us pretty free to say whatever the hell that we want."

"Haven't you seen the man called Easan before?" said Eliam. He gulped. "How he treats those who talk badly of him?"

"I've spoken with him before," said Keo. "And anytime I've ever said anything negative about him, he'll either retort with a dumb comeback or just glare and scowl at me."

"That's not what he did to me," said Eliam. "But of course, I see why he would do that to you. He probably didn't want to show his *actual* power to the public."

"Actual power?" said Keo. "What are you talking about?"

"I am talking about what he did when he interrogated me," said Eliam. He actually shuddered, which was the first time Keo had ever seen the mad Magician do that. "The shadows listened to him in a way that I have never seen them act before. And his eyes … they became as red as blood. And he seemed to be able to hear me even when he wasn't around, which is why I said to be careful about what you say about him even in private."

"Red as blood …?" Keo repeated. He stopped speaking, frozen by the implications of Eliam's description. "No … it can't be …"

"What can't be?" said Eliam. "Do you know what was wrong with Easan?"

Keo bit his lower lip. He thought about telling Eliam what he suspected, but he decided against it. Eliam wasn't a friend or a trusted acquaintance. He wasn't even sure how much knowledge about the return of the demons that Eliam had. If Keo's theory was right—and he hoped to the Good King that it wasn't—then that meant that Easan was working with the demons. That meant that Easan was behind the demonic attack in the Throne Room, and might have possibly even been behind the attack of that other demon back in the border between South Lamaira and the Old Kingdom.

And if Easan is working with the demons, or is maybe a demon himself, then he can't be allowed to be crowned the King of Lamaira, Keo thought. *If he is, there's no telling what he will do, but I doubt it will be good for anyone other than the demons.*

That made it more urgent than ever for Keo to escape his cell. He had to confront Easan and make him confess his alliance with the demons to the Keepers. But then Keo remembered again that he was stuck down here, with no way to escape. It didn't matter, then, that Keo now understood who the real threat to the Kingdom was, because as long as he remained down here, he would never be able to escape and thus would never be able to tell the Keepers what he knew.

But Keo was not going to give up just yet. He looked around his cell again, searching for anything, anything at all, that he could use to escape, but his cell seemed pretty escape-proof from what he could see. The people of the Old Kingdom, it seemed, were very good at designing escape-proof cells, though that did not mean that Keo had to give up just yet.

Then Keo remembered the golden flames he had summoned around Gildshine. He wondered if those might be able to help him break free. He had no idea if he could use the golden flames without Gildshine, mostly because he had never even tried to use them like that, but he had to give it a shot. He did worry that the golden flames might count as magic, and therefore be unable to burn through the antimagi that coated his cell, but he would not know until he tried.

So Keo stood up and walked over to the door of his cell as best as he could with his restricted, awkward movement. He put his hands on the door and closed his eyes, focusing as hard as he could on the fire that he knew existed deep within himself. He didn't know if Eliam was watching him or not, but he didn't care, because at the moment all he cared about was getting out of here before Easan's plan succeeded.

But despite Keo's best efforts, he could not feel the fire within him at all. It felt like the fire wasn't even there. He focused again, hoping that maybe he had somehow overlooked it, but the longer he stood there, with his hands wrapped around the coarse bars of the door and his eyes closed and his wrists and ankles starting to ache from the weight of the shackles on them, the clearer it became that he could not access his fire right now.

Opening his eyes, Keo looked down at his hands. He didn't know why his flames were not appearing. He suspected that it had to do with the fact that he didn't have Gildshine, which confirmed his theory that he could only use his flames when he had his sword, but it could just as easily have been because he was still unused to using his golden flames.

Whatever the reason, the fact was that Keo had no way of escaping at this point. The bars were too strong to knock down or pull apart, the door was locked, and he did not have Gildshine or his golden flames to free himself.

So Keo—his shoulders slumped—turned and walked back to his cot. He sat down on it and looked down at the dark and grimy floor of his cell, certain at this point that his journey had finally come to an end, and a rather inglorious one at that.

"Succumbed to depression?" said Eliam, who sounded a little

bit disappointed. "I thought you were stronger than that."

Keo looked up at Eliam in annoyance. "Why are you disappointed? I thought you'd be happy to see me 'weak.'"

"Because I was hoping you'd free me, too," said Eliam with a sigh. "But I can see that we are both going to spend the rest of our days down here. Oh, well."

Eliam stepped away from the bars of his cell and back into the shadows. Keo heard Eliam sit down on his own cot, and then there was silence in the dungeons once more.

Thus, Keo was left alone with his thoughts ... thoughts that just made him more depressed than ever.

It looks like this is the end, Keo thought. *I just hope that I am executed before the demons return, at least.*

That was when Keo heard a metal door open and close somewhere nearby. He assumed that it was probably the door to the dungeons being opened and closed by a Knight, who was probably coming to check on the prisoners. Maybe the Knight was even delivering food to Keo and Eliam, although Keo wasn't very hungry at the moment.

But oddly enough, Keo did not hear the usual clanking of armor that he always heard whenever the Knights were walking. Instead, he heard the pattering of leather shoes, which made Keo assume that it was probably one of the servants, then, and not a Knight. Not that it mattered either way, seeing as neither the Knights nor the servants were likely to free Keo.

Then a woman's voice said, in the quiet of the dungeons, "Keo? Are you awake?"

Keo's head snapped up. The voice sounded like the voice of a middle-aged woman and, although he was certain that he had never heard it before, there was something about it that sounded familiar for some reason.

Then a woman appeared in the hallway outside his cell. She was a middle-aged woman with dark, gray-streaked hair, wearing black robes, but they were not Magician robes, because they looked coarser than those robes. She looked like one of the Castle's maids, but there was something about the way she looked at Keo—with a sense of urgency, like she feared being caught—that made him think that she was not a member of the Castle's staff.

"Who are you?" said Keo, staring at the woman in surprise. "And how do you know my name?"

"My name isn't important," said the woman, shaking her head. "You are not even supposed to even see me, but I had to intervene because all of Lamaira depends on your freedom."

"Wait, what are you even talking about?" said Keo. "What do you mean, I'm 'not supposed to see you'? Why not?"

"There's no time to explain," said the woman. She drew closer to the bars, concern in her eyes. "Tell me, are you injured? Can you walk on your own?"

"I think so," said Keo. He glanced at the shackles around his wrists and ankles. "But I can't get very far with these shackles on me."

"I just needed to know that you can still walk on your own," said the woman. "I'll free you and get you out of here before it's too late."

"Do you have the keys to my cell?" said Keo, although he didn't see them in her hands.

"I don't have the keys, but that's because I don't need them," said the woman.

Before Keo could ask her how she planned to free him without the keys to his cell, the woman raised her hand and brought it down hard on the lock. A loud *snap* followed and, in the next instant, the lock itself fell to the floor with a *clunk*.

Keo's eyes widened as the woman pulled open the door to his cell. "Did you just break that lock with your bare hand?"

The woman entered Keo's cell and walked up to him. She didn't look that much stronger or larger than any other middle-aged woman Keo had seen in his life, but if she could break thick metal locks like that without effort, then she was obviously much stronger than she appeared.

"I did," said the woman, though she didn't sound as impressed by it as Keo, like she broke thick heavy locks every day. "Now raise your hands so I can remove the shackles."

Without arguing, Keo raised his hands. The woman tore the shackles off his wrists and tossed them to the side, while Keo started rubbing his now-aching wrists. And then the woman stomped on the shackles around his ankles, freeing his legs as well.

"Now you are free," said the woman. She glanced over her shoulder, like she thought someone might be following her. "Now we must go. Quickly, because the guard will be back soon to check up on Eliam and you."

Keo still had no idea who this woman was, but considering how she had gone out of her way to save him, he decided that he could live without knowing her identity for the moment. He just stood up and followed her out of his cell, but then Eliam said, "Wait!"

Keo and the woman stopped and looked at Eliam's cell. The Tracker was right up against the bars again, looking at them both with pleading eyes.

"Are you going to let me out as well?" said Eliam. "I have also been unjustly imprisoned, so—"

"No," said the woman flatly, shaking her head. "You are not important. I don't care what they do to you."

With that, the woman turned and left, walking down the dungeon hallway. Keo followed, trying his best not to listen to the string of curses that was coming from Eliam behind them as they walked.

Chapter Eighteen

THE WOMAN LED KEO out of the dungeon and into the Old Castle's dark hallways, but rather than lead him deeper into the Old Castle, she led him through a secret passageway behind a statue of the Good King that took them outside of the Old Castle. They emerged outside into the cold night air of the Old Castle's Garden, which Keo had seen a few times during his stay at the Castle, but had never actually visited until today.

The Garden was located in the back of the Castle and was separate from the rest of the Castle grounds with its own walls, although they were not as tall or thick as the walls that surrounded the Castle itself. A clear pond stood in one corner, while a dazzling variety of flowers that Keo could not identify due to being unfamiliar with their species were scattered here and there. There were also a good variety of fruit trees, which smelled great, but like with the flowers, Keo could not identify the trees' species.

Not that Keo was thinking about the trees, though. He was more concerned with being seen and caught by the Knights, the Castle servants, or someone else. Granted, it was probably midnight, so most of the Castle was most likely asleep at the moment, but Keo knew that the Castle had night guards, as well as servants who worked at night.

The woman, however, didn't seem to be very concerned about being spotted. She just walked along the stone path of the Garden, not saying a word, keeping ahead of Keo all the while, even though Keo was younger and taller than her. She didn't even look over her shoulder to see if Keo was following her, though he supposed that that was unnecessary because there was no way he would stop following her and risk getting caught.

Then the woman led Keo off the path, toward a thick grouping of fruit trees that looked quite old, and squeezed inside them. Keo, hesitating for a split second, followed her inside, wondering why they were going in here.

As soon as Keo entered the trees, he saw that they were not alone. Illuminated by a small but bright candle, Dlaine and Maryal looked up when Keo and the woman entered the trees. Jola was probably there, too, but as always, she was invisible.

"Keo?" said Maryal. She looked unharmed, but a little shaken up, no doubt due to having been arrested and jailed like him. She smiled and stood up. "It's great to see you. I thought I'd never see you again."

"Dlaine? Maryal? Jola?" said Keo, looking at them both in surprise. He kept his voice to a whisper, however, just in case someone was out there. "How did you three get out here?"

"I got them out before I rescued you," said the woman, standing to Keo's right. "I knew that they were your friends, your trusted traveling companions, so I decided to rescue them with you. That way, you would not need to travel by yourself."

"She's real impressive," said Dlaine, gesturing at the woman. "Broke the locks on our cells without a sweat. And she got us out of the Castle without being seen, too."

"You do not need to thank me," said the woman, shaking her head. "I did only what I had to do."

"Well, thanks anyway," said Keo. Then he looked at the others urgently. "Did you guys hear anything about Easan?"

"No, we haven't," said Dlaine, shaking his head. "All we know is that the Keepers are going to crown him King of Lamaira tomorrow. Or is it later today? I lost track of time down there."

"I think it's either late at night or early morning at the moment," said Keo. "But it doesn't matter. Back in the dungeon, Eliam told me that Easan could control shadows and also had red eyes and seemed to be able to hear people talk about him whenever he's not around."

"Is Easan a Magician?" said Maryal in surprise. "Because that sounds like a Magician to me."

"No," said Keo, shaking his head. "At least, I doubt it. I think that Easan is working with the demons, who gave him his powers in exchange for helping them destroy the Old Kingdom."

Dlaine and Maryal exchanged concerned looks, while the woman did not react to that at all. Either she knew that Easan was working with the demons or she had already suspected it herself, but Keo did not think that the woman was willing to share what she knew with them, so he didn't bother to ask for her input.

"But why?" said Maryal, looking at Keo again. "Why would Easan ally with the very creatures that wish to destroy all of humanity?"

"I don't know," said Keo. "Maybe the demons promised to make him King of Lamaira. Or maybe they're possessing him and he doesn't have any free will anymore. All I know is that letting Easan become the King of Lamaira is a *very* bad idea, no matter how you look at it."

"Then we need to interrupt the coronation," said Dlaine. "But unfortunately, I don't know where it is supposed to take place."

"At the Grand Arena, most likely," said Keo, nodding. "That's where our duel was supposed to be and I can't see them deciding not to use it at the last minute, not after going through all of the trouble of preparing it for our duel. We just need to find out what time the coronation is supposed to start so we can get there in time."

"No," said the woman, causing all three of them to look at her. "You must not go after Easan. Instead, you must flee Tain and the Old Kingdom. And never look back."

Keo, Dlaine, and Maryal looked at the woman in confusion. Keo thought that she must be joking, but the woman's expression looked very serious, as if she meant every word she said.

"Excuse me?" said Keo. "Did you just say we should *leave* the Old Kingdom? And let Easan be crowned the King of Lamaira?"

The woman nodded. "Yes. That is exactly what I said."

"And you are serious?" said Dlaine, who sounded just as disbelieving as Keo.

Again, the woman nodded. "Quite."

"Okay, lady, I don't think you were listening to anything we just said over the last five minutes, so I'm going to repeat it to you slowly," said Dlaine. He leaned forward, looking her straight in the eye. "There is a good chance that Easan is working with the demons. And if Easan is crowned the King of Lamaira, then that will give the demons control over yet another country. But if we can stop him—"

"I was listening to every word that you said," said the woman, interrupting Dlaine and glaring at him with a cold stare. "But that doesn't change the fact that you need to leave. You cannot defeat Easan and hope to save the Old Kingdom yet, not when most people believe you all to be criminals who want to kill the Rightful Heir."

"But—" said Keo.

"And you don't even have proof to back up your claims," the woman pointed out. "You have only suspicions and assertions, neither of which will fly with the citizens of Tain. You will only succeed in earning the ire of the Tainians and likely getting arrested again, perhaps even killed entirely if you fight back against the Knights."

Keo would not admit it, but the woman did have a point. It would be hard to prove to the Tainians that their hero, Easan, was in fact a villain. And it would be beyond dangerous to confront Easan directly, who likely had demonic powers that Keo and the others didn't even know of yet.

"What should we do, then?" said Maryal, rubbing her hands together anxiously. "You said we should leave the Old Kingdom, but you didn't say why or to where."

"You must head northwest," said the woman, pointing in that direction. "To the Upper Mountains. There you will find the help you need, the help that will ensure your victory against the demons."

"What is in the Upper Mountains?" said Dlaine. "Why should we go there? What kind of 'help' can we expect to find?"

"I cannot say, because I was not even supposed to show myself to you," said the woman, shaking her head, "but now that I am here, I have to tell you this explicitly. I am just as concerned about the rise of the demons, but you must understand that it will take more than just the correct King on the Throne to defeat them. You humans don't have all of the facts about the demons and how to ensure that the seal remains closed."

You humans? Keo thought. *Why is she talking to us like—*

Then it suddenly all clicked together in Keo's head. The talk of going to the Upper Mountains ... finding the help they needed ... the woman's inhuman strength ... it all made sense now.

Keo looked at the woman, this time with understanding, and said, "You are a Dracone, aren't you?"

The woman returned Keo's look and Keo saw in her eyes a burning fire that was definitely not human. He suddenly felt far less safe around her than he had moments before, because he remembered just how strong she had shown herself back in the dungeons and he knew he was no match for a woman with her strength.

"Yes, I am," said the woman. "I see you have figured it out."

"So you were the dragon I spoke to back in the Good King's Tomb," said Keo. "I can't believe it. Why are you here? I thought the Dracones lived in the Upper Mountains. Why did you come all the way down here? Are there more of you nearby?"

The woman folded her hands behind her back. She looked quite embarrassed by these questions, as if she could not answer them. Or, perhaps far more likely, because she did not want to answer them, though why, Keo couldn't guess.

"I cannot answer those questions," said the woman. "I have already done too much by helping you as much as I have. All you need to know is that you *must* head to the Upper Mountains and, yes, speak to the Dracones, who will help you."

"Wow," said Dlaine, looking at the woman with a new found interest. "A real live Dracone. I'd have never guessed you were one of those. Thought they didn't really exist."

"Yes, I know," said the woman, sighing in exasperation. "But again, it doesn't matter. What matters is going to the Upper Mountains and seeking out the rest of my people. They are waiting for you, even if they don't know it yet."

"But why can't we stop Easan and then go to the Upper Mountains?" said Keo, folding his arms over his chest. "That way, the demons won't get the Old Kingdom and we'll still be able to get the Dracones' help."

"Because I already explained why," said the Dracone woman. "It is impossible to stop Easan at this point. You will need to return later, after you have learned your true power and have gained my people as allies and supporters. I know it doesn't seem like it, but this is the best chance you have for yourselves and for the Kingdom as a whole."

"No," said Keo. "We are not leaving until everyone in Tain knows the true nature of Easan. Until then, we are staying here, where we will stop him before he gets the crown placed upon his head. And there is nothing you can do to stop us."

The Dracone woman looked at Keo in surprise, as if she had not expected him to speak so strongly against her. And there was a look in her eyes, like she was worried for Keo, but in a way that was far deeper than a stranger would worry for someone she barely knew.

But then the Dracone woman nodded and said, "Very well. I see that I cannot convince you to leave while you have the chance. If you left tonight, you could make it out of Tain before anyone even realizes you're no longer in your cells, but it is clear to me that you are not going anywhere until you've confronted Easan."

"Right," said Keo. "You're free to help us, if you wish. I think having the aid of a Dracone could be useful."

The Dracone woman, however, stepped back. "No. If I tried to help you, I would likely only make things worse for us all, both in the short and long term. I must head back to the Upper Mountains myself, because I've done what I needed to do here."

"All right," said Keo, who was a bit disappointed, mostly because he had hoped to see the power of a Dracone in action. "Hopefully we'll see you again soon, after we defeat Easan and save the Old Kingdom."

"As long as you do not get killed while doing it," said the Dracone woman. "But before I leave, I think you will need this."

The Dracone woman stuck her arm into the hollow of a nearby tree and pulled out Gildshine, still in its sheath, from within. She handed the sheathed sword to Keo, who took it in both hands, looking down at it in surprise. He pulled the sword partway out of its sheath to make sure that it was Gildshine. There was no mistaking that iron blade for any other.

Sheathing the sword back into its scabbard, Keo looked up at the Dracone woman again and said, "Thank you. How did you get this?"

"I stole it from the vault where confiscated weapons are kept," said the Dracone woman. "I was planning to give it to you when you came with me back to the Upper Mountains, but I've decided to give it to you now because its yours and you will need it if you are going to stop Easan."

Keo reattached Gildshine's sheath to his belt. "Again, thank you. I will remember your help always, even if we never see each other again."

The Dracone woman looked away, as if she was going to cry and did not want him to see. "Thank you. Now I must leave, but I will be waiting for you back at the Upper Mountains, should you survive."

With that, the Dracone woman made to leave, but then stopped briefly and said, without looking at them, "Oh, and you can leave the Garden by going through a hole in the walls. There is a certain spot with removable bricks that you can use to open a hole for you to crawl through so you can get into the rest of the city. It is marked with a small, faint *x*."

Before Keo or the others could say anything else, the Dracone woman stepped between the trees and vanished instantly. Keo did not even hear her footsteps in the trees, but he didn't care. He knew that she would be able to get out of the city on her own without being seen or caught.

"All right," said Keo, looking back at Dlaine and Maryal. "The coronation is tomorrow, right? So we need to be there to expose Easan and stop him before he is crowned the King of Lamaira."

"Right, but how do we do that?" said Maryal with a frown. "I'm not nearly as much of a downer as that Dracone lady was, but she did have some valid points. At the moment, everyone in the city thinks we're accomplices to a bunch of demons and murderers of Knights. We don't really have any friends on the outside who could help us."

"Maryal's right," said Dlaine, leaning against one of the trees, his hands in his pockets. "And then there's actually getting into the Grand Arena, which will undoubtedly be heavily guarded by the Knights, especially once they learn that we've escaped from our cells."

"That brings up another problem we need to consider," said Maryal. "Once the Knights find out we're missing, they'll probably search the whole city for us. That means we need some place to hide, some place where we know the Knights won't search for us."

Keo rubbed his chin, considering the problems that Dlaine and Maryal had brought up. Then he looked down at the locket hanging off his neck and an idea occurred to him. He wasn't sure it would work, but if it did, then he would solve several of their problems all at once.

"Let me try to contact Hesera," said Keo. He pointed at his locket. "She told me that I could contact her through this locket, because it is a magical artifact with a twin that she owns. She likes me, so she might be willing to help us if I explain to her what the current situation is."

"Are you sure about that?" said Dlaine. "Just because she liked you before doesn't mean she still likes you. No doubt the rest of Tain already knows that we've been arrested for possible crimes against the Old Kingdom. She might not be willing to help us if she believes that we're as bad as Easan says we are."

"She's our only contact on the outside who would be even willing to consider helping us," said Keo. "Besides, you two don't have any better ideas, do you?"

Based on their silence, Keo took that as a yes.

So Keo grabbed his locket and flipped it open, hoping that Hesera was still awake at this time and that she still liked him. Because if she didn't, then he was probably going to ruin their escape attempt before they even got out of the Garden.

Now Keo was not exactly sure how this locket worked. Right now, he only saw his own reflection in its tiny mirror. He looked the locket over briefly, but he did not see any instructions that might tell him how it worked.

Maybe I need to say Hesera's name to make it work, Keo thought.

So Keo said, "Hesera?"

As soon as he said her name, the mirror flashed. One minute, he was looking down at the reflection of his face in the mirror; the next, he was staring at Hesera's own beautiful features.

And before he could even say anything, Hesera said, "Keo? Is that you?"

Keo nodded. "Yes. Glad to—"

Hesera let out a happy squeal that made Keo, Dlaine, and Maryal wince. It also made Keo cover the locket briefly in order to mute the sound, even though he was pretty certain that there was no one else in the Garden aside from them right now.

Then Hesera stopped squealing, causing Keo to remove his hand from the locket as she said, "Oh, I can't believe you actually contacted me! This is so amazing. I didn't expect you to try to contact me so soon. But why so late at night? Not that I'm complaining, of course, but I didn't take you for a night owl."

"Because something bad has happened that I can't explain right away," said Keo. "Did you hear that my friends and I were arrested for treason?"

"Of course," said Hesera. "I heard it, but I didn't believe it one bit, because I know that from experience that you're a good man."

"Good," said Keo. "That's because it's completely false. We were framed by Easan."

"Easan?" said Hesera. She scowled. "I always knew there was something off about that man, and it wasn't just his choice in fashion."

"Yeah, but we managed to escape the Old Castle and need some place to stay," said Keo. "Can we stay at your place for the night? We'll explain the details and our plans to you when we get there."

"But of course," said Hesera, flashing Keo a brilliant and beautiful smile. "My mansion isn't far from the Old Castle, about five blocks or so. Just head down West Street for five blocks and you should see it. You can't miss it."

"Thanks," said Keo. "We'll head there now. See you soon."

Hesera nodded and then Keo closed the locket on her face. Looking at Dlaine and Maryal, Keo felt a rising sense of anticipation, but knew that there was no time to waste and that they had to leave now if they wanted to get to Hesera's mansion before the Knights discovered their escape from the dungeons.

Chapter Nineteen

THE NEXT DAY, WHEN the sun was high in the sky, Keo—along with Dlaine, Maryal, and Jola—walked along with Hesera's servants to the Grand Arena. It was a massive building located on the northern end of Tain, where it was visible over the tops of the other buildings. The Arena was normally used for jousting tournaments for the Knights, but according to Hesera, it had also been used by the Keepers to make public announcements to the citizens of Tain due to its massive amount of seating (at least 5,000 seats, according to Hesera) and spacious interior. That was probably why it had been chosen as the place of Easan's coronation, because it would give many of Tain's citizens a good view of the event.

Hesera said that she had received an invitation to the duel, which had been hastily changed to the coronation at the last minute, and that she had been intending to go regardless of what the event turned out to be. She had then offered to help Keo and his friends get into the Arena disguised as her servants. This would work because Hesera almost always traveled with a large crowd of servants who did whatever she needed them to do; thus, it was unlikely that anyone would notice anything off about a few extra servants no one had seen before.

Keo looked down at his clothes as they walked. He wore plain tan servants' robes, which covered his body well. Gildshine was strapped to his side, which made walking somewhat awkward, but also ensured that the Knights would not see it and thus recognize him for who he really was. Keo also had a hood over his head, which hid his face very well.

Dlaine and Maryal were dressed similarly, though Dlaine had gotten a haircut and Maryal wore a veil over her own face, which was apparently a traditional veil that single women of the Old Kingdom wore to these sorts of big public events. Men didn't, but Hesera assured Keo and Dlaine that as long as they wore their hoods and acted inconspicuous, then it was unlikely that the Knights would pay any attention to them. She said that the Knights rarely paid attention to her servants, mostly because she was, in her own words, 'far more interesting to them' than her servants were.

Even so, Keo didn't feel very relaxed. While he walked as calmly as ever, he kept expecting the Knights to run up to him at any moment and arrest him again. He remembered how, earlier that morning, the Knights had put out a warning to all citizens of Tain to watch out for the 'escapees' and to report them to the nearest Knight if they saw them. Keo had even seen a few Knights patrolling the streets outside of Hesera's mansion, though none of them ever actually came up to the front door and demanded to be let in.

Just keep your cool, Keo, Keo told himself as he, Hesera, and the others joined the throngs of people heading into the Grand Arena, which looked even bigger up close. *As long as you don't behave in a strange or suspicious manner, you shouldn't even be noticed.*

But now that they were actually about to enter the Arena, Keo suddenly found himself wishing that he had accepted the Dracone woman's offer last night and left with her to go to the Upper Mountains. He knew that was a foolish feeling and that it would go away on its own soon, but a part of him was still worried that he had made a terrible mistake.

After all, he knew very little about the full extent of Easan's power. If Easan was working with the demons, then that meant that he likely had many dangerous powers that Keo might not be able to handle. Keo had killed demons before, but he had never killed another human being, much less one with demonic powers at his command.

But Keo pushed those thoughts and feelings from his mind in order to focus on the present. He knew that he was doing the right thing and that it would all work out, but he just needed to be smart about it and not let his emotions get the better of him.

Up ahead, at the entrance to the Grand Arena, were four Knights with green highlights on their armor standing on both sides of the crowd. Though their visors were down, Keo knew that these Knights were keeping an eye out for him and the others. No doubt Easan knew that Keo was most likely going to try to crash the coronation, but there was no way that Easan or the Knights could possibly have guessed that Keo and his friends would be sneaking in through the front doors in plain sight.

Even so, Keo didn't lower his guard at all. He did not meet the visors of the Knights as they passed by them, but it was hard not to because his every instinct was telling him that they were in danger of being found out. Yet none of the Knights said a word to Hesera or any of her 'servants' as they entered the massive Arena lobby, which was full of people.

Some of these people were merchants, selling food and drinks to people who had come to view the event, but most of the people in the lobby were normal citizens making their way to their seating in the stands. Keo did not see Easan or any of the Keepers anywhere, but that made sense. Most likely, Easan was backstage, preparing for his coronation, never suspecting that Keo and his friends were going to crash it.

But rather than head to the stands, Hesera led her servants to a doorway off to the side. There were two Knights—Blue Order, based on the blue highlights of their armor—standing before it. They were huge, their muscles obvious even underneath their plate armor, and they both carried swords that looked as big as broadswords, along with shields as tall as a small child.

But Hesera didn't seem intimidated by them. She just walked up them, smiling as beautifully as always, and said, "Hello. I'm Hesera, here for the coronation of the *shelmai*. I was invited to sit in the upper seating."

"Show us your invitation," said one of the Knights in a low, rumbling voice. "Otherwise we can't let you up. Arena policy."

Without hesitation, Hesera pulled out a card from her bag and handed it to the Knight. The Knight took the card, glanced at it, and then handed it back to her as he said, "All right. But what about your servants? Do they have invitations, too?"

Keo bit his lower lip, but tried not to look suspicious. He glanced at Dlaine and Maryal, but they were looking straight ahead. He wished that he was the invisible one now, rather than Jola.

Hesera threw back her hair and said, "What a silly question. My servants didn't need invitations to past events and they certainly don't need invitations to the most important event since the founding of the Old Kingdom itself two decades ago. They are with me, and if any of the Keepers or Easan or anyone else has a problem with this, just point them in my direction and I'll be happy to talk to them about it."

Keo looked at Hesera in surprise. She had always come across as rather ditzy to him, but she was obviously a lot craftier and aggressive than she appeared. Of course, Hesera was said to be the most popular actress in all of the Old Kingdom, so maybe Keo was seeing some of her acting skills in action right now.

The Knight—despite being at least three times as large as Hesera—held up his hands and said, in an apologetic voice, "I am so sorry, Miss Hesera, I forgot that your servants do not need invitations to enter. Please forgive my mistake."

"It's fine," said Hesera, waving off the Knight's apology like it was nothing. "I just wanted to make sure that the Arena's policy hadn't changed. I understand that you were just doing your job; in fact, if I see the Keepers, I'll mention to them what a good job you are doing here, making sure that only people who were actually invited to the event get to enter."

"Oh, thank you, Miss Hesera," said the Knight, who sounded relieved that Hesera was no longer angry with him. "I would like it very much if you told the Keepers that. I only asked for identification for your servants because of the recent escape of the false *shelmai* Keo and his friends. The Keepers fear that the false *shelmai* will try to sneak into the Grand Arena and disrupt the coronation of the Rightful Heir Easan, so we were given special orders to be especially careful about who tried to enter the upper seating."

"Well, I can tell you right now that that awful and vile Keo and his merry band of stupid friends is certainly not among my loyal and trustworthy servants," said Hesera, who managed to sound like she really did think that Keo and his friends were vile and bad. "I mean, wouldn't they be risking getting found out if they tried to do that? Besides, I know the names and faces of each and every one of my servants, so if they tried that, I would have known well before I even left my mansion."

"Yes, yes, of course," said the Knight, nodding. "Anyway, we will let you inside now. Here you go."

The two Knights stepped aside, though not before opening the door to the upper seating. Hesera flashed another brilliant smile at both of them before entering, with Keo and the others following behind her, keeping their faces straight ahead to avoid being recognized by the guards.

As they climbed the staircase, Keo sped up until he was walking right next to Hesera. Seeing as they were alone in the staircase, he said, "That was some quick thinking back there. I thought that the Knights might decide to check us out anyway, just to be sure that we weren't us."

"Oh, it was incredibly easy, because I am a natural actress, which is why I've been so successful in my career," said Hesera, though she looked pleased at Keo's compliments just the same. "Anyway, we're in, so all you need to do now is get down to the Arena field and confront Easan, correct?"

"That's the plan," said Keo as they passed a locked door to their right. "Jola should be contacting us any second now to tell us how to get down there without being spotted."

"You mean you haven't heard from her yet?" said Hesera,

looking at Keo in surprise as they climbed closer and closer to the upper seating.

"Not yet," said Keo. He looked over his shoulder at Dlaine. "Dlaine, have you heard from Jola yet?"

"Nope, but I'm not worried," said Dlaine, shaking his head. "Jola's smart and won't get herself caught. Should be just a matter of time now before she contacts us."

Keo nodded, but he still felt uneasy about this part of the plan. Due to Jola's constant invisibility and good sneaking skills, it was decided that she should go to the Arena ahead of the others to scout out a path for Keo and the others to use that would allow them to reach the Arena field without being seen or caught by the Knights or anyone else. While Keo was well aware of Jola's talent for sneaking around unnoticed, he was still worried that something might go wrong and Jola might get caught anyway. He was thinking about Easan, who might have had another demon hidden in the Arena to take down Keo and his friends.

Of course, I haven't actually seen *any hint that this demon might exist, but that doesn't mean much, considering how easily demons can hide themselves if they want,* Keo thought. *I bet Jola will tell us if she sees any hints of a demon, anyway. She's smart that way.*

When they reached the top seating, they discovered that several people were already here. Most of them appeared to be from Tain's upper class: men in fine golden robes, women in silver dresses, and servants of both genders waiting upon them both. There were a handful of Knights here as well, with purple highlights on their armor, which told Keo that they were Purple Order Knights. Now Purple Order Knights may have been the lowest Order, but the fact was that they were still above ordinary Knights, which meant that the Keepers and Easan must have sincerely believed that Keo and the others might pose a dangerous threat to the lives of the people in the Arena.

Wonder what kind of crap Easan has been selling the Keepers about us, Keo thought with a scowl. *Maybe they think we're psychotic explosion-obsessed mass killers like Eliam. If so, they're about to be highly disappointed.*

Hesera took a seat near the back of the upper seating, next to a middle-aged man who looked like he must have been a handsome man in his youth, but had lost much of his handsomeness in his old age. Hesera, however, immediately started chatting with the middle-aged man like she had known him for years, though Keo didn't pay very much attention to that. He was focused on the view of the Arena field that the upper seating gave him.

The Grand Arena's field was huge. It was mostly dust and sand, with a few patches of brown grass here and there. It reminded Keo of the Knights' training grounds, except far, far larger. It looked like you could put two massive armies there, with enough room for camps for both.

The thousands of seats below were mostly empty, but they were filling up quickly as people from Tain and the surrounding area filed in from the lobby. Keo had known that the Grand Arena was said to be big enough to hold 5,000 people, but until this very moment, he had not known what an Arena full of 5,000 people might look like. He guessed that the cheering of the people, once it started, would be absolutely deafening.

On the opposite end of the Arena stood a massive statue of King Riuno himself. The statue stood with the tip of its gigantic sword resting in the plinth, its hands folded over the sword's handle. The statue's gaze-less eyes were staring straight ahead and looked so lifelike that Keo felt his father's gaze judging him, even though he knew that the statue was just that and nothing more.

Below, at the feet of the statue, were six thrones arranged similar to how the thrones of the Keepers back in the Old Castle were arranged. And, despite the distance, Keo could clearly see that the Keepers were already emerging from behind the statue to sit upon their thrones. There were also a dozen Knights with them, including Sir Abohji, who was recognizable due to the distinctive red highlights of his armor, while the other eleven Knights had blue highlights to indicate that they were members of the Blue Order.

Of course the Keepers would get the best protection, Keo thought. *The Blue Order is only one rank below the Red Order, but with Sir Abohji leading them, Easan might not even have to do anything to stop us.*

But Keo did not let that deter him. He just looked for Easan, but apparently the traitor had not yet emerged into the Arena. He guessed that Easan was probably preparing for his grand entrance, which would undoubtedly be met with tons of applause from the spectators. That would have made Keo grind his teeth in anger if he hadn't been trying to avoid drawing attention to himself, but he found it hard to remain calm whenever he thought about how Easan had framed them and made everyone in the city think that he and his friends were criminals. It reminded Keo far too much of South Lamaira, where he and his friends really *were* considered criminals due to the Magical Council's hatred of them.

But unlike there, I am in a position to prove our innocence once and for all by exposing Easan before the Keepers and everyone else in Tain, Keo thought, a smile crossing his face despite his best efforts to keep his expressions neutral. *Just need to wait for the right moment and then strike.*

At that moment, Keo felt a familiar presence enter his mind—Jola's presence—and heard Jola say in his head, *All right. I've found a way for us to reach the Arena floor without being spotted. But you will need a distraction first so you can leave without being seen.*

Keo looked at Dlaine and Maryal. Based upon their expressions, they must have heard Jola's words as well.

I've got an idea, Keo said to Jola, though he was sure that Dlaine and Maryal could hear him as well. *Just hold on.*

Keo bent over forward to Hesera's ear and whispered, "Jola called. We need to leave."

Hesera—who had still been avidly chatting with her older friend—looked at Keo and said, "Ah, yes. Please go and fetch me some refreshments from the lobby, if you will, but you can take your time, since it doesn't look like Easan will be coming out any time soon."

Of course, Keo understood that Hesera was providing the distraction for him. By telling Keo, Dlaine, and Maryal to go get her some refreshments from the lobby, that gave Keo and his friends an excuse to leave, but at the same time, also made it so that no one would suspect that they were about to crash the coronation. Again, Keo marveled at just how quickly she could make up a convincing excuse on the spot like that. He made a mental note to try to catch one of her plays these days, if only to see if she was just as good an actress on the stage as she was in real life.

Nodding in understanding, Keo stood up and walked back down the staircase, gesturing for Dlaine and Maryal to follow him, which they did. The Purple Order Knights in the upper seating did watch them leave, but neither of the two Knights followed them, which made Keo feel a bit more relaxed, because that meant that those two Knights did not suspect him or the others of being up to anything they should stop.

As they walked down the stairs, Jola said, *Go through the locked door on the right side of the staircase. You passed it earlier when you were going up to the upper seating.*

Keo, Dlaine, and Maryal found the door quickly, because it was the only door in the staircase besides the entrance at the bottom. Keo opened the door and quickly stepped inside and then stepped aside to allow Dlaine and Maryal to enter. Once they were inside, he closed the door behind them, immediately plunging them into darkness.

But it was only for a moment. In the next moment, a small but bright flame suddenly flickered into existence, which Keo knew was the work of Jola, even though he still couldn't see her. The light of her flame revealed that they were standing a dark and dry hallway, with thick layers of dust on the walls and floor. It stretched on ahead out of sight, making it impossible for Keo to know what might be waiting for them.

"What is this place?" said Maryal, looking around at it in curiosity. She coughed loudly, probably after she got some dust in her lungs. "It's so dirty."

Maintenance tunnel, said Jola. *There's an entire system of tunnels like this in this place. I think the Arena's caretakers use it to get around the place quickly and without being seen. But don't worry; I scouted out this particular tunnel and learned that it hasn't been used in years, but it will definitely take us to the Arena field, where we can confront Easan.*

"All right," said Keo. He took off his servant robes and dropped them on the floor. "Won't be needing these anymore."

Dlaine and Maryal followed his lead, but before they could take even one step forward, there was a sudden loud sound of muffled cheering from outside the door. It was followed by a single loud voice whose owner Keo was unable to identify due to the fact that it was muffled by the walls, but he looked at Dlaine and Maryal in worry anyway.

"What was that?" said Maryal, looking around the maintenance tunnel in alarm.

"Sounded to me like the crowd was cheering," said Dlaine. "And I bet that voice belonged to one of the Keepers, who is probably speaking to the audience."

"Then we have no time to lose," said Keo as he removed Gildshine from its position against his body and reattaching it to his belt. "Let's go."

With Jola's fire in the lead, Keo and the others walked down the long maintenance tunnel as quickly as they could. There was no reason to be quiet about it; the walls and ceiling of the tunnel were too thick for sound to escape through. And even if they weren't, the loud cheers of the crowd above would have drowned out any noise they made.

Again as they walked, Keo could not help but feel anxious. He had no idea what was going to happen when they got to the Arena field. He was sure that the Knights would try to stop him and his friends, but maybe they would be able to expose Easan before that. Keo wanted to show the Tainians Easan's true colors. He didn't even care if they still hated him, though he figured that the peoples' opinion of him would probably rise once they learned the truth about Easan.

There's still time to leave, the scared part of Keo said, the part of himself that he usually tried to ignore in times like this. *Leave, and go to the Upper Mountains where the Dracones live. If you leave now, you will be long gone by the time the Knights realize you're no longer in the city.*

But as always, Keo ignored it, because in truth, there really *wasn't* any time to leave and never look back. They had come this far, so there was no turning back now, regardless of what happened or how Keo felt.

A few minutes of walking down the tunnel later, Keo and his friends found the exit, a locked wooden door similar to the one they had taken to get here. Jola unlocked the door with her magic, but before they stepped out, Keo peeked his head out the door just to make sure that there were no Knights or anyone else on the other side waiting for them.

The door led to one of the entrances to the Arena field. There were three Blue Order Knights standing with their backs to the door, keeping an eye on the field like they thought Keo and his friends were about to burst out of the ground at any moment. None of them had heard Keo open the door, but Keo did not want them seeing him, so he pulled his head inside and whispered to Maryal, "Three Knights. Knock 'em out."

Maryal nodded and stepped out of the maintenance tunnel into the Area entrance. She raised her hands toward the Knights and balled her hands into fists.

Immediately, the three Knights started gasping for breath. They dropped their weapons and clutched their throats, but in a couple of seconds they collapsed onto the ground, unconscious from the lack of air.

As soon as all three of them were down, Maryal gestured for the others to step out of the tunnel. Keo, Dlaine, and Jola exited the tunnel, closing the door behind them, and then walked up to the exit to the Arena field to get a good look at what was going on out there. But the four of them clung to the walls, hiding in the shadows to avoid being spotted by anyone in the stands or out on the field.

From what Keo could see, there were easily one hundred Knights from every Order gathered in the center of the Arena field, with Sir Abohji leading them. It looked like the Knights were performing a ceremony, because they were marching in formation, but Keo did not know what ceremony they were doing. He did, however, note that all one hundred of those Knights were well-armored and well-armed, particularly Sir Abohji, who carried a massive broadsword in both hands that looked almost as big as Jola.

Then Keo looked up at the plinth of his father's statue. All six Keepers were seated in their thrones now, as well as Easan, who was seated in a larger throne right in the middle. That almost made Keo think that Easan had been crowned King already, but then he noticed that Easan was not wearing a crown on his head. He was, however, wearing the golden Ceremonial Armor, with its dragon-like helmet resting on his lap. He was watching the Knights' ceremony below with amusement, though he also looked a bit impatient, as if he wished he could skip the formalities and go straight to the crowning.

Too bad we'll never get to the crowning, once I expose you for who you are in front of the Tainians, Keo thought.

"Should we run out there and confront Easan now?" said Dlaine in a whisper, even though the clanking of the Knights' armor and the cheering of the crowd meant that it was unlikely that anyone could have heard him even if he had been screaming at the top of his lungs. "I didn't know there was going to be one hundred Knights."

Keo shook his head. "Not yet. If we run out now, Sir Abohji will just have his men capture us. We need to wait for the perfect moment, and then we will strike."

But even as Keo said that, self-doubt was gnawing at him again. All one hundred of those Knights were members of elite Orders. Even if they waited until the Knights left the field, Easan and the Keepers might just order the Knights to come back and arrest him and his friends anyway, without giving them a chance to speak.

As always, however, Keo pushed that self-doubt out of his mind and focused on the present. He continued to watch as the Knights marched before the cheering crowd, which went on for a couple more minutes before they stopped and then bowed, first at the audience, and then at Easan and the Keepers. Then Sir Abohji led the hundred Knights off the field and into another entrance that was thankfully nowhere near where Keo and his friends were.

But even when the last of the Knights left the field, the people continued to cheer and shout, at least until Aster stood up from his throne in front of the statue of King Riuno and raised his hands.

The crowd immediately went silent, which Keo found amazing, because Aster looked rather small in comparison to the thousands of people gathered in the Arena today, though they had likely turned silent due to Aster's authority.

Then Aster lowered his hands and spoke. His voice was loud and authoritative, easily heard even from a distance. Keo wondered if Aster had a little magical power in himself that allowed him to increase the volume of his voice, because he could not see any device on the Keeper that made his voice loud enough for the entire Arena to hear.

"Welcome, citizens of Tain, to the momentous event that we have been waiting over twenty years for!" Aster said, his tone joyous. "I would first like to thank Sir Abohji and the Hundred Knights, who, per tradition, performed the excellent and beautiful March of the Brave to open the coronation. They have put us all in the correct mood for the coronation of the *shelmai*, the Rightful Heir, Easan, the long-lost son of the legendary King Riuno himself."

Behind Aster, Easan was still smirking, while the other Keepers looked pleased at the way things were going. The crowd was still silent, listening to Aster's speech. After all, almost everyone in this place had been awaiting the return of the *shelmai* and so were willing to endure the formalities if it meant that they would have the first King in two decades at the end of it.

Unfortunately, it looks like they're going to have to wait a little while longer before that happens, Keo thought, but he did not yet leave his spot in the shadows. He just listened to the rest of Aster's speech.

"It is sad, however, that this day must be marred by the

knowledge that the false *shelmai* and traitor to humanity, Keo of the Sword, and his co-conspirators somehow fled the Old Castle dungeons and are still on the loose somewhere in this beloved and ancient city of ours," said Aster. "Nonetheless, I can assure all of you that you are all as safe or even safer than if you had chosen to stay home today. Brave Sir Abohji is in charge of the two thousand Knights of the Old Kingdom protecting this building. Should the evil Keo and his friends attempt to interrupt the coronation, they shall be swiftly dealt with by our valiant defenders."

Keo frowned. *Evil? I thought that Aster said we were going to get a trial. Easan must be corrupting the Keepers' minds with his demonic magic.*

"But let us not think about such sorry news for the moment," said Aster. "Crown-bearer, please come forward."

A young boy—probably no more than ten and sweating profusely, even though it wasn't very hot right now—stepped forward from the right of Aster's throne. The young boy carried a large purple pillow in his hands and upon the pillow was a golden crown with miniature dragon wings built into its temple.

Aster gestured at the crown sitting upon the pillow. "Behold, my fellow Tainians, the Ancient Crown, said to have been crafted by the Good King himself upon the establishment of the Kingdom of Lamaira. It has been worn by every single legitimate King of Lamaira since that day, including by the last King, King Riuno, although it has been two decades since it was last worn by a member of the Lamairan Royal Family. But today, that drought shall end."

Aster carefully lifted the crown off of the pillow and walked over to Easan's side. Easan was smirking as smugly as ever, but Keo did not walk out just yet. He glanced at Dlaine and Maryal, who looked ready to interrupt the coronation, but Keo didn't think the time was yet right to reveal their presence yet.

"Easan of the Golden Flames," said Aster, holding the Ancient Crown in his old, veined hands. "Do you vow to honor and protect the Kingdom of Lamaira, to work to restore the Kingdom to its original glory, and to restore the power to the seal that your great ancestor placed upon the demons a thousand years ago, as the prophecy states you must?"

Easan nodded. "Yes, Keeper Aster, I do. I will reunite the war-torn kingdom and restore Lamaira to its original glory among the nations. And I will do everything within my power to ensure that the demons of legend remain just that and never take the life of even the humblest of lives in my kingdom so long as I live."

Though Easan spoke humbly, Keo saw right through his lies. He knew that Easan didn't care if the demons were free, just as long as he got to rule the Kingdom.

And that infuriated Keo. It infuriated him so much that he felt the fire burning hotly within him again, that same fire that had he always had trouble accessing consciously. The fire compelled him to draw Gildshine from its hilt, which he did not hesitate to do.

Then he looked at Dlaine and Maryal and nodded at them and they nodded back in understanding. And then he ran onto the field just as Aster raised the Ancient Crown over Easan's head, shouting, "Wait!"

Keo's shout echoed throughout the Arena. It was so loud that many of the spectators jumped in their seats, while others looked around in confusion for the source of the shout. Aster froze when the Ancient Crown was partway to Easan's head, while Easan himself looked down at them and gasped.

"You!" Easan shouted, pointing at Keo and the others as they ran onto the field. "How did you get in here without being seen by the Knights?"

Keo and his friends stopped in the center of the Arena field and Keo glared up at Easan. The spectators in the seats were whispering and murmuring among themselves at this unexpected development, but Keo ignored them in order to focus on Easan. He pointed Gildshine at Easan, which immediately burst into golden flames without Keo even thinking about it.

"It doesn't matter how we got into here," said Keo, shaking his head. He raised his voice as loud as he could so he would be heard by everyone in the Arena. "What matters is that we are going to stop you from being crowned the King of Lamaira, because we know your *true* nature, Easan, friend of the demons!"

Many people in the stands gasped when Keo said that, while Easan shouted back, "Friend of the demons? I am no friend the of demons. I am the *shelmai*, the Rightful Heir, and I loathe anyone who desires to destroy the Kingdom, whether human or demon."

"You can say that all you like, but that doesn't change the fact that you are not the true *shelmai*," said Keo. "You tricked the Keepers and the people of Tain into thinking you were on their side, when in fact you have been working with the demons this entire time. You are trying to take over the Old Kingdom so you can prevent its people from stopping the return of the demons."

More gasps and even a few cries of, "Liar!" from the people, but again, Keo did not look at them. He looked directly at Easan the entire time, his focus never wavering. The false *shelmai* looked enraged and offended by Keo's accusations, but he had not yet denied them, though that was probably because he was so angry at his true nature being revealed in public to answer.

Then Aster, who seemed to have recovered from the shock of Keo's sudden appearance, pointed at Keo and his friends and said, "Guards! Capture the traitor and his friends and take them away from this place! Throw them back into the dungeons, where they will await their final fates until the coronation is over and Easan is crowned King of Lamaira!"

Keo suddenly heard the sounds of dozens of suits of armor clanking against each other and looked around. From every entrance in the Arena came five hundred or so Knights, all of them armed to the teeth. They blocked off every exit, making it impossible for Keo or the others to flee the Arena. Dlaine raised his fists defensively, while Maryal held her hands in preparation for a spell, but Keo knew that there was no way they could defeat so many Knights, especially because all of the Knights appeared to belong to the Purple Order and up.

But then Easan raised a hand and shouted, "Halt!"

Without hesitation, all five hundred or so of the Knights stopped their march toward Keo and the others. Puzzled, Keo looked up at Easan, a smug expression on his face.

"Easan, what is this?" said Aster, looking at Easan in surprise and anger. "Why did you order the Knights to halt? The traitor and his friends must be caught before they can harm you or anyone else in the Arena."

"I understand, Keeper, and I will let the Knights do their duty soon, but first, I wish to duel Keo," said Easan. "Then the Knights can lock away these liars in the dungeons to let them rot and you can crown me King, as I rightly deserve."

"Duel Keo?" said Aster. He sounded genuinely confused as he looked from Easan to Keo and back again. "But why? You do not need to duel him. Everyone knows that you are the true *shelmai* and that he is the false one. You do not need to prove anything."

Easan glared up at Aster. "I want to prove that I am Keo's superior, that the people of Tain can trust in me. If they see me defeat the traitorous foreigner who has deceived us all, then that will erase any doubt in the minds of the Tainians as to who is superior. Besides, it will be quick, because I am the better swordsman and fighter."

"But—"

Easan pushed the crown in Aster's hands away and stood up. "I don't care about your objections, Aster. I will fight Keo and I will beat him and then I will be crowned the King of Lamaira, as is my destiny."

Aster scowled, but he did not say anything else. He just stepped back, while the other Keepers exchanged worried looks like they were not sure how to react to this sudden turn of events. But none of them objected, either, and Keo understood, because —although he'd never admit it—Easan truly did look as authoritative and royal as any king. He looked like the kind of ruler you did not question or doubt, otherwise you risked getting thrown out of his court and into his dungeons.

Holding his helmet under his arm, Easan looked down at Keo again, his blue eyes burning with anger. "Keo! I challenge you to a duel, between you and me only, here and now, in front of the entire audience of the Grand Arena. Your friends may watch, but they may not intervene or help you at any point, no matter how bloody or brutal the duel may get. And the winner will be crowned King of Lamaira. Do you accept?"

Keo lowered Gildshine, but nodded and said, "I do. Bring it on."

Easan nodded, but then looked at the audience watching in silence. He drew Shadowbane from its sheath and held it above his head. The sword burst into golden flames, much like Gildshine, as Easan shouted, "Citizens of Tain! Today, you are going to witness the true might of the *shelmai*, as foretold by the prophecy! When this duel is over, you will see that your trust in me is justified and that there is not a force on the face of the planet that can stop me or threaten my people and expect to get away with it."

The crowd immediately burst into wild applause, while Keo looked at his friends. They nodded to show their support and then stepped back several feet away from Keo in order to give him the room he needed to fight Easan. Dlaine gave Keo a thumbs up, while Maryal rubbed her hands together anxiously like she was worried that Keo might be in over his head.

As for Keo, he ignored his doubts and turned to face Easan again. Easan put his helmet on his head and then jumped off the plinth. He flew through the air for a brief moment before landing on the Arena floor on both feet as naturally as if he did that every day.

Now Keo and Easan stood opposite each other, their swords drawn and burning, while everyone in the Arena—Dlaine, Maryal, and Jola, the Knights, the Keepers, and the spectators— watched in anticipation for the duel to start.

Then, without warning, Easan dashed toward Keo, holding

Shadowbane before him, and then Keo dashed toward Easan, holding Gildshine before himself as they ran to meet each other in the middle.

And when their swords clashed, it created a massive cloud of fire that briefly obscured them from the spectators.

Chapter Twenty

THE CLASHING OF GILDSHINE and Shadowbane created a fireball of golden flame that rose up into the air above Keo and Easan, where it exploded, raining sparks and fire down upon them both. Easan's armor protected him from it, but Keo had no armor, so he had to grimace as the tiny sparks bit at his skin and created tiny, burning holes in his clothes.

But Keo did not have the luxury of lying down to rest. He pushed back against Easan, who was surprisingly strong despite appearing less muscular than Keo. The two pushed back against each other as hard as they could, but they were almost evenly matched in terms of sheer physical strength. Gildshine and Shadowbane also seemed to be matched evenly, because both swords did not crack or strain under the impact of the blow.

The heat from the swords' flames washed over Keo and Easan, but Keo barely felt it. He just focused all of his effort into forcing Easan back, ignoring the heat and the pain from the sparks that had fallen on his body. Through the flames and through the eye holes of Easan's helmet, Keo saw Easan's eyes, which were glowing with anger. He wondered if Easan was getting overheated in his armor, but decided to ignore that in order to focus on winning the duel.

But Easan suddenly stepped to the side, causing Keo to stagger forward. Easan raised Shadowbane to bring it down on

Keo's head, but Keo turned the stagger into a roll, rolling away from Easan as his sword fell into the ground. Rolling back to his feet, Keo turned to face Easan, who had yanked his sword out of the ground and was now walking toward Keo again with his flaming sword at the ready.

All around Keo, the people chanted, "Easan! Easan! Easan!" over and over again. Keo tried to ignore that, but the peoples' shouts were so loud and so insistent that he found that a difficult task. The hardest part about it was knowing that most of the people in the Arena were on Easan's side, but Keo pushed that thought out of his mind. Whether the people supported him or Easan, it didn't matter, because Easan was a threat to everyone in the Arena and needed to be put down before he could gain the power he could use to destroy everyone.

Then Easan pointed Shadowbane at Keo and fired a stream of fire at him. Keo dodged it and then fired a fireball at Easan, which flew too fast for Easan to dodge.

But Easan deflected it with Shadowbane, sending the fireball flying into the sky, where it exploded above their heads. Even as more sparks and flame fell to the blackened earth around them, Easan dashed toward Keo again, moving fast despite his heavy armor, and swung his sword at Keo.

Keo blocked Shadowbane again and the two started trading blows, swinging their swords at each other ferociously. Each blocked blow sent more sparks flying, but the two paid no attention to that, because even a brief moment of distraction would be enough to cause a quick and painful defeat for the one who got distracted.

But then Easan missed just once, giving Keo the opening he

needed. He slashed at Easan's arm, but the Ceremonial Armor blocked the blade from cutting through Easan's flesh. Still, the blow connected and caused Easan to stagger back, allowing Keo to move in to get in a few more blows. He slashed at Easan's chest, striking his opponent's chest plate and even denting it slightly, while Easan almost dropped Shadowbane.

Keo went in for another strike, this one aimed at Easan's head, but Easan dodged it and struck at Keo, who had left an opening for Easan to exploit. Keo, however, managed to dodge the worst of it, but Shadowbane still cut through Keo's shirt and abdomen, which caused Keo to cry out in pain as the wound in his abdomen bled and burned.

Staggering away from Easan, Keo looked down at his wound. It wasn't very deep, nor was it bleeding very much, but it did hurt and it was bleeding enough to worry Keo. He had no way of staunching the bleeding at the moment, but he would need to, because if he bled enough, then Easan wouldn't even need to beat him in order to win this duel.

Clutching his bleeding abdomen, Keo looked up at Easan, who stood there looking at Keo with triumph in his eyes.

"Do you want to give up?" said Easan, his tone mocking. "I don't really want to kill you, so if you give up now, I will spare your life and have one of the Castle's Healers heal your wound … in the dungeons, of course, where you will rot away the rest of your pathetic days."

"Never," said Keo, wincing at the pain in his wound. "The demons and their allies are a bunch of liars. I know you want to see me dead more than anything. I can see through your lies."

Easan shook his head. "I have no idea why you think I have

anything to do with the demons, but I guess you think that if you tell a lie often enough, it will become the truth. Too bad you aren't going to remain conscious long enough for your lie to become a truth."

With that, Easan moved forward, still holding Shadowbane before him as its golden flames burning as hotly and brightly as ever. Still clutching his wound, Keo stepped backwards, thinking quickly about how to end this fight. Even though his abdomen wound was not very deep, the fact was that it was bleeding and bleeding fast when he wasn't covering it with his hand. Easan, on the other hand, was uninjured and ready to keep fighting.

If this fight lasts any longer, I'll probably die of blood loss, Keo thought, biting his lip as he kept walking backwards. *That means I need to end the battle now. But how?*

That was a question to which Keo had no answer and he did not have time to come up with an answer to it, because Easan was upon him again. Easan raised his sword and brought it down on Keo, but Keo raised Gildshine to block it. But Easan forced him to the ground and Keo had no choice but to let him do that because Keo was unable to push back. As he sank to the ground, Keo tried to keep Shadowbane from coming any closer, but Easan was pushing down hard and it wouldn't be long before his blade sank into Keo's head and killed him.

Must ... find ... a ... way to fight back, Keo thought, but even his thoughts were strained, because he had to hold Gildshine with one hand, which was all he could spare against Easan's doubled-handed grip on Shadowbane. The combined heat of the flames made him sweat, which added to his difficulty thinking. *Cannot ... lose ...*

Through the golden flames of Shadowbane and Gildshine, Keo saw Easan's blue eyes gleaming from within his helmet. Easan looked pleased at the way this battle was going, pleased that he was going to win, and pleased that he was going to get to kill Keo in front of five thousand people.

The idea of Easan being happy about deceiving so many people angered Keo. He was already angry due to being wrongfully accused of working with the demons and thrown into the dungeons for a crime he didn't commit, but seeing Easan's smug eyes and knowing the source of Easan's happiness only added to the flame burning deep within Keo's soul.

In fact, the flame did more than merely burn. Keo felt it flow through his body, the same as it had during his battle with the demon in the Citadel at Capitika. Rather than burn his innards, however, the flame gave him strength unlike any he had known before. It even made the pain in his abdomen, where Easan had cut him, go away.

Growling with anger—and it was a deep, inhuman growl that Keo had never heard himself make before—Keo started forcing Shadowbane up. Easan's eyes went from smug and triumph to confused and even frightened as Keo pushed against him.

Inch by inch, Keo pushed back Easan's blade, until soon Keo was standing upright again. He continued to push back against Easan, whose eyes now showed anger rather than confusion or fear.

"Impossible," said Easan, a tinge of fear in his voice. "How have you recovered? Where did this strength come from?"

Keo did not answer. Instead, he drew upon more of the fire deep within, the burning flame that made Gildshine into a force to be reckoned with and gave him strength greater than he had ever known, and used it to increase his strength. With an inhuman roar, Keo shoved Easan back as hard as he could.

Knocked off balance, Easan swung his arms wildly through the air to avoid falling backwards. That left him open for an attack by Keo, who slammed Gildshine's burning flames against Easan's right hand, knocking Shadowbane—which immediately lost its own golden flames—out of Easan's hand and sending it flying out of his reach.

Then Keo kicked Easan in the chest, knocking his opponent flat off his feet. And before Easan could recover from that, Keo slammed his foot down on Easan's chest, actually denting Easan's chest plate, and pointed the tip of Gildshine's still-burning flames at Easan's throat. Easan, who had grabbed Keo's ankle in an attempt to throw him off, froze when he saw how close Gildshine's flames were to his face.

"Now, Easan," said Keo, panting hard, his eyes never leaving his fallen opponent, "just whose lie will not become truth anytime soon?"

Easan glared up at Keo, but he did not try to get up or do anything else. He looked like he had given up, but Keo wasn't happy with that.

He pressed down harder on Easan's chest, causing Easan to groan in pain. "Say you surrender, you monster. Say it!"

"I … surrender," said Easan, his voice weak underneath the weight of Keo's foot. "Please … take your foot off my chest. I can't breathe …"

Keo, however, did not remove his foot just yet. He looked up at the rest of the Grand Arena. In the stands and seating above, thousands of people watched Keo and Easan in complete and utter silence. Sir Abohji and the five hundred Knights all stared as well, though with their visors down, it was impossible to tell what they were thinking. Dlaine and Maryal were staring at Keo as well, but unlike everyone else, they seemed happy about his victory.

"Do you see what happened to your precious *shelmai*?" Keo shouted, his voice echoing in the silence. He pointed at Easan. "He has been defeated. If he was the true *shelmai*, he would have been able to defeat me without any issue. But the fact is that his power comes from the demons of old, who have used him to weaken the Old Kingdom from within and destroy anyone who attempts to stop them."

"Why do you keep insisting that I am working with the demons?" said Easan. His voice was much higher now, probably because he was afraid. "Until I saw that one demon in the Throne Room, I hadn't even *seen* a demon before. Where is the proof that I work with the demons?"

Angered at Easan's constant lies, Keo looked down at the traitor. He looked into Easan's eyes, expecting to see the fear of a coward and deceiver whose lies had finally been exposed to the people.

But to Keo's astonishment, he saw honesty in Easan's eyes. Yes, Easan was clearly afraid that Keo was going to kill him, but Easan looked less like a deceiver whose lies were exposed than a frightened man who thought he was going to be killed for something that he had not done.

It must be a trick, Keo thought, though he didn't really believe that thought. *Easan has to be the one who worked with the demons. The evidence adds up.*

Now that Keo thought about it, though, he realized that he really didn't have any proof that Easan was the one who had let that demon into the Old Castle. Sure, it seemed suspicious that the demon had attacked at the same time that Keo and his friends arrived in Tain, but Easan hadn't even been in the Throne Room at the time. Even if Easan had been the one to get him locked up, it was probably because Easan had seen Keo as a threat to his own ascension to the Throne, and not because he was doing the bidding of the demons.

True, there was Eliam's description of Easan's red eyes and apparent control over shadows, but Eliam had already lied once about working with Keo. What if he had lied about that, too, just to make Keo think that Easan was the real enemy?

But ... if Easan isn't the traitor, then who is? Keo thought.

Then Keo heard a deep, aged voice behind him shout, "No!"

Looking over his shoulder, Keo saw that the shout had come from Aster. The aged Keeper still held the crown in his hands, but his hands were shaking, like he was so angry that he could barely contain it. He was staring at Easan with hate and disbelief in his old eyes and he looked like he was about to have a stroke.

"Aster?" said Seria, who sat on the throne nearest him. "What is the problem? You know getting worked up isn't good for your —"

"Silence, woman," Aster snarled, his voice briefly becoming distorted, like he was speaking through a rushing wind. "This was not how this was supposed to happen. Easan was supposed to win, *not* lose to some stupid kid from the south!"

The other Keepers gasped, while Keo removed Gildshine from Easan's throat and turned to face Aster. He raised his sword and pointed it directly at Aster, who stepped back in fear, like he thought Keo was going to attack him.

"So … *you* are the traitor," said Keo, raising his voice high enough for everyone in the Arena to hear. "You were the one who let that demon into the Old Castle, the one who caused all of this trouble for everyone."

Aster's hands continued to shake, but when he spoke, his voice was far steadier, though still angry. "I see no reason to hide the truth anymore, then. Yes, Easan was never anything more than a puppet. A useful one, easy to manipulate due to how arrogant and entitled and jealous he is, but a puppet nonetheless, one whose strings I always intended to cut at some point."

The spectators in the stands and seats immediately started muttering and murmuring among themselves about this. The Knights all looked to Sir Abohji, whose body language told Keo that he was just as surprised by this sudden turn of events as his subordinates. Maryal had clasped a hand over her mouth, while Dlaine stared dumbfounded at Aster.

As for the other five Keepers, they were all staring at their leader in pure shock. Seria even looked like she was about to have a heart attack.

"How long have you been this way?" said Keo, his sword never wavering.

"How long have I been a traitor?" said Aster. He snorted. "A year. I was contacted by the King of Demons himself in a dream. He told me that the demons were going to rise again, and if I wanted to survive, then I should help his people return from where they had been banished. He promised me complete and absolute power over the Old Kingdom—power I would not have to share with the other Keepers or give up to the son of some long-dead King no one cares about anymore—so I accepted."

Even though Aster was clearly without any allies in the Arena, he did not sound like he was afraid. He spoke smugly about the deal he had struck with the King of Demons, which made Keo think that Aster must have lost his mind.

"Were you always planning this?" said Keo. He gestured at Easan behind him, who still lay on the ground where Keo had knocked him down. "Always planning to have Easan become the King?"

"Not always," said Aster, shaking his head. "I spent a good deal of time searching the Old Kingdom for a suitable false successor to the Throne. It took a while, but eventually I found Easan, who bears a striking resemblance to the late King Riuno despite not being related to him."

Keo heard movement behind him and looked over his shoulder to see Easan standing up again. Only this time, Easan did not look like he was going to fight Keo. Instead, he removed his helmet and stared up at Aster, disbelief and shock etched into his features.

"But I came to Tain of my own free will," said Easan, pointing at himself. "No one told me to come to Tain to tell everyone that I am the *shelmai*."

"But Easan, don't you recall what made you think that you might be the Rightful Heir?" said Aster. He pointed at Shadowbane, which still lay several feet away from Easan. "You discovered Shadowbane, the Good King's sword, in the middle of an ancient forest near your hometown. But do you know how Shadowbane even got there in the first place?"

Easan shook his head.

"I put it there," said Aster simply. "I rediscovered Shadowbane when digging through the vault shortly after I agreed to work with the King of Demons, even though Shadowbane had been said to be missing ever since King Riuno's death. I took the sword and hid it from my fellow Keepers until I could find a use for it, and I believe that using it to trick an insecure orphan into believing that he is the long lost son of the last King of Lamaira is a good use for it, wouldn't you say?"

Easan's eyes widened. He looked down at the helmet in his hands for a moment before looking back up at Aster. "Are you telling me that my father is *not* King Riuno?"

"That is exactly what I am telling you, Easan," said Aster with a dark chuckle. "I don't know who your real parents are, but I do know that you are not the *shelmai* and never have been. As I said, you are nothing more than an orphan suffering from severe insecurity."

"Then what about Shadowbane?" said Easan. "What about the golden flames that I can summon?"

"Shadowbane is a magical sword in its own right, with the ability to summon those golden flames around it irrespective of who wields it," said Aster. "You are not more special than any other mortal just because you were able to use its power like that, though I admit it was very helpful in furthering your own delusions and the delusions of the rest of the Tainians."

Easan looked absolutely crushed by this revelation. He dropped his helmet and fell down to his hands and knees, his face displaying extreme despair. In fact, he looked so despairing that Keo actually felt sorry for Easan, which was the very first time he had ever felt that way toward him. A small part of Keo was glad, however, that he and Easan weren't actually related, if only because he couldn't stand the idea having Easan as a brother.

"Trust me, Easan, I am just as disappointed in you as you are right now," said Aster, shaking his head. "I had hoped that, by installing you as the King, I could keep the Old Kingdom from being a threat to the demons' rise, but now that you've lost to Keo, I can see that I was mistaken to think you were anything other than a needy orphan who just wanted to be told that he was special."

Again, Easan said nothing in response to those harsh words. He seemed to have completely lost all interest in the rest of the world, as if his whole universe had been completely shattered by Aster's revelation.

Keo looked up at Aster, his hands trembling in anger. "So you played Easan and the entire Old Kingdom this entire time. Why? Why did you do this? I thought the Keepers were supposed to *protect* the Old Kingdom, to preserve its traditions and laws, for the return of the *shelmai*. Not ally with demons for their own personal gain."

Aster laughed. It was a long, mad laugh, one that made the rest of the Keepers look quite terrified. It just annoyed Keo, however, who continued to glare at Aster until the old man's laughter died off.

"I have led the Keepers for over two decades in leading and ruling the people of the Old Kingdom," said Aster. He spread his arms as if to indicate all of the spectators in the Arena right now. "For two decades, I have protected this country from the Magicians from the south and the Divinians in the east. I did it at first because I fervently believed in the return of the *shelmai*, that if we could just get the right King on the Throne, then all of our problems would be saved." He scowled. "But that was terribly naïve on my part."

"Naive?" Seria said. She looked like the only Keeper who had the courage to speak; the others were practically cowering in their thrones. She leaned forward, looking at Aster with shock. "Aster, our duty as Keepers is to preserve the laws, customs, and traditions of the Kingdom of Lamaira until the return of the *shelmai*. There is nothing naïve about that."

"Are you certain?" said Aster, glaring at her. "Look at what two decades' worth of waiting has gotten us. Endless war against two enemy nations that would like nothing more than to wipe out our very way of life … the deaths of countless young men, our sons and nephews and grandsons … and for what? For a King who will never come, rather than taking power ourselves?"

"But the Rightful Heir *did* come," said Seria. She pointed at Keo. "Easan may not be the true *shelmai*, but Keo most definitely is. That means that our job is almost over and that soon, the Kingdom will rise again."

Aster shook his head. "Do you honestly believe that a kid who grew up in the middle of a backwater in an enemy nation is fit to lead anything? Keo was not there when the Kingdom of Lamaira shattered. He was not there when the Magical Council and the Chosen Three took over the south and the west and declared war on us."

Aster sounded genuinely angry and heartbroken at all of this, which made Keo realize that Aster was likely suffering from some severe stress after ruling the Old Kingdom for so long without any real hope. Not that that made Keo feel any sympathy toward him, but he better understood where Aster was coming from, at least.

"But he is still the *shelmai*," Seria insisted. "That means that he belongs on the Throne, whether you think he is fit to lead or not. He must sit on the Throne if we are to reunite the Kingdom."

"And how do you know that he will be able to do that?" said Aster. "He has already admitted that the Magical Council of his home country hate him. And I doubt that the Chosen Three will be willing to give up their power to some dumb kid who isn't even half the man that his father was."

"Then who should rule?" said Seria. "You?"

Aster nodded. "Yes. And I will do it with the power of the demons. The demons will rise again. No one can stop them … in fact, no one *should* stop them. They have promised to end the wars that have engulfed our once great Kingdom since King Riuno's death. The King of Demons said that he will end the wars and allow me to rule the newly-restored Kingdom of Lamaira in peace."

"But demons are liars," Keo said. "I don't know what the King of Demons said to convince you to side with him, but I can assure you that it is a lie. The demons, including their King, just want to kill us all. They are lying to you to get you to do what they want and don't care about you or your well-being."

"No, they are telling the truth," said Aster. "But even if they are not, I am tired of endless war, tired of waiting for a King who will never be as good a ruler as me. I would rather risk the return of the demons, whose rise will end the wars one way or another, than give a dumb kid like yourself the kind of ultimate power that the King of Lamaira used to wield."

"Then you're making a huge mistake," said Keo. "One you will not live long enough to regret."

"You may believe that, but that does not automatically make it true," said Aster. "What is true, however, is that, though you may have ruined my plan to install Easan as the puppet king that I would rule through, you cannot stop me now."

"What are you talking about?" said Keo. He gestured at everyone in the Arena, from the spectators in the stands and seating to the Knights on the field. "Everyone heard your ranting. Everyone knows that you are a traitor to the Old Kingdom. And no one here is going to stand by and let you get away with it or escape to try again another day."

"The Rightful Heir is correct," said Sir Abohji, whose voice was still somewhat muffled through his visor. "Keeper Aster, it is the job of the Knights of the Old Kingdom to defend the safety of the people from any threat, internal or external. And that includes dealing with corrupt leaders like yourself, whose plans, if put into action, would surely end in the deaths of countless innocent people, both here and in the other countries to the south and to the west." He held up his sword. "That means that we must arrest and throw you in the dungeons, where you will spend the rest of your life for crimes against the Old Kingdom, its people, and the *shelmai* as well."

"Sir Abohji and Keo are correct," said Seria, who sounded a lot more confident now. "Brother, you are alone. There is nowhere for you to run to now. I suggest giving up peacefully so that the Knights can take you in without needing to use violence. There is no point in resisting, not anymore."

Aster, however, did not look ready to give up. He dropped the Crown to the floor, but rather than run away, he looked down upon everyone with wrath in his eyes.

"Do you really think that I am alone?" said Aster. He laughed. "Of course not. The demons did more than simply promise to make me ruler over the Kingdom of Lamaira. They gave me the power I would need to make that happen if I couldn't do it on my own."

Aster raised his hands above his head. As he did so, his shadow behind him started to twist and turn. Then something rose from within it, at first nothing more than a formless shape, before it sprouted arms and a head as it grew taller and taller behind him. The shadow's arms were bulky and large, like tree trunks, while its face was stretched back over its skull, like a mask pulled over its face. It had long, sharp white teeth and deep blood-red eyes, in addition to a slimy, black tongue that darted out from between its teeth.

The demon rose higher and higher, until it towered over everyone in the Arena. The spectators screamed and started to flee, jumping out of their seats and stampeding toward the nearest exits. The Knights stood their ground, but a few of them shook in fear when they saw the demon, while Keo, Dlaine, and Maryal took up fighting stances as well. Easan looked up, his eyes widening when he saw the demon, but that was all he did, most likely because he was still distracted by the shattering of his world.

"Behold and despair," said Aster, his voice loud and mad, his eyes glowing the same blood-red as the demon's. "For this is the power that will allow me to rule the Kingdom of Lamaira."

The demon raised its own hands as well, which had claw-like fingertips. The demon looked down on Keo, his friends, Easan, and all of the assembled Knights, a hungry and deadly grin on its face.

This was easily the largest demon Keo had ever seen in his life, but that did not make him run away. He held Gildshine in both hands and it immediately burst into golden flames again, while Sir Abohji and his Knights took combative stances and Dlaine and Maryal also got ready for battle. Only Easan seemed unlikely to fight, but Keo hadn't expected him to anyway.

Aster pointed at the assembled heroes and said, "Do you really think that all of you can defeat my demon? How amusing. Let Shadow of Death show you just how outmatched you are."

Without warning, the demon let out an inhuman roar that made Keo and everyone else cringe. It raised its hands and dark shadow walls rose up all around Keo, his friends, and Easan, cutting them off from Sir Abohji and the Knights.

"What?" said Maryal, looking around at the massive shadow walls surrounding them on all sides. "Where'd these come from?"

"From Shadow, of course," said Aster, his voice now utterly mad. "He could have destroyed all of those Knights in one blow, but it isn't the Knights who messed up my perfect plan. It is you, Keo, and your three friends who ruined everything I have been working toward for a year, and it is you who will die first."

The Keepers rose from their thrones, but before they could escape, more shadow walls appeared around them, cutting off their escape. The Keepers cried out in fear, but there was nothing that Keo or anyone else could do to save them at the moment.

"Die!" Aster shouted.

Shadow's fingers extended like tree limbs toward Keo and his friends, forcing them to scatter. Half of the fingers struck the ground without hitting anyone, but one of them slammed into Dlaine, knocking him off his feet, while another hit Maryal, also knocking her out. And then Keo saw yet another strike something invisible, most likely Jola, and probably knock her down, because he did not hear her get back up. As for Easan, he had managed to dodge the one that had come after him, but he still didn't look like he was going to fight back against Aster and Shadow yet, if ever.

So Keo, brandishing Gildshine before him, looked up at Aster and Shadow. The demon retracted its fingers as it turned to look at Keo, a deep growl emitting from its throat. Or maybe it was emitting from Aster's throat; it was hard to tell, because the two seemed to be intimately connected.

"Now, Keo of the Sword, you are on your own," said Aster. "I should, perhaps, kill your friends, but I first want to kill you, because you have done more to harm my plans than any of your silly friends have. Though to be honest, your friends will die, too, once I am finished with you."

Keo didn't answer that. Instead, he said, "Then bring it, Aster! I'd rather have you fighting me than my friends anyway."

"Very well," said Aster. He pointed at Keo. "Shadow, kill him."

Shadow's hand shot toward Keo at an astonishing speed. Keo slashed at it with Gildshine, but Gildshine's golden flames hardly seemed to hurt the demon. Instead, Shadow knocked Gildshine out of Keo's hands and then wrapped tightly around his body. Immediately Shadow started trying to squeeze the life out of him, causing Keo to gasp for air even as he struggled to break free, though Shadow's grip was too tight for him to fight against.

"Yes ..." said Aster, glee in his voice, which was starting to sound less human and more demonic. "Feel your life leave you. You may be the *shelmai*, but even the *shelmai* can be killed. May you be reunited with your father in the next life. I wonder how disappointed your father will be when he sees that you failed to save your Kingdom."

Keo's vision was fading in and out rapidly. He found it hard to access the fire deep within himself that had given him the strength he needed to defeat Easan earlier, as if it had gone out. He continued to struggle against Shadow's hand nonetheless, even though it was clear that there was no way he could free himself.

But then, without warning, a blade wreathed in golden flames slashed through Shadow's wrist. The demon let out an inhuman scream of pain as the sword severed its hand from its arm, causing the shadow hand to dissipate immediately at the same time that the demon pulled its arm back closer to its body.

Without the demon crushing him to death, Keo breathed in as much air as he could. As he did that, a familiar voice to his left said, "You dropped this."

Keo looked to his left and saw Easan—who was now wearing his helmet again—standing there, holding Gildshine in his right hand. Easan also held Shadowbane, which was burning with golden flame, in his other hand.

"Thanks," said Keo as he took Gildshine from Easan. He briefly looked over it once to make sure it was okay before looking at Easan again. "Did you save me?"

Easan nodded. "Of course I did. But don't look too deeply into it. I am only helping you because I hate Aster even more than I hate you. It was quite pleasant to see Shadow killing you, but I realized that if I was going to get my revenge, I'd need your help."

"Uh, thanks," said Keo, although he wasn't sure what to say. He then raised his own sword and summoned the golden flames, which burst into existence around Gildshine's blade as usual.

"Easan!" Aster shouted, causing both Keo and Easan to look up at him. "So you've decided to work with Keo to defeat me, eh? That is exceedingly foolish of you, but I should have expected nothing less from a spoiled brat like yourself. You have never taken well to being told that you are not special."

Easan scowled at Aster, but said, "I don't care if I am special or not. What I care about is the fact that you had manipulated me. And I hate being manipulated."

"Whatever the reason for your sudden bravery, I will slaughter you both like livestock," said Aster. "And then the line of the Good King will truly end once and for all, ensuring that the demons will rise again ... and this time, without opposition."

Chapter Twenty-One

THE DEMON EXTENDED ITS fingers at them again, forcing Keo and Easan to separate to avoid getting hit. At the same time, Keo and Easan raised their swords and fired off two bursts of golden flame, which struck Shadow in the chest and caused it to hiss in pain. Aster hissed with it, even though he hadn't even been touched by the flames. That told Keo that Aster and Shadow really were connected to the point where they felt the same things.

So Keo shouted at Easan, "Aim for Aster! He and Shadow are connected and share the pain."

Easan nodded and aimed Shadowbane at Aster. He fired another burst of golden flames, but this time Aster and Shadow dodged it, allowing the flame to go past them. Aster thrust his hands in Easan's direction, causing Shadow to swipe at him, but Easan dodged the demon's claws.

While Shadow was distracted by Easan, Keo aimed Gildshine at Aster and fired his own golden flame burst. The sparkling flames shot through the air, but Keo's aim was off and the fire struck the ground in front of Aster, exploding and sending flames flying into his face. Aster raised his arms to block it, but his robes caught fire, which he hastily put out as quickly as he could.

"Shadow! Kill them both!" Aster cried out.

All of a sudden, Shadow retracted back into Aster's shadow.

Then Aster's shadow detached from his back and slithered across the plinth and onto the ground, where the demon rose to its full height again. This time, however, it sprouted an extra head and another set of arms, allowing it to focus on Keo and Easan at once while Aster stood there on the plinth watching the battle play out below.

Shadow slashed at Keo, but Keo deflected the blow with Gildshine and responded by firing another burst of golden flames at the demon. The flames struck Shadow dead on, causing it to shriek in pain this time, but it didn't give up. Its fingers extended straight into the ground, moving through the earth until they exploded out of the ground around Keo, surrounding him on all sides.

But Keo, moving fast, held Gildshine out and spun in a circle. Gildshine's golden flames cut through Shadow's fingers as easily as butter, earning yet another shriek from the demon. It also gave Keo an opening to run around the demon. He wanted to join Easan, who seemed to still be holding his own against his half of Shadow, but before he could successfully get around the demon, a wall of darkness appeared in his path, forcing Keo to come to a halt to avoid running into it.

As soon as he stopped, Keo looked to the left and saw that his half of Shadow was coming at him again. There was nowhere for Keo to dodge, so he redoubled his grip on Gildshine and slashed through the wall of shadow that had appeared in his path. Gildshine cut through the wall easily, creating a gap large enough for Keo to jump through.

Without hesitation, Keo leaped through the hole, barely avoiding Shadow's claws. Landing on his feet, he ran over to

Easan, who had just managed to blast away some of Shadow's fingers, and then stood by his side. Turning to face Shadow, Keo said to Easan, "Scored any major hits just yet?"

"Not sure," said Easan, the sounds of panting coming from his helmet in between sentences. "I've never killed a demon before, but I think it's getting weaker."

Keo nodded as the two halves of Shadow reformed into its original large self. "Hopefully, but I think we should aim for the head or heart. I've found in my experience that demons can be killed if you stab them in the head or heart, just like normal beings and creatures."

"Why don't we aim for Aster instead?" said Easan, nodding at the old man, who had not moved from his position on the plinth. "He's undefended, and if he's connected to Shadow like you said, then killing him should kill Shadow as well."

"We don't want to kill him, though," said Keo. He fired a burst of flame at Shadow for a moment to keep its claws away before continuing. "We want to kill Shadow and then let the Knights arrest Aster and put him on trial for his crimes."

"Are you crazy?" said Easan in disbelief. "Who cares if Aster lives or not? It's the only way we can defeat Shadow. Sorry if that offends your delicate sensibilities."

"My sensibilities aren't delicate," said Keo in annoyance. "I just think that—"

"If you won't do it, then I will," said Easan. "Cover me."

Easan dashed past Keo, while Keo shouted, "Hey!"

But Easan paid no attention to Keo's protests. He ran toward the plinth, Shadowbane at his side, while Shadow reached out toward him, most likely to stop him from reaching Aster. So Keo fired another fire blast at Shadow, striking it in the face and causing it to look at him in anger, even as Aster shouted, "No, you fool! Get Easan!"

Keo expected Shadow to turn back to Easan, but instead it extended its fingers toward Keo again. This time, all five fingers came from slightly different directions, so that when they came close enough, Keo had to swing Gildshine around in several different directions to block each blow.

This left Keo unable to cover Easan, who had reached the foot of the massive plinth. He pointed Shadowbane upwards, aiming it at Aster, but before he could shoot, Shadow pointed the fingers of its other hand at him. They shot toward him as fast as possible, prompting Keo to shout, "Easan, watch out!"

Easan must have heard Keo, because he jumped to the side, but he was too slow. One of Shadow's claws caught his leg and he fell on the ground, but before he could get up, two of the claws slammed down into Easan's wrists, forcing him to let go of Shadowbane and cry out in pain as Shadow pinned him to the ground.

"Easan!" Keo shouted.

Unfortunately, Easan's fall had distracted Keo, which allowed Shadow's other claws to slash at Keo's face. Keo tried to dodge, but the claws nonetheless cut his face, causing him to stagger backwards. The claws then slapped Gildshine out of his hands and immediately wrapped around his body, pinning his arms and legs together against his body. Shadow raised Keo off the ground and then slammed him back down. The impact left Keo's head spinning, dazing him for a moment.

The demon's grip around him tightened, to the point where he found it almost impossible to breathe. He struggled against the demon's grasp, but it was impossibly strong and he lacked the strength to break free. Nor could he reach Gildshine, even though it lay only a few feet away, because his hands were stuck firmly to his sides.

He looked in Easan's direction. Easan was struggling to free himself just as much as Keo was, but he was having the same amount of luck. And everyone else was either unconscious, like his friends, or still kept out of the battle by the shadow walls that the demon had summoned, like Sir Abohji and the Knights.

As for Aster, he was rubbing his hands together eagerly. He himself was looking more and more demonic, with his beard becoming darkening and his fingers becoming like Shadow's claws.

"Yes, Shadow, kill them both," said Aster, mad glee in his voice. "Do it slowly, but painfully. Show them the true power of the demons, the power that will end all wars and bring about everlasting peace to Lamaira."

"Peace?" said a familiar voice that Keo had not expected to hear. "You mean war."

Aster whirled around and Keo raised his head to see a middle-aged woman in dark clothes standing behind him. Keo's eyes widened when he saw the woman, because he recognized her as the Dracone woman who had rescued him and his friends from the Castle, which was strange because he had not heard her arrive.

"Who are you?" said Aster, who seemed both surprised and annoyed by the Dracone woman's sudden appearance. "And how did you get in here without me knowing?"

"That's irrelevant," said the Dracone woman, shaking her

head. "All you need to know is that you picked the wrong *shelmai* to try to kill, though you won't live long enough to regret that decision."

Aster laughed. "Why should I be afraid of you? You're nothing more than a middle-aged housewife who should be back in her home preparing dinner for her husband."

The Dracone woman let out a deep growl that was definitely not human. Her body started to change. Large, leathery wings extended from her back, her skin became plated and leathery, her face extended, her hair retreated into her head, her hands became sharp claws, and her entire body grew, until in seconds the woman was gone. She was replaced by a large black dragon, the same dragon that Keo had seen back in the Good King's Tomb, only this time, the dragon looked far more feral and ferocious than before.

Aster suddenly stopped laughing. He stepped backwards, raising one hand before himself as he said, "Impossible ... a Dracone? I thought they were—"

Aster did not get to finish his sentence, because in the next moment the Dracone woman opened her mouth. A huge, blue-colored stream of fire erupted from her mouth, bathing over Aster before the Keeper even got a chance to scream. Aster was immediately lost under the flames, which burned so hotly that even the stone of the plinth melted under its heat.

Shadow roared in pain. Its claws that had been pinning down Keo and Easan vanished immediately, freeing both of them, but Shadow itself was not yet gone. It turned toward the plinth, but its movements were far more sluggish than before even as it raised its claws to attack the dragon.

But as Shadow raised its claws, the demon started to melt back into the ground. The shadow domes that had appeared over the other Keepers vanished, showing that all of them were unharmed, although they all appeared equally frightened and traumatized by the experience. Meanwhile, the shadow wall keeping the Knights out slowly started to fade, although Keo still couldn't see the Knights themselves just yet.

Shadow's form became more and more faded, but the demon attempted to save its master anyway. It tried to move toward the plinth, but its movement was jerky and slow and it grew smaller and smaller every second, until soon Shadow had completely melted back into the earth, leaving no sign that it had been there even a few minutes ago.

Then the dragon closed her mouth, cutting off the powerful flames that had engulfed Aster. When the flames disappeared, the only thing that was left of Aster was his skeleton, which stood over a pile of ashes at its feet before it fell over backwards with a *clunk*.

As soon as Aster's skeleton hit the plinth, the shadow wall surrounding the area vanished, allowing Keo to see Sir Abohji and the Knights. Based on the way that the Knights were lined up with their weapons out, it looked like they had been trying to break through the wall to get in. They froze as soon as the shadow wall vanished, likely taken aback by this sudden turn of events. They seemed especially startled by the appearance of the Dracone woman, who had not moved from her position on the plinth.

As for Keo, he sat up and looked back at the plinth. He met the eyes of the Dracone woman, who was still in her dragon form. They looked at each other for only a moment, but it felt like a much longer time, because the Dracone woman's eyes were a question and an offer.

A second later, the Dracone woman nodded and then, with one massive flap of her wings, shot into the air and through the opening of the Grand Arena's ceiling above.

And in seconds, she was gone, leaving Keo and everyone else in the Arena alone.

Chapter Twenty-Two

ONE WEEK LATER, KEO stood in the Throne Room of the Old Castle, along with Dlaine, Maryal, Jola, and Sir Abohji. The remaining five Keepers were there also, sitting on their thrones, but the sixth throne—Aster's throne—was empty and had been so for a week. Keo had been told that the Keepers were searching for a replacement for Aster, but that it was difficult because there were very few people in the Old Kingdom who were as qualified to hold the place of Keeper as Aster had been. But Keo suspected that the Keepers were too traumatized by Aster's betrayal to replace him that quickly, which he understood, because Aster had been their leader and a friend to all of them. Had Keo experienced a similar betrayal, he would have likely reacted similarly.

Sir Abohji, as usual, stood just to the right of the Keepers, though his helmet was off at the moment, held underneath his arm. The removal of his helmet showed that he looked quite stressed, which Keo also understood, because this week hadn't been an especially kind week to any of them.

Right after the Dracone woman killed Aster and Shadow, Sir Abohji and the Knights had gone to check up on Keo and the others. The remaining Keepers had not been harmed by Shadow's darkness, but Keo, Dlaine, Maryal, Jola, and Easan had required immediate medical attention. The Knights had transported them to the Old Castle, where the city's best Healers healed the various injuries that Keo and the others had suffered during the battle. Thankfully, the Healers had managed to heal them all and had informed Keo and his friends that they were probably not going to suffer any permanent or long-lasting effects from the injuries.

That had been nice to hear, but that hadn't changed the fact that the leader of the Keepers had been revealed to have been in league with the demons. Although Keo had spent the week in the Old Castle and its grounds, he had heard from Knights and servants that the entire city of Tain was angry and that there had even been a few riots that the Knights had been forced to put down. While it was common knowledge that only Aster had been a traitor and that the rest of the Keepers were innocent, there was a loud and angry minority of Tainians who were demanding the resignation of the other Keepers, because they had no way of knowing if they could even trust the other Keepers anymore. So far, those ideas belonged only to that loud minority, but it certainly had not made calming down the citizens any easier. There were even rumors of a revolution in the works, though so far no one had tried anything yet.

As for Easan, he, too, had healed from his injuries, but had not left his room in the Old Castle since being transported there by the Knights. Not only that, but Easan completely shunned all contact with everyone else, accepting only meals and nothing else from the Castle's servants. Keo figured that Easan was still traumatized by the revelation that he wasn't actually the *shelmai*, which actually made Keo feel sorry for him. He had no idea what it must have been like to have your entire world shattered so abruptly like that. He wished that he could talk with Easan about this, but no one knew when or if Easan would ever emerge from his room or his depression, so Keo doubted he would get an opportunity to talk with him about it.

As it turned out, the Knights in the Grand Arena had not been the only people to see the dragon. According to several witnesses, when the dragon had emerged from the Grand Arena, it had flown around the city once before heading north. Many people, including Castle servants, could not believe that there had been an actual dragon sighting in the city, but many Tainians reported seeing the dragon flying around Tain. From what Keo had heard, this had also added to the tenseness of the situation, because most Tainians had not known if the dragon was on their side or not. Even after reports came out that it had been the same dragon that had slain Aster and Shadow, many Tainians apparently still worried that the dragon was the first of many that would invade the Old Kingdom, even though there was no evidence to suggest that such a thing would ever happen.

Now Keo and his friends stood in the Throne Room, where the Keepers had summoned them to discuss their next course of action. The atmosphere in the Throne Room was depressing and somber, largely due to the fact that Aster's throne was empty. It felt a little strange to see Aster's throne so empty, but Keo chose not to focus on that for now.

"Well," said Seria, who as far as Keo could tell was the leader of the Keepers for now, "Keo, I am sure you are wondering why we summoned you and your friends here today."

"I am," said Keo, nodding. Then he glanced at the Throne. "But I can guess."

Seria also glanced at the Throne before looking back at Keo.

She brushed away strands of her white hair and said, "We know now that Easan is not the *shelmai* and is not related in any way to King Riuno at all. That means that you, Keo of the Sword, are the Rightful Heir, which means that you will inherit the Throne left by your father the King."

Keo nodded. He still found it hard to accept that he was the son of King Riuno himself. He had grown up not knowing anything about his parents, living in a humble manner with Master Tiram, never suspecting that he was royalty. He knew he'd get used to it eventually, but for now it was hard to wrap his head around.

"Moreover, the people of Tain are willing to accept you as king, as, I am sure, the rest of the people of the Old Kingdom are," Seria continued. "There are a few people who would prefer Easan over you, but even they acknowledge the importance of following the laws and traditions of our ancestors, which state that only the firstborn son of the King can inherit the Throne unless he voluntarily gives up his inheritance to someone else."

"What are you asking me, Seria?" said Keo, although he knew what she was about to ask even before she said it.

"We, the Keepers, are asking you to accept your inheritance and be crowned the King of Lamaira, as is your birthright," said Seria, gesturing at the Throne. "We still have the Crown, so we can set up another coronation if you wish. Or we could skip it entirely, seeing as the coronation is a mere formality and does not bestow any real authority on you. I think that may be wise, considering what happened at the last coronation, I doubt that the citizens of Tain would complain if you skipped yours. They have waited many years for your return and certainly would not want to wait another second for you to take your rightful place."

Keo looked at his friends. Dlaine had his hands in his pockets, while Maryal had hers folded behind her. Jola, as always, was invisible, but he knew that she was likely standing somewhere near Dlaine. He had talked with all three of them about their plans for the future over the past week, had asked them for their opinions on how Keo should react if offered the Throne, but they had all said that they would go along with whatever Keo chose to do.

"And we do need a king," Seria said. "The people of Tain don't trust us Keepers as much as they used to. If you ascended to the Throne and chose a new Keeper to replace Aster, then that might avert a possible revolution by the people. It seems like the people trust your judgment far more than ours, now that they know the truth."

Keo looked at the Throne again. He could just imagine himself sitting there, wearing the Ceremonial Armor and the Crown on his head, giving orders to the Knights and Keepers and deciding how to defeat the demons.

But Keo also remembered what the Dracone woman had told him, about how if they wanted to actually defeat the demons, then they would need the help of the Dracones. He had been thinking hard about what the Dracone woman had told him and his friends that night in the Garden, wondering if there was any truth to her words. At the time, he hadn't seen any reason to believe her, mostly because he had not been sure that she was actually on their side. But after seeing the Dracone woman kill Aster and Shadow, he realized that she was indeed their ally, even if he still didn't know who she was or what her real motives were. He was especially interested in what the Dracone woman had meant about unlocking his 'true' power, which he suspected had something to do with the golden flames that he could summon but which he still did not even understand even now.

"What will happen if I refuse?" said Keo, looking at Seria.

"We Keepers will remain the ultimate authority in the Old Kingdom, but you will still have the freedom to sit on the Throne at some point if you wish," said Seria. "But I and the other Keepers urge you to sit on the Throne right away. The Kingdom of Lamaira has gone too long without a proper King and it should not have to wait any longer than is necessary for its new one."

Keo folded his arms across his chest. "While I know how important it is that I take my rightful place as the King of Lamaira, I am afraid that I will have to put that action off for a little while longer."

The Keepers exchanged shocked glances, while Sir Abohji stared at Keo as if he could not believe his own ears. But Dlaine and Maryal (and probably Jola, too) did not look surprised, because they had already discussed this with Keo during the week.

"Excuse me?" said Seria. She leaned forward in her throne, looking at Keo as if she was not quite sure that she had heard him correctly. "Did you just say that you want to put off taking your birthright?"

"Yes, I did," said Keo.

"But why?" said Seria. "Not only do we need a King who can reunite the Kingdom, but we need a King in order to strengthen the seal on the demons and keep them from rising again. What reason could you possibly have for putting this off for even another day?"

"I need to go to the Upper Mountains, where the Dracones live, and get their help," said Keo. "And I cannot do that if I am sitting on a throne in a castle all day leading a Kingdom."

"The Dracones?" Seria repeated, briefly exchanging surprised looks with the other Keepers. "Do you mean like that dragon that killed Aster? There are more of them?"

"Yes," said Keo, nodding. "I have spoken with that Dracone woman before. She told me that if we are to defeat the demons once and for all, then we will need the help of the Dracones to do it. Not only that, but she said that I could not unlock my true power unless I went to the Dracones, who could help me with that."

"But can't you become King and then send an envoy to the Dracones offering them an alliance instead?" said Seria. "Surely that would be easier and be much less dangerous."

"No," said Keo, shaking his head. "As I said, I want to unlock my true power. I believe that the Dracones will be able to answer some questions about myself that I don't know the answers to, which is why I must go myself, rather than send an envoy in my place."

"How long will you be away?" said Seria. "Do you know?"

"I don't," said Keo. "According to the research I've done, it will take at least two months to travel to the Upper Mountains on foot. And the demons will rise again in five and a half months."

"But you must also factor in the return trip," Seria said. "Even if you stay in the Upper Mountains for only a day, and then start the return journey the next day, by that time there will only be a month and a half left before the demons rise again. Can you truly reunite the entire Kingdom of Lamaira in that short a time, assuming you are successful in forming an alliance with the Dracones?"

"I don't know, but I do know that this is something I have to do," said Keo. "The Dracones have an important role to play in stopping the demons. I don't quite know what that role is right now, but I do know that it would be foolish of us to ignore them."

Seria's shoulders slumped. "Then I assume that there is nothing that I or any of the other Keepers can say to convince you to stay."

"Nothing at all," said Keo. "I want you guys to keep the Old Kingdom safe while I'm away. You can pick out a new Keeper if you want to replace Aster, and just keep things going the way they were before Easan arrived until I return."

Seria looked like she wanted to argue with that, but then she nodded and said, "Very well, Your Majesty. We'll continue to protect and guide the people of the Old Kingdom until your return. When will you leave for the Upper Mountains?"

"Tomorrow morning, at the crack of dawn," said Keo. "We want to leave right away so we don't waste any time."

"Who will be traveling with you?" said Seria. She looked at Dlaine and Maryal. "Your friends?"

"Just the four of us," said Keo, gesturing at himself, Dlaine, Maryal, and Jola.

"You mean, just the *five* of us," said a voice behind Keo, causing him to look over his shoulder to see who had spoken.

Easan was walking toward them. He was no longer wearing the Ceremonial Armor. Instead, he wore a long dark traveling cloak with the symbol of the Old Kingdom stitched into the right shoulder. He also walked with a long, thick staff, with Shadowbane nowhere to be seen. His wrists looked normal, having been healed from Shadow's claws, but he did limp slightly, like he had not yet fully recovered from their battle with the demon a week ago.

"Five of us?" said Keo, turning around entirely to face the approaching Easan. "What are you talking about? Who is the fifth person?"

Easan stopped and rolled his eyes. "That would be me, though I'm not surprised you didn't catch that, seeing as you've never shown yourself to be particularly quick-witted. That's surprising, considering how King Riuno was said to have a quick wit, but I guess you didn't inherit everything that belonged to your father, huh?"

Keo scowled in annoyance, while Dlaine said, "Wait a minute. Who said you could come along? I don't remember inviting you." He looked at Maryal. "Maryal?"

"Wasn't me," said Maryal, holding up her hands defensively. "I've barely even talked with Easan, much less invited him to come with us to the Upper Mountains."

And I didn't invite him, either, for the record, said Jola. *So don't ask me where he got that idea from.*

"No one invited me," said Easan, shaking his head. He put one hand on his chest. "I invited myself."

"Why?" said Keo, looking at Easan suspiciously. "I thought you hated me and my friends. Why do you want to come with us?"

"Because there is nothing else for me here in Tain or the Old Kingdom," said Easan. "Because I am not the Rightful Heir, I have nowhere else to go and nothing else to do. But I *do* want to help defeat the demons."

"Why?" said Keo.

"Because they, through Aster, manipulated and lied to me," said Easan. "And I hate being manipulated. I don't consider you or your friends to be friends of mine, Keo, but I believe in the old saying, that the enemy of my enemy is my friend. So I want to travel with you guys to put an end to the demons once and for all, if that's what you are trying to do."

Keo looked at Easan closely. Easan did not seem to be lying, and indeed, Keo couldn't think of any reason for Easan to lie to him. He still considered rejecting Easan's offer anyway because he didn't like Easan, but then he realized that having a swordsman with Easan's skill on his side would be a huge advantage, especially if they ran into any more demons on their way there.

"If we let you come along, will you be able to take care of yourself?" said Keo. "Because we are not going to meet your every need, you know."

"Of course I will take care of myself," said Easan. He jerked a thumb at his chest. "Prior to coming to Tain, I had no one I could rely on except for myself. Trust me, I won't be deadweight."

Keo nodded and glanced at Easan's waist and noticed that Shadowbane wasn't there. "What about Shadowbane? Will you be bringing that with you?"

"No," said Easan, shaking his head. "I'm leaving it here. I only wielded it because I thought I was King Riuno's son, but now—"

"Then go and get it," said Keo, interrupting Easan and pointing behind him.

Easan looked at Keo in annoyance. "Go and get what?"

"Shadowbane," said Keo. "If you are going to come with us, then you'll need that sword if you intend to kill any demons we run into along the way. All right?"

"Wait," said Easan. "Are you saying you will let me come with you?"

"Yes," said Keo, nodding, albeit reluctantly. "I don't know what we'll run into up north, so I figure it can't hurt to have some more help in case we run into anything we can't deal with on our own."

Easan frowned, like he was not sure if Keo was pulling his leg or not. But when he realized that Keo was not lying, Easan said, "A wise decision, Keo, perhaps the only genuinely wise decision you've ever made. I can assure you that you will not regret it. Now if you will excuse me, I must grab Shadowbane so I can be ready for our journey tomorrow morning."

With that, Easan turned and walked toward the exit. When he left, Dlaine looked at Keo and said, "Are you sure you will be able to tolerate Easan for two months?"

"I will," said Keo, "because we'll be too busy trying not to die in the wilderness to kill each other."

"Well, I hope you're right," said Dlaine, though he sounded quite doubtful about that.

"I think I am," said Keo. "Anyway, it's time for us to go now. We need to get our supplies in order for the journey tomorrow morning. I want all of us to be ready to leave tomorrow, because I have a feeling that this is going to be the most important part of our journey yet."

Chapter Twenty-Three

MAGICIAN NESMA PACED BACK and forth in front of her desk in her office in the Citadel in Capitika. She had been doing this for a good half hour now, as it was a habit she indulged in whenever she got nervous. And she got nervous whenever she realized that things were not going the way she wanted them.

Like now. She was listening to her assistant Gers, who had just finished reading aloud a report from one of the Magical Council's spies in Tain. This particular spy, of course, answered directly to her, because Nesma was in charge of capturing Keo and his friends and needed to know their every move so she could figure out how to counter them.

"Tell me what that report says again," said Nesma, without looking at Gers. "I just want to make sure I didn't miss any important details."

Without any complaints, Gers looked down at the letter in his hands and said, "The report states that Eliam the Tracker was unsuccessful in killing Keo and his friends. Eliam was captured by the Knights of the Old Kingdom, who imprisoned him in the dungeons beneath the Old Castle in a cell coated with antimagi. And Aster, one of the Keepers of the Old Kingdom, was revealed to be an agent of the angels and was killed by a Dracone woman, who then fled the city of Tain shortly thereafter."

Nesma had already known that one of the Keepers was on the side of the angels—Love of Light had told her so before his untimely and unjust death at Keo's hands—so she did not show any surprise at that.

"And where are Keo and his friends going again?" said Nesma, brushing back some of her hair, which was starting to get messy because she had been so focused on stopping Keo.

"To the Upper Mountains," said Gers. "Allegedly, they are going there to form an alliance with the Dracones, who are said to dwell there. They believe that the Dracones could help stop the rise of the angels."

"And Keo is the Rightful Heir, the long-lost son of King Riuno, right?" said Nesma. "That's what the report says?"

"That is indeed what the report says," said Gers, nodding. "The report says that Keo's identity was confirmed by the Keepers, although he's not going to sit on the Throne just yet."

"Which means that, if Keo becomes the King of Lamaira, he might be able to ally the Restorationists with the Divinians," said Nesma, running her hands through her long, dark hair, "and then ally with the Dracones to invade South Lamaira and make it part of the Kingdom. And even worse, stop the angels from rising again."

"The situation does indeed seem quite grim when you put it that way, Miss Nesma," said Gers. "I have not yet sent out this report to the other members of the Council. Do you want me to?"

"Not yet," said Nesma, shaking her head as she continued to pace back and forth. "They might act hastily if we did that. They might even demand that I give up chasing Keo after this utter failure and will demand that we focus on increasing our military strength instead."

"I see," said Gers. "Then what *should* we do, Miss Nesma? Allow Keo and his friends to continue their journey unopposed and allow them to create a confederation that will overwhelm the Magicians?"

"No," said Nesma. "We need to send someone else after them. Someone who has never failed to kill an assigned target, who the Magical Council has relied upon in dark times like these."

"Are you speaking of the Brothers White Blood?" said Gers. There was dread in his voice when he spoke that name, a dread Nesma understood, because she experienced it herself whenever she thought about them.

"Yes," said Nesma with a suppressed shudder. "Send them a message telling them that we have a job for them that will take them abroad for a while. And don't delay, because I know Keo and I know he isn't the kind of person to waste time whenever he sets his mind to complete some task."

"Yes, ma'am," said Gers, bowing.

He turned and walked over to the door, but before he left, Nesma said, "Gers?"

Gers paused, one hand on the doorknob. He looked over his shoulder and said, "Yes, Miss Nesma?"

"Tell the Brothers not to eat Keo when they kill him," said Nesma. "That's disgusting."

Based on Gers's grimace, Nesma could tell that he agreed. "Yes, ma'am, of course."

With that, Gers opened the door and left, leaving Nesma all alone in her office, hoping that she had not gone too far this time in her quest to make sure that her misguided friend did not make the terrible mistake that he was deliberately trying to make.

Continued in: Kingdom of Dragons

As the demons grow more and more powerful, Keo travels to the mountains in the north, seeking the aid of the legendary Dracones, a race of shape shifters who can change from dragon to human form and back at will. He also seeks answers to his own true nature, which he believes the Dracones can give him.

But receiving the aid of the Dracones becomes difficult when Keo learns of the sordid history between humanity and the Dracones. In addition, he soon finds himself caught between the remnants of the Dracones and a small but determined group of humans who claim the mountains as their own territory and will not give it up without a fight.

Keo must find a way to bring peace between the Dracones and humans before all-out war breaks out between them. If he fails, then it may be impossible to stop the demons from rising again.

Available in ebook and trade paperback wherever books are sold!

About the Author

Timothy L. Cerepaka writes fantasy as an indie author. He is the author of the Mages of Martir fantasy novels, the Two Worlds science-fantasy series, and the Tournament of the Gods fantasy novels. He lives in Texas.

Find out more at his website at www.timothylcerepaka.com.

Other books by Timothy L. Cerepaka

Prince Malock World:

The Mad Voyage of Prince Malock

The Return of Prince Malock

The New Era of Prince Malock

The Coronation of Prince Malock

Mages of Martir:

The Mage's Grave

The Mage's Limits

The Mage's Sea

The Mage's Ghost

Two Worlds:

Reunification

Alliance

Allegiance

Retaliation

Desinence

Tournament of the Gods:

Gathering of the Chosen

Betrayal of the Chosen

Invasion of the Chosen

Ascension of the Chosen

The War-Torn Kingdom:

Kingdom of Magicians

Kingdom of Heirs

Kingdom of Dragons

Standalones:

The Last Legend: Glitch Apocalypse

www.ingramcontent.com/pod-product-compliance
Lightning Source LLC
Chambersburg PA
CBHW052021020726
47501CB00004B/1172